THE SIREN AND THE DARK TIDE

FAIRYTALES FOREVER
BOOK TWO

EVIE FINN

All rights reserved, including the right to reproduce this book or portions thereof in any form, except quotes for review purposes.

Evie Finn © 2024

Cover: MerryBookRound

❦ Created with Vellum

CHAPTER 1

The tide pulled gently at Riella's hair, creating a silvery cloud around her face. The reef was warm from the relentless Zermetic summer and she lingered in the sun-dappled outcrops of coral with her two best friends. Tiny orange fish darted playfully around her tail while she collected rubbish from the sea floor.

"I miss wrecking their ships," Galeil Sent via siren telepathic connection.

"We all do," Sent Mareen in reply. "But we must hold back from aggression, as the elders ordered. Against pirates, at least. Slavers are still fair game."

"Killing slavers is fun," Sent Galeil. "But pirates put up more fight." She paused. "What if we *accidentally* punched a hole in the hull of a Dark Tide Clan ship?"

"Then you would *accidentally* start another war," replied Mareen, sending an impatient sigh alongside her telepathic words. "And really, the elders are right. We belong in our world and the land-walkers belong in theirs. We ought to leave each other alone. If only they'd stay out of the sea." She unhooked a piece of garbage from the coral and grimaced. "What is this?"

Mareen flicked it into the steadily growing pile of garbage they were collecting in a discarded fishing net.

"Who cares?" retorted Galeil with a giggle, a stream of bubbles erupting from her mouth like a string of pearls in the aquamarine water. "Do you miss fighting, Riella?"

Riella forced herself to concentrate on the conversation running parallel to her private thoughts. She rolled over in the water to face her friends.

Mareen's vivid orange hair flickered in the light like an underwater flame while she meticulously removed fishing hooks from the fins of a nurse shark. Mareen's purple tail was three times the length of her upper body, beating rhythmically and instinctually against the current to keep her stationary. Thin ribbons of blood rose from the shark's wounds, dissolving into the saltwater.

Meanwhile, Galeil turned backward somersaults through the water, her dark hair touching the end of her green tail to form a perfect circle.

"I don't miss holding wounded sirens in my arms," Sent Riella.

"I suppose," Sent Galeil, coming to a stop. "But surely you miss attacking their ships. Tearing up their sails. Singing to them," she added, with a vicious gleam in her piercing violet eyes.

Riella giggled. The others joined in, and soon their giggles transformed into unhinged cackling. Singing to a male human, when a siren was angry enough, shredded his eardrums.

"It *was* entertaining," conceded Riella, sweeping her lightly-webbed hands through the water, enjoying its cool, gentle resistance. She smiled. "I always enjoyed making them scatter like rats across the decks of their ships."

Mareen released the shark, now free of hooks. It nudged the siren's hand in thanks before swimming away into the cobalt-blue depths. "Ah, you speak like that, but you're soft on humans, Riella. You linger on their vessels whenever you get the chance. You converse with them. And no one listened more avidly than you during our land-walker lessons with the elders. Don't pretend otherwise."

"I'm not soft on them."

"You *are*," chorused Galeil and Mareen. "The only words we should reserve for humans are threats," added Mareen. "To be swiftly carried out."

Riella fixed them with a glare. "Curiosity isn't the same as being soft. I believe it's a good idea to understand the enemy, that's all."

Her friends raised their brows at each other.

"Here," Sent Mareen, swimming to the garbage net and tying it closed with a length of fraying rope. "Since you love humans so much, you can be the one to deliver this to the boat we passed a way back. But hurry, because we must return to Zydenthis for Thera's ceremony. Every pod from the realm will be in our city."

"Our little Thera has come of age," Sent Galeil, smiling wistfully. "She really needs to hurry up and get her first kill."

Riella and her friends had their first kills before coming of age at twenty-one. That was three years ago, and they'd had many kills since, thanks to the bloodiest war between sirens and pirates in living memory. The war had ended, but grudges remained.

"She will in time," Sent Mareen, darkly. "If anything's certain in our world, it's danger. That's what happens when we allow humans to traverse our waters."

Riella grabbed the top of the net. "For now, I'll return this garbage to them. See you both soon."

She swam off with the net in hand, her powerful tail and

body undulating to propel her through the crystalline water. Her long blonde hair streaked along behind her like a pale ghost and schools of fish shifted around her in synchronized harmony.

The boat was a shadow on the surface, floating over deep waters. Half a dozen lines ran from the vessel and disappeared into the blue abyss.

A mischievous giggle escaping her mouth in a bubble, she tugged one of the lines. The humans responded quickly, the line growing taut as they tried to reel her in, believing she was a catch. She held the line steadily in place, toying with them.

Then, without warning, she yanked the line hard. A fishing rod splashed onto the surface of the water, the line going slack. She cackled, knowing the sound would travel up to the men. By now, the humans would know a siren was in their midst. They would haul in the lines, or perhaps simply cut them, and head straight for shore.

As the dropped fishing rod sank near her, she caught it, along with the line, and swept them into her net. The boat still hadn't moved. Riella frowned, wishing to chase them. It was more fun when there was a chase. The humans would do everything in their limited power to make haste in their vessel, while she swam lazy laps below until she felt like making her presence fully known.

But this boat would not move. What in the seven seas were they doing?

With an aggrieved sigh, she kicked her tail to propel herself straight upward, the water turning clear as she neared the surface. She kept going, breaking through with a delighted shriek. Dragging the garbage net with her, she leaped through the air and caught hold of the largest mast. Blinking her eyes to adjust to the harsh sunshine, she tossed the net indiscriminately on the deck of the boat, making sailors dive out of the way.

Her tail shone, her fins and scales iridescent blue and pink in the sun.

"Siren!" yelled one of the men. "Siren!"

She wrapped her tail around the mast and slid down it, surveying the scene before her. It was a fishing boat, with nets and rods and a pile of dead-eyed flounder growing stinky in the heat. The men were probably from Klatos, the nearest port city. In the distance, the brown and green land shimmered on the horizon like a mirage.

"You will dispose of this garbage," she said, her musical voice bouncing off the water. "Now. Or I will eat you for my supper."

She burst into laughter at the mens' reactions to her presence. Several jammed their hands over their ears, fearing Sirensong. Others wore expressions of wide-eyed desire as they gazed at her body. It never ceased to amuse her, the ridiculous contradictions of the male nature.

A siren's first weapon was her beauty. Even as the men feared for their lives, they gave in to the temptation to stare at her bare gleaming skin, ocean-blue eyes, and pouty pink lips. Her wet silvery-white hair clung to her shoulders and pert bust. To disarm them further, she gave a slow, smirking smile. The men covering their ears dropped their hands, their mouths going slack.

One sailor stepped forward, pulling his battered hat from his head and holding it in front of him with both hands, as if it might protect him. He was older than the others. The captain, perhaps.

"I, uh—" He gulped. "We're from Klatos. Our boat, uh—"

Riella slid farther down the mast and leaned forward, so that her face was level with his.

"Speak up, human," she said in a teasing voice.

He cleared his throat and tried again, sweat pouring from his bald head. "Our rudder was destroyed on the reef. We're unable to return to port."

Riella bared her teeth and hissed, making the man stumble backward in fear. "Surely you *meant* to say that you damaged the reef with your rudder?"

His face crumpled. "Yes. I am sorry. Sorry. I'm sorry."

"Shut up!" she howled, her voice scaling several octaves. She could feel the Sirensong bursting to spring forth from her throat. "Save your breath, for you will need it when I fling you into the ocean as an offering to the sacred beauty you feel so entitled to desecrate."

He fell silent, quivering.

Riella considered her options. She was supposed to return to Zydenthis soon for the ceremony. But the boat would sink sooner or later if she left the men here. She scanned the horizon again. No other boats or ships were visible in the afternoon glare.

She hissed in frustration. "Withdraw your lines. I'll pull you to the nearest shore."

The man stammered in shock. "Th—thank you."

Riella rolled her eyes. She pushed off from the mast, snapping it in half out of spite, and dove cleanly into the water.

"What's the delay?" Sent Mareen, from a distance, having sensed Riella return to the water. "Were you tormenting the sailors? If so, why didn't you invite us to join in?"

The lines started to move through the water. Riella swam out of the way, lest the hooks snag her as they flew past. "They're stranded with a faulty boat. I'll take them to shore."

Mareen and Galeil reacted with indignant cries. "They don't deserve our help! Let's sink them and be done with it."

"And pollute the water even more?" countered Riella. "The boat would sit on the ocean floor, spreading filth."

She knew they understood the logic. Their protestations were the sirens' obligatory rebuke of any human foible, no matter how big or small.

"Do you need assistance?" Sent Galeil when her scorn had ebbed away.

"No, the boat isn't large. Return home and I'll follow you shortly."

"Alright." Mareen sighed exaggeratedly. "Promise you'll terrorize them a little, for your trouble."

A thick rope splashed into the water at the bow of the boat, spiraling downward until Riella caught it. She gave a firm tug, to ensure the men had secured it properly. The rope held.

"If I have time, I promise to ruin their day," she Sent.

Soon she was out of communication range, swimming swiftly through the blue expanse with the boat in tow. The water became warmer as she neared the shore, the shallows heated by the mid-summer sun. Only when waves curled ahead, making spectacular white dips and rises, did she relinquish her hold on the rope.

She surfaced, beating her tail to stay in place. The waves picked up the boat and carried it to the beach. The men shouted their thanks from the stern and she responded only with a glare. As the vessel washed up on the sand, the fishermen jumped out, dragging the boat past the tide line.

The weather had turned. The sky was steel-gray and a stinging wind whipped across the surface of the water. Knowing she should already be on her way home, she dawdled just beyond the swell, eyeing the land. It was a remote stretch, with only a few small settlements dotted along the coastline, and the dizzyingly high Black Cliffs to the right. A good place to wreck a ship.

Klatos was many leagues to her left, out of sight. The men would likely struggle to return to the city, but that was not her concern. What mattered to her was the boat was out of the ocean.

Unbidden, she wondered, not for the first time, what it would be like to walk the streets of Klatos. To go places beyond the endless blue desert of the sea. She ought not to have wondered such things, for no good could come of it. Sirens did not belong on land.

Cursing her curious nature, she dove underwater and surged out to sea, moving with incredible swiftness now that she was free of the boat.

Rain was coming. Perhaps even a storm. She could tell by the way the fish behaved, tightening their pods and seeking shelter.

A thrashing movement caught her eye, on the surface above her. At first glance, Riella thought it was a feeding frenzy—a shark devouring prey without mercy.

Her instincts tingling, she drew closer. Something was not quite right, she could feel it. This was no ordinary frenzy. Sure enough, the commotion was not caused by a shark, or any sea creature at all.

Human legs kicked madly, heavy in sodden trousers, arms flailing wildly. Riella hissed in disbelief. How many good deeds did she have to do for the land-walkers today?

Mareen and Galeil would leave him to drown. They may've even dragged him under, for amusement. Her friends would mock her for even thinking about saving him.

But, Mareen and Galeil were not there.

Riella rose quickly and latched onto the man's wrist. It was not until she broke the surface that she realized her dire mistake. Before she could fight, or swim away, the human who baited her had already cast the spell.

Her vision went black. She lost the ability to move her tail or arms or even open her mouth. All she could do was drift, like seaweed. With her head out of the water, she couldn't send a long-range distress signal to her friends. The man grunted with exertion as he tied ropes around her body and hauled her into his boat, which was invisible moments ago.

As her mind slid into unconsciousness, dread engulfing her, she had one last thought:

Mareen and Galeil were right. Humans didn't deserve her help.

CHAPTER 2

*R*iella awoke to darkness spliced by flickering orange.

Submerged in salty water, she instinctively kicked her tail, only to have it hit a hard, flat surface. She was in a tank. Heavy manacles pulled on her wrists, attached to thick chains bolted to the sides of the tank. She kicked upward, breaking the surface of the water, looking around wildly.

A grid of sturdy metal bars crossed over her head. Her throat burned, like she'd swallowed fire, but she was otherwise unscathed. Hazy and disoriented, memories flooded back to her like a nightmare.

The thrashing man in the water was a lure. He'd cast a spell and now she was a prisoner in a tank in the middle of a cave. The walls were jagged black rock and the roof was wooden slats, leaving the cavern half open to the warm night air. The crash of waves reached her ears.

She squinted into the shadows of the cave. The only light came from torches in brackets on the wall. Her senses were slightly duller out of the water, because she was less attuned to the environment. The cavern was unoccupied, apart from her, and seemed to be a workshop.

A table sat near the tank, piled high with parchments and books and glass bottles of varying fullness. There were also sharp metal objects, lying neatly on a tray, and a mirror with a gilded frame. The rest of the cave had only a desk and chair, and smelled like sulphur. A banner hung on the rocky wall, showing a lightning bolt through a circle.

Upon closer inspection, Riella found the tank was not made of glass at all. It was clear natural crystal, far thicker and stronger than any material a human could make. She would not let that stop her from escaping, though.

A siren's physical strength waxed and waned with the moon. It was currently a dark moon, to her disadvantage. Nevertheless, if she could remove the manacles, she would try with all her might to strike the crystal until it broke.

Movement from a shadowy corner of the cave made her freeze.

"Who's there?" she demanded. "Show yourself."

A pale figure stepped into the shifting orange light, chained at the ankle. Riella suppressed a gasp. It was not the man who'd captured her. The creature was completely colorless, with lank hair, pale lips, gray irises. She had the features of a young woman, except for her ears, which were pointed, like an elf.

But that was impossible. For this creature—dressed in a fraying plain shift—was devoid of the divine vitality that characterized elves. The elven affinity to nature was a trait shared by sirens. The two races couldn't be more different in disposition, though. Elves were peaceful, and sirens were the warriors of the ocean.

"He'll be back soon," said the pale creature, pressing her white palms against the tank. "You have to get out of here. I'll help you any way I can, but he is powerful."

"Who are you? Why are you in these caves?"

"I'm Seraphine, an elf from the Emerald Mountains. Polinth kidnapped me, and now he drains my life force to keep his terminal Rotting disease at bay. But the others he captures are not so lucky. You must escape. He'll continue experimenting on you until your body gives out."

"Experimenting," repeated Riella in horror. "What did he do to me?"

"I don't know, but he was muttering about needing a siren's Voice."

"So, how can we escape?"

Seraphine hesitated. "We?"

"I won't leave you here, of course."

The elf shook her ankle, the heavy manacle clanging against the floor. "I would dearly like to see my family again before I die. He kidnapped me from the forest, and none of my people will know what happened to me. But I believe I won't last until then. He's drained so much of my life force already."

"You aren't going to die. Not here in this vile cave, and not any time soon. I promise."

"There are stairs down the side of the mountain." She glanced at Riella's tail. "But I suppose you'll want to return straight to the water." Seraphine pointed to the mouth of the cave. "The cliffs are right outside. Can you jump?"

The siren nodded. "Then let's—"

"Ah, I'm so glad my two special beauties have met. My sun and moon."

Riella whirled to the right. A man wearing blood-red robes appeared from the gloom, his thin hands folded in front of him. His wizened features and bald head glowed with vigor, despite his advanced age.

She opened her mouth to Sing. He watched with a serene expression as she buckled in pain from the stabbing sensation in her throat. She couldn't Sing, at all. The Sirensong was simply gone. A pained rasp was all that came out.

"What have you done to me?" she hissed at him.

The man gave a genial smile. "You'll find you are in perfect health, my dear. At least, for the time being. I require your Voice for some very important work I'm doing."

Riella processed his revolting words. Seraphine was right. The mage had taken her Sirensong, by force. By magic. She hadn't even known such a thing was possible.

With renewed anger, she tugged at the manacles and bashed the tank walls with her tail, to no effect. Perhaps it was the aftereffects of his spell, but she felt weaker than usual. Her strength seemed to be ebbing away more and more, like the tide at dawn.

For the first time since she regained consciousness, she noticed a small red wound in the crook of her left arm.

Riella fixed him with an accusing glare. "You are a ghoul. You experiment on living beings. You keep a prisoner and feed on her life force."

He clicked his tongue and shook his head, as if they'd had a friendly misunderstanding. "I'm at the forefront of the mystical arts. I am breaking barriers. For that, I need my health. Seraphine is a small price to pay. As are you." Polinth clapped. "But you can relieve Seraphine of her duties. Tell me, siren, what do you know of the Amulet of Delphine?"

Riella blinked in surprise. The amulet was a myth, a curio sirens told stories about, but it did not actually exist. "Nothing," she spat. "I know nothing about it. Want to hear what I *do* know?"

He raised his eyebrows, smiling, as if greatly anticipating the answer. "What do you know, my dear?"

"You are going to die. You will be flayed alive, screaming, and I'll watch."

Polinth bounced on his feet in delight. "Ahh, that's the

siren spirit." Riella bared her teeth at him, but he kept going, unperturbed. "Truly, you're a magnificent creature. You've given me the means to retrieve the amulet, with your Voice, and allowed me to push the laws of Nature, with your body. The charlatans at Starlight Gardens will be forced to accept me as their superior."

Riella had no idea what he was talking about, but she'd never had to listen to a male human speak this long in her life, and the experience was causing her immense irritation and rage.

With renewed determination, she crashed her tail against the tank and wrenched at the chains, ignoring the pain in her wrists. She screamed and wailed, but the sound was only a strained echo of her Sirensong. What did he plan on doing with this alleged amulet? What did he plan to do with *her*?

Polinth held his hands up to placate her, which only made her fight harder. The water lapped over the edge of the tank, splashing the front of his robe. He stepped back, dragging Seraphine with him.

"I shall let you calm down," he said to Riella. "I have some cataloging to do in my storeroom, anyway. We can talk again when you feel better, and I'll explain your situation fully. I'm afraid I did have to make certain compromises to achieve your transformation. But you will surely live longer than the last one."

"What?" she shouted in disbelief, her fury multiplying with every sentence from his mouth. "What are you talking about? What have you done?"

He did not reply, clamping his hand on the elf's arm and hauling her from the room, the long chain dragging behind her.

Riella gritted her teeth and kicked the crystal wall with her tail. If she'd not been weakened by whatever foul sorcery he disabled her with, she would've quickly demolished the tank.

Going by his ominous words, she would grow weaker still. This would likely be her only chance to escape, as no one knew her location. The waves pummeled the rocks below, calling to her. If she could just return to the healing power of the ocean, away from this monster, she would regain her strength.

The crystal remained intact. Riella switched her focus to the manacles, pulling them with as much strength as she could muster. But the chain links were thick and she howled in frustration when they refused to budge.

To bolster her strength, she pictured Polinth's smug face beaming at her.

With a grunt of hatred, she finally managed to rip both manacles from the tank walls, the heavy chains falling into the water with a splash. She cackled in delight and anticipation. Wrapping her fists in the chains, she punched the crystal wall, over and over again.

A fracture formed in the middle of the tank, splintering the smooth surface like a branch of lightning. Her freedom was so close she could taste it. With her next blow, the crystal broke apart with a deafening crack. Chunks of the wall crumbled to the cave floor and the salty water poured out, like a dam breaking. Riella squeezed herself through the gap, dragging the chains with her.

Polinth lurched into the room, the water washing over the hem of his robes. His smile had vanished. Behind him, Seraphine limped into the room, her gray eyes wide.

"No," he cried. "You don't know what you're doing."

Leaning on her hands, Riella angled her body toward him. "Yes, I do. I'm killing you."

He backed up. "Please, listen to me. If you return to the ocean, you will die. Allow me to take care of you."

The siren answered by flinging one of the heavy chains at him. The links hit him square in the chest, making him crash to the floor, winded.

Suddenly dizzy, Riella's arms buckled. Her body ached all over and when she breathed, her insides felt too big and airy. Panic seized her. What was going on? If she didn't return to the ocean soon, she wouldn't survive.

Seraphine tugged at the long chain around her ankle, bolted to the rock wall. The siren grasped the chain and yanked, pulling the bolts from the stone and freeing the elf. If they could leave before Polinth recovered, they might have a chance of escaping.

"Let's go!" said Seraphine, looking over her shoulder at Polinth, who clutched his chest and gasped. "Once he casts magic, we're done for."

The elf ran from the cave, her gait lopsided from the chain dragging at her ankle, while Riella pulled herself along the floor to the black rocks outside. The briny wind whipped her face. After the claustrophobic constriction of the tank, the air was refreshing.

Light from the torches cast a faint glow on the rocks. To the side of the cave, a set of rough-hewn stairs disappeared down the mountain. Beyond the edge of the cliff, where Riella would go, was only a long, long drop to the ocean.

"Will you be alright?" asked Seraphine from the top of the stairs.

"I will—" Her words were interrupted by an unprecedented jolt of pain in her chest, making her cry out. "Once I'm in the water, I'll feel better."

Inside the cave, Polinth rose to his feet, fixing his manic gaze on Riella. Seraphine was around the corner, out of sight. The siren steeled herself in preparation for the jump she'd have to make. Anything was better than staying here with him.

Seraphine melted into the shadows, hurrying down the stairs. Riella turned and pulled herself along the craggy rocks. Just before she reached the rocky overhang of the cliff, one of the chains around her wrist caught and jerked her backward.

Crying out in fear, she tried to free herself, but the end of the chain was wedged between two rocks. The harder she pulled, the more the chain became stuck. Polinth's silhouette loomed in the mouth of the cave.

He lifted his arms and began to chant.

"No!"

The voice belonged to Seraphine, who'd come back for her. The elf darted from the stairwell and lunged for the stuck chain, wrenching it. The chain went blessedly slack on Riella's wrist, liberating her.

"Jump!" shouted Seraphine, crouching on the rocks. "Jump now!"

Pain spasmed through Riella's tail and her chest tightened. There was no time for hesitation. She pulled herself over the cliff's edge, praying Seraphine could flee to the nearby stairs before Polinth cast magic.

But, a moment too late, Riella registered a flash of red light, followed by Seraphine's piercing scream. The sound haunted Riella the whole way down, the force of the wind stinging her face and body.

The siren crashed through the surface of the seething water. Having expected relief, she was alarmed to find herself sinking rapidly. Another shock of pain wracked her body. She sank farther, the heavy chains making her drop like a stone.

Water slipped through her hands too easily. The webbing between her fingers was gone, making it impossible to paddle to the surface. She kicked her tail, which felt agonizingly splintered.

Nothing happened. She kicked again, and now she felt no tail at all.

In the starlit water, she looked down, confusion and terror engulfing her. What she saw made no sense. Where her tail had been just moments ago, there were two slender, flailing appendages.

Riella had human legs. And judging by the rate she swallowed water, human lungs, too.

CHAPTER 3

"Nah. She can't be."

"I'm telling you, that's a siren."

"Are you daft? She's got legs. Same as me or you."

"Her legs are a good deal nicer than your gnarly gams, Berolt."

Riella became aware of a steady rocking sensation. A hard surface beneath her body. Voices above her, male and rough. It was still nighttime, firelight tinging her vision.

She tried to speak, but coughed instead. Saltwater spewed from her mouth. She pushed herself up, hands clawing at the wooden surface.

The rocking almost toppled her sideways. More water came up from her stomach in a heave—a seemingly impossible amount for her to have swallowed.

Metal dug into her wrists. She narrowed her eyes, trying to focus her vision. Manacles.

Everything came back to her. The mage named Polinth captured Riella. Seraphine the elf traded her freedom to save the siren. And *Riella had legs.*

"I reckon we throw her back in the water. Last thing we need are the sirens thinking we kidnapped one of their own. It'd start another war."

"She'd drown, numbskull. You want them to think we killed one of their own, instead?"

"What do we do with her then, if you're so smart?"

Riella chanced a look at her legs. They were definitely real—pale and strange and useless. They were not some horrible nightmare.

Her body was tangled in a net, seaweed clinging to her naked body. Without her tail, she felt exposed in a way she never had before. And without the ability to use Sirensong, she was trapped.

Her hands grappling with the slippery deck of the ship, she sat up. Dawn was coming, a mauve tint beginning to supersede the darkness of night.

Riella's legs flopped around awkwardly. She tried to move them, like she would her tail, and they splayed at the knee, causing her to gasp in pain. Human legs were so terribly angular and hinged. How did they manage to walk around on these things?

The manacles felt several times heavier than when she'd been in Polinth's cave. She tried not to think about what that meant—about how much he'd weakened her. Poor Seraphine was still at the sorcerer's mercy. Riella had abandoned her, only to end up in a possibly worse situation. What a waste of the elf's sacrifice.

"Oi, she's awake."

Not wanting to look up at their faces, she stared at the legs surrounding her. Male human legs, dressed in grubby trousers. One of the men squatted in front of her, attempting to put his face to hers. On instinct, she lashed out at him with her hand, swiping with her diamond-sharp talons. At least she still had those.

"Jeez!" The man skittered backward in panic. "Yeah, that's a siren alright."

She bared her teeth at him. His face was weathered and he was missing a chunk of his ear. Tattoos covered his arms. Her blood turned to ice when she recognized one in particular. The mark of the sirens' most sworn enemies.

Heart thumping, she forced herself to look up at the masts, confirming her grim suspicion.

Atop the highest mast, above the flapping white sails, was a black flag bearing a pair of crossed cutlasses. She'd been fished out of the ocean by Dark Tide Clan pirates. Perhaps she fought some of these very men during the war.

The pirates stared at her, but she avoided meeting anyone's eye. What in the seven seas was she going to do? If she jumped overboard, she'd likely drown. But she didn't know anyone in the human world, unless she counted Polinth, which she absolutely did not. Where was she supposed to go?

"Say what you want about sirens," one of them murmured. "But no one could ever accuse 'em of being ugly."

Several wheezed with amusement.

"Pity she'd bite your pecker clean off," said another one.

All roared with laughter this time, Riella's head pounding as she struggled to suppress her anger.

Never in her life had she been forced to swallow her rage. She had always had an outlet. Singing. Fighting. Swimming. Polinth had completely neutered her. All because he wanted some amulet that may or may not exist, and to find out what happened when you magicked away a siren's tail. If only she'd heeded her friends and not troubled herself with human affairs. She'd be with them right now, safe and whole, having celebrated Thera all night.

"So what do we do with her?" asked one man.

"Take her down to the brig."

"Are you kidding? Those bars won't keep a siren. She'll rip a hole in the hull trying to get outta there, and sink us."

"You got a better idea? Captain'll be back soon, and he won't want to deal with this. Not when—"

"Brig it is, then." The man knelt, well outside of the striking distance of Riella's talons. "Can you walk, little fishy?"

Picking up the chain attached to her wrist, she flung it at him. He seemed to be ready for it, though. He ducked out of the way, the chain lashing the deck instead.

"Pass me that sail over there," he said to one of the other crew members. "Help me grab her."

With the voluminous sail in his hands, the man came at Riella like she was a wild animal. Tangled in the net, she couldn't fight off the pirates when they descended on her. They wrapped her in the thick fabric while she wailed and thrashed. Grunting and swearing at each other, they hauled her down a narrow set of stairs.

Below deck was dark and humid and smelled like the sweaty, unwashed bodies of male humans. Riella retched from the stink as they dumped her on the floor. She wriggled partway out of the sail, glaring up at the three men eyeing her warily. They'd brought her to a cell with iron bars, and the gate was open. She could still escape.

"Don't even think about making a break for it," said a man with red hair and a scruffy beard. "Be easier on us if we slit your throat, and that's exactly what we'll do if you don't stay calm."

A dilapidated mattress stuffed with moldy straw was the sole furnishing of the cell. There were no portholes, and the only light came from a few sputtering candles and a lantern held by a bald man with beady eyes. The lantern swayed in time with the rocking of the ship, causing the shadows in the cell to do an eery dance.

"Here, put this on," said the red-haired man.

He removed his shirt, a cotton long-sleeved garment that perhaps one day had been white, and threw it at her. She grimaced, making no move to pick it up. Better to be naked than to wear a pirate's smelly shirt.

"She needs pants, too," said the third man, who was tall and wiry and wore a large silver hoop earring. Riella felt the intense urge to rip it out.

"Yeah, go get her some pants, Berolt," said the bald man, his eyes on the siren. "I ain't giving her mine. How about you?"

The red-haired man shrugged and plodded up the stairs, leaving her alone with the other two pirates. They gave each other a long look while seeming to silently debate something between themselves. A chill of premonition came over Riella, and she twitched the cotton shirt off the floor, after all.

She pulled the garment over her head and body, feeding the chains through the oversized sleeves and letting the hem fall. The ballooning fabric covered her body to the knees. Riella had never worn clothes before, and she did not like it. But she disliked the sick, uneasy feeling these men evoked in her more.

The bald man took a step toward her. He held the lantern aloft, emphasizing the cragginess of his face. The tall one glanced at the stairs, before huddling next to his friend and bearing down on Riella.

"I ain't never seen a siren with legs before," said the bald man while leering at her body. "Have you, Lovel?"

"Nah, Terrick. Me neither."

Riella tensed, readying herself for a fight. Weakened or not, she would not tolerate foulness from these men. But her legs buckled when she tried to stand and she fell painfully to her knees. Were these limbs faulty? Or was she just not used to them?

Terrick leaned in closer. "Show us a look between yer legs, why don't you?" he breathed. "If you're shy, I'll be a gentleman and show you mine first."

Riella grasped the lantern, ignoring the scalding heat of the glass, and smashed it into his face in a blaze of orange. He shrieked, trying to put out the flames with his flailing arms. The fuel from the lantern doused his clothes, his frantic movements making the fire spread.

As the other one, Lovel, lunged at her, she ripped out his stupid earring. Blood spurted across the cell wall and she cackled, despite herself. He bellowed in pain, groping at the handle of the dagger on his hip.

Before he could seize it, she slammed him bodily into the iron bars. It took a considerable amount of her effort, and he had not died on impact like she'd expected. She was shocked at how weak she was now—she was nearly as weak as a man.

Terrick stumbled from the cell to where a pail of water caught leaks from the deck above. He upended the bucket on his head, shouting in relief as the flames went out. Red welts covered his face and neck, his skin steaming.

"Siren, you are dead!" shouted Lovel, his shoulder drenched in blood.

He charged at her with outstretched hands. She punched him in the face before he could touch her, then spun him around and slung one of the chains tightly around his neck, strangling him. He gurgled in panic, his legs kicking wildly.

Distracted, Riella hardly registered the heavy footsteps descending the stairs. An immense shadow loomed over her, blocking the candlelight. Terrick still cursed and hollered from outside of the cell.

A large hand clamped down on her shoulder and jerked her backward. Lovel scurried to the corner of the cell, coughing and massaging his throat. Riella was lifted into the air by the mountain of a man who'd arrived in the brig without a word.

He dragged her up, level with his eye-line, crashing her wrists into the wall over her head and holding them there. Her already-useless legs reached new levels of uselessness as they dangled in the air, far off the ground.

To her disbelief, she could not throw him off, no matter how hard she bucked her body. His arms seemed to be threaded with steel, the muscles under his tanned, heavily tattooed skin bulging. She screamed in his face in frustration and tried to bite him.

He reacted by slamming her wrists harder against the wall.

"Stop moving." His deep, low voice washed over her body, like a wave. "And stop trying to kill my men."

Emboldened, Terrick jeered at her while edging nearer. "Yeah, it's bloody rude. I reckon we ought to teach her a lesson. Right, boss?"

Lovel closed in too, a vicious smile spreading across his blood-splattered face. Riella fought against the large man's grip, to no avail. If he was the boss, that meant he was the captain of this ship. No man became a leader of the Dark Tide Clan without claiming the title through ruthless violence. Her situation had drastically worsened.

Although he looked and smelled cleaner than the others, she suspected that had to do with his rank. His square jaw was stubbled and his dark hair was disheveled by sea spray and wind. Tattoos covered his broad chest, peeking through the material of his shirt, and a heavy gold pendant hung on a chain around his neck. The symbol stamped on the pendant was familiar, but she had bigger concerns than his jewelry. He likely stole it, anyway. The man was a pirate.

"Now, what are we going to do with you?" he muttered as he inspected her.

His green-gray eyes swept over her face and down her body, which was mostly hidden in the baggy borrowed garment.

As the other two men gawped at her, true fear bloomed in Riella's chest. She was completely at their mercy. Desperately, she tried to conceal this new and unwelcome feeling, but her face betrayed her. Lips trembling and brows knitting together, she squeezed her eyes shut, just for a moment, to collect herself.

Willing herself to be strong, she opened her eyes and jutted her chin. In defiance, she glared directly into the captain's eyes. She may not have had a tail or been at full strength, but she was still a siren. She would show this brute exactly what that meant.

He frowned thoughtfully, returning her gaze. She sensed that he was distracted by whatever was going through his mind. She decided to make the most of it, and that the situation was dire enough to utilize her siren charm.

Seduction was always a last resort for Riella, because she much preferred the simplicity of fighting. But now, running her tongue across her bottom lip, she gazed deep into his eyes, praying she'd retained the ability to hypnotize and lightly stupefy mortal men.

"Come closer," she whispered, so that he would not quite hear her over the creaking of the ship and the rush of the waves. "I bid you, come closer."

Obediently, his eyes slid unfocused. He leaned toward her, even as his hands remained clamped on her wrists. Seizing her chance, she head-butted him as hard as she could, making the bones in his face crack. Blood sprayed across her skin and his grip on her finally loosened. The man grunted, screwing his eyes shut and reaching for her.

But she was too quick. Riella snatched up the sharpest,

longest shard of glass from the broken lantern. Then she rose, driving the point of the shard into the man's chest.

With satisfaction, she felt the glass breach his ribs and plunge directly into his heart.

CHAPTER 4

*R*iella killed the man. She knew she had. So, why wasn't he dying?

Her back against the wall, she watched in confusion as he swayed on the spot, grasping at the shard blindly. His eyeballs had turned entirely black and hazy, like storm clouds. Lovel and Terrick backed away.

"Oh, you're in trouble, girl," said Terrick with a sneer.

The tall man gritted his teeth.

"Sirens will be the bloody death of me," he said, closing his fingers around the shard and pulling. "I will end you for that."

Blood spilled out as he dislodged it, dripping down his linen shirt like liquid rubies. But there was less bleeding than there should've been. Right before her eyes, the wound began to close, his body healing itself.

He raised his stormy gaze to her. With a jolt, she realized she was now in more danger than ever. Not only was this man enormous and strong, but apparently he was invincible, too.

Without looking away, he barked an order at his men.

"Leave us."

"But we wanna watch you gut her—" started Terrick with a whine.

"Now!"

Lovel and Terrick stomped up the stairs, muttering to each other.

The man snatched up her wrists and slammed them into the wall again. Despite knowing she could not kill him, she struggled against his grip. She had never been this close to a man, except briefly and during active combat. The way he seemed to pin her down with not only his hands but also his intense gaze was unnerving.

Grudgingly, she could see why he was the boss, with a quality like that.

"I've never put fear in a siren's eyes before," he said in a quiet voice. His lips curled into a wicked smile. "And not for lack of trying."

He shook his head as if shooing a fly and his eyes cleared, returning to a normal color.

Riella exhaled through her nose and looked away, her cheeks flushing. "If you kill me, you'll restart the war with the sirens."

She didn't know if this was true. No one was even aware she was on the ship, except the pirates. He could easily kill her and dispose of her body without anyone finding out.

"That's a risk I'm willing to take." He tapped his thumbs against her wrists, like a pulse. "Now, how do you want to go? Should I repay you in kind with glass to the heart?"

Riella shifted under his grip. Her hands were going numb.

"Coward," she spat. "You would corner me in a cell and kill me in the dark, where no one can see? Where is your honor?"

"I don't owe you honor." He snarled at her and drilled her

wrists harder into the wall. "Your kind slaughtered my closest friends."

"And I hope their deaths were painful! You don't belong in the ocean, you imbecile!"

He laughed in her face, catching her by surprise. "Nor do you, any longer, so it seems."

A set of footsteps came down the stairs. The ginger-haired man, Berolt, returned with a garment in his hands. He tossed it to her from outside the cell, staying safely behind her tormentor.

"Here you go," he said. "Courtesy of Drue, our cabin boy. He's the only lad on board whose clothes I thought might fit ya. They're clean enough, I think," he added, although he sounded doubtful.

Overhead, boots crossed the deck. There seemed to be far more than before, causing a twinge of anxiety in Riella. Her eyes darted from the trousers to the pirate who'd pinned her.

"Are you going to kill me or not?" she asked him, raising her brows. If she was going to die, it wouldn't be with fear in her eyes or heart. "Because I would welcome death over staring into your face for a moment longer. Get on with it."

Berolt cleared his throat loudly. "Ah, Jarin?"

"What?" replied the man without turning around.

"A word?"

"Siren," he murmured in her face. "I will filet you if you try anything."

While maintaining stern eye contact, the man named Jarin slowly loosened his iron grip on her wrists. She fell to the floor, her strange new limbs crumbling under her. They *had* to be faulty. There couldn't be the same legs every other human walked around on with such ease.

Keeping the siren in his peripheral vision, he pulled Berolt aside.

"How'd it go?" he asked in a low voice.

"Ah, I believe he got what he was looking for. Still dunno what it is. You might have more luck getting it out of him. He loves you like a son."

Jarin grunted. "And hates me like a rival."

"To be fair, you are. But I have an idea—"

Berolt lowered his voice further while Riella fumbled with the trousers. The first time she tried putting them on, she somehow managed to get them backward. They did fit well enough, though, staying up over her hips once she had them on the right way.

After hearing Berolt's words, Jarin paused, glancing over at Riella. For some time, he continued muttering back and forth with his crew mate, and she heard very little of it. Not that she cared about the plotting of pirates. She only cared about leaving this ship. And decapitating Jarin, if she could manage it. See if he could survive *that*.

Berolt darted up the stairs and returned less than a minute later, handing tools to Jarin.

"Siren," he barked, striding to her with a mallet and chisel. He stood over her, pointing the mallet. "I'm going to remove your manacles. If you attack me, I will cave in your pretty little skull."

She glared up at him, grinding her teeth. It wasn't like she had a lot of options. With a jerk of her head, she nodded her assent.

"There's been a change of plan." He squatted in front of her. "I'll make you a deal. I will let you off this ship when we arrive at Klatos, if you kill the captain. Artus."

"You're not the captain?"

"No. Second in command."

Riella blinked. "So, you want me to kill . . . the leader of the Dark Tide Clan?"

She would've done that for free, and for fun, but she kept that to herself.

"That's right. I need him dead, and none of us can do it."

"Why not?"

"Blood oath. You wouldn't understand."

She scoffed. "Because pirates are so mysterious and complex. No one could *possibly* fathom the depths of your stupid rules and covenants."

He shrugged. "Take it or leave it. But I'd still owe you death, siren, to be clear."

Despite her rage and annoyance, Riella thought of Seraphine. The elf would perish if Riella left her with Polinth. She had to get back to the Black Cliffs.

"Sure, I'll kill him," said the siren. "But then you'll take me to the Black Cliffs. And if you want to kill me, it's in a fair fight. Not while I'm slumped in the brig of your stinky ship."

A flash of curiosity crossed his features. "What's at the Black Cliffs?"

"Yes or no?"

He grabbed both chains with one hand and wrenched her toward him without warning. She pitched forward, barely catching herself with her knees. Her feet and toes grappled with the dirty floor, trying to gain purchase while he held the chains steady.

"You've got a deal," said Jarin, lining up the chisel over the bolt of one of the manacles.

Berolt looked on in silence.

The commander drew the mallet high over his head. As he brought it down on the chisel, she willed herself not to flinch. The mallet made perfect contact, driving the chisel into the bolt. The manacle fell open like a clamshell. He opened the second one with the same precision.

Riella wrested her hands away, rubbing the raw skin of her wrists and sighing with relief. She prodded at the lily-white soles of her feet with her fingers, wondering how she'd get around on them. They'd be a disadvantage when fighting the captain, but she'd just have to make do.

The commander collected the chains and tools and slung them out of the cell, where they landed in a pile with a clatter. He got up and went to leave, but stopped at the last second. "How'd that happen, anyway?" he asked. "Your legs?"

"Sorcery," she replied with a grumble.

He folded his arms, the veins prominent over his tanned muscles. "Polinth?"

CHAPTER 5

Riella did a double-take. "Yes, it was Polinth. How'd you know?"

"I knew someone he studied with. His reputation precedes him." He frowned at her as she struggled to stand. "You better work out how to use your legs, if you're to hold up your end of the bargain. You'll save me a mutiny, and you get to live another day."

"How generous of you."

"Hey, you stabbed me in the heart. I'll seek retribution however I see fit. It'll give me immense pleasure to slay you grandly, and in broad daylight, for all to see."

"You are your mother's son, alright," mumbled Berolt, half to himself.

The commander gave him a sharp look, but said nothing.

Riella pulled herself onto her feet by gripping the wooden panels of the wall. The ship hit a wave, sending the bow high and the floor rocking. She stumbled and fell forward onto her hands and knees, causing her to hiss and spit in frustration.

"Gods, I better make sure you can walk," said Jarin. "Artus

is no puppy-dog and you'll need the use of your legs. Go to the helm, will you?" he added to Berolt, who nodded and left up the stairs.

"I don't need your help," she replied, standing. "Ouch!"

The soles of her feet were uncomfortably sensitive and she'd stepped on a rock. The pirate offered his hand and she ignored it.

"Take my hand, for gods' sake. It won't kill you to touch a man, you know." His gravelly voice became serious. "You need to be able to defend yourself, don't you?"

"You threatened to kill me a minute ago!"

A deep frown creased Jarin's brow. "Yeah. But I'm not talking about death. I'm talking about what Terrick and Lovel would do to you."

"Oh." Riella's face grew warm. "Well, I was handling it."

His frown cleared and he snorted. "That you were." After contemplating her for a moment, he offered his hand again. "Here."

She pushed up the sleeves of the oversized shirt and took his hand. His skin was warm and his palms were slightly calloused.

"Clothes are so uncomfortable," she said, to distract from the strangeness of holding a man's hand. "I don't understand why you all wear them. Bodies aren't shameful and they shouldn't be something to cover up."

"In your opinion. I don't want to see what my crew are rocking beneath their clothes."

Riella gained her balance, her feet flat on the rocking floor. Holding onto Jarin's hand did help keep her steady. Her core muscles tensed, distributing her body weight evenly on her legs.

"Good point," she conceded. "I don't, either."

"Go on. Take a few steps."

Riella walked several shaky steps, frowning fiercely down

at her pale feet in concentration. Jarin's boots moved alongside her.

"Makes it all the better, though," he murmured. "When a member of the fairer sex finally does take her clothes off for you."

Caught off guard, she looked up at him mid-step. A wave buffeted the hull and sent her sideways. Jarin broke her fall with his arm around her waist, hauling her back to her feet.

While the waves subsided and the floor stopped careening, Riella held the pirate's muscular forearms. For some reason, he didn't make her skin instinctively crawl, the way the other men did, despite that he'd promised to kill her. Why was that? Because he was handsome? She would never be that shallow, would she?

She'd always thought men were all the same—probably because she'd never had cause to distinguish between them. If they were in the ocean, they were the enemy. It was simple.

But now, forced to consort with men up close, she was fast realizing it was helpful to gauge them as individuals. Polinth was vile. Berolt had shown her kindness. Terrick, vile. Lovel, vile.

Jarin? Remained to be seen. He *had* blackmailed her into killing someone.

"Who's the sorcerer you know?" she asked, wanting to break the loaded silence between them. Jarin was so close she could feel the steady in and out of his breath. "The one who studied with Polinth."

"What's at the Black Cliffs?" he repeated, conspicuously dodging her question.

"Someone who I promised would live. And someone I promised would die. Who's the sorcerer you know?"

A horn blared outside, sending a shiver through Riella's body. She'd heard that ominous sound many times before. During the war, the Dark Tide Clan would use it to signal to each other's ships that sirens were attacking. To her, it meant a fight was imminent.

Were sirens approaching the ship? Was it possible that her friends had somehow found her?

The effect of the signal on the commander was instantaneous. He released her hand and gathered up the tools and chains.

"Kill Artus the first chance you get." He slammed the cell door shut with Riella inside. "Doesn't need to be anything fancy—just get it done. Alright?"

"Why's the horn sounding?" she asked, pressing her face against the cold bars.

Without answering, he took the stairs two at a time, leaving the siren alone.

Before long, she had her answer anyway. The floor tilted sharply from the force of shifting water, and men shouted. Another ship was approaching.

"Ahoy!" someone yelled. "Incoming!"

There was swearing and yelling and men running. They did not seem to be under attack, like she hoped. Indeed, some of the men whooped with glee.

To her relief, no one else came down the stairs. It seemed the Dark Tide Clan were well and truly distracted. She practiced walking while she waited to learn what was happening on deck.

The iron bars were helpful, giving her something to hold as she wobbled along the filthy floor. Sunlight beamed down the stairs as the sun rose. With relentless practice, the siren could do laps around the cell. She still felt like a mutant, but at least she would be a mutant who could walk.

The rowdiness on the deck died down, yet no one came to the brig. She was left alone for so long that she began wishing for another fight with a pirate, just for something to do.

The ship was definitely moving, and rather quickly, it seemed. Were they going to Klatos, as the commander said? He was a pirate—he very well could've lied. Perhaps they were en route to one of the many island hideouts controlled by the Dark Tide Clan, and he'd told her a lie to placate her.

A deserted island might not have been so bad for Riella, though. It'd be easier to locate her friends from a secluded beach than the crowded city of Klatos. Sirens avoided the city's bay, as a rule. Humans befouled the water and the rudders of their vessels were dangerous.

At long last, boots stomped down the stairs.

An unfamiliar man approached the cell, his hands behind his back. Another figure stood in his shadow. Despite the man's calm, impassive expression, Riella's skin broke out in goosebumps as he surveyed her.

His black hair was graying at the temples, his cheeks were pockmarked, and his body was huge and barrel-chested. The copious tattoos and sun-worn skin told the story of a man who'd sailed the seas for a long time. He wore a red and blue jacket, frayed at the cuffs, with silver buttons.

The man smiled and she was reminded of a sea-snake, the way no warmth reached his eyes. A gold tooth glinted from one side of his mouth.

"I'm Artus, Captain of the Pandora. This is Fletch." Riella assumed he meant the man behind him, though Artus made no gesture at him. "Jarin said I'd want to meet you." His eyes traveled slowly down her body and up again. "He was right about that."

When Artus looked at her, he somehow made her feel like she was still naked. She barely resisted the urge to grab his jacket collar through the bars and smash his face into them. The only reason she held back was because she didn't trust that Jarin would keep his word once she'd killed the captain.

"Where's Jarin now?" She flexed her fingers behind her back, ready to attack Artus when she got an answer.

"He's carrying out my orders." Artus produced a key from his pocket and opened the cell gate. "I'll be seeing you safely to your destination."

Her fingers relaxed fractionally. "My destination?"

"We're about to dock at Klatos. I'll take you ashore. Somewhere pleasant and fine, where you can be aided. You're in luck, because I planned to visit this particular establishment anyway, so I'll take you myself. Grand, is it not, to be escorted by a captain?" He beckoned, a note of impatience entering his voice. "Come, now."

Riella chewed her lip, weighing her options. Perhaps she was better off disembarking with this captain. Unlike Jarin, Artus was offering to take her ashore without her needing to do anything in return. Once in Klatos, she could find her way to the Black Cliffs. After all, if she killed the captain now, then what? She was still in the brig of a ship crawling with pirates.

Fletch watched her through one watery eye, a patch over the other. He stood with a pronounced lean and had frizzy hair.

"Fine," she said. "Take me ashore."

Let Jarin kill the captain himself. She owed the commander nothing. And if he really wanted that fight with her, he could find her.

Bracing herself against the rhythmic tilt of the ship, she took a few tentative steps from the cell. A square of blue sky emerged as she climbed the stairs, seagulls floating on the air currents. The gulls meant that land was indeed nearby.

Artus poked her in the back with his finger, making her clench her fists.

"Up you go," he said. "The city awaits."

CHAPTER 6

*J*arin climbed the stairs from the brig, leaving the siren in the cell.

Had his luck finally changed? Would she dispense with Artus, leaving him to take command of the ship? A siren was one of the few beings strong enough to kill Artus. Nor was she bound by the Dark Tide blood oath that dictated no pirate could slay the captain. It couldn't hurt to make her try, anyway.

The fear in her eyes when he pinned her wrists confused him, though. He hadn't known a siren could fear humans. They were like the ocean made sentient, in all its majesty and untamable rage. As a sailor, he knew well enough to fear and respect the ocean. Never had he known it to fear him in return. Polinth sure did a number on her. Jarin would almost feel sorry for her, if she'd not plunged a shard of glass into his heart.

He put the siren from his mind. There were bigger concerns, like the cryptic words the old Seer, Ferrante, muttered to Jarin the last time they saw one another. The old man said that fate itself would rest on this expedition and the trinket Artus sought.

The deck was a hive of activity as the captured ship drew nearer. Jarin grimaced when the ship's flag came into view, tattered and half-burned on the mast. Artus had taken a royal Zermes ship, which the captain swore he wasn't going after. He said he was setting out for a Hataran merchant vessel, lest they attract the ire of the royal navy. But then, when had Artus ever kept his word?

The captain valued infamy more than he valued gold. As a pirate, that made him weak. Artus was driven to conquer and command and bring everything to heel, including the ocean. His arrogance was a threat to the entire clan. Jarin planned to neutralize that threat, but for the moment, he had to go along with the captain. When he got the chance, he'd send Artus below deck to be mauled by the siren.

The captain's most trusted lackeys climbed rope ladders onto the Pandora, hauling crates of artifacts from the royal ship. Artus had already returned to his usual spot at the helm of the Pandora, laughing with Terrick, whose neck was stained with blood from the siren attack.

Jarin cracked the lid of one of the crates, finding a random jumble of artifacts inside: stone tablets, scrolls, brass instruments, and embroideries. Artus had received a tip-off about the shipment in a bar, the last time they docked at Klatos. Based on that tip-off, he mounted the attack. But for what?

"Jarin, my boy."

Artus swaggered across the deck toward him, shoving crew members out of the way. As always, Fletch tailed him like a pet jackal. Berolt had been right about Artus's mood. He grinned broadly, his gold tooth catching the sun, and spread his arms wide.

"I see you held down the ship in my absence," he said,

clapping Jarin on the back, like a father to his son. "Good lad."

Jarin rubbed the back of his neck, nodding at the crate. "This is what we baited the wrath of the Crown for?" He picked up a burnished candlestick and turned it in his hand. "Looks like a pile of junk to me."

"Ah." Artus leaned in close, lowering his voice. The stench of stale tobacco washed over Jarin. "This is but the leftovers of the real feast." He patted the pocket of his red and blue jacket. "Got myself an honest to gods' treasure map. It'll take me to the Amulet of Delphine, worth more than any amount of gold."

The Seer Ferrante had predicted that Artus would pilfer such a trinket. A *rare ocean jewel*, he'd said, that would alter the fate of Jarin and the whole clan.

He folded his arms. "And what's the amulet for?"

The captain wheezed with laughter. "It gives life."

Jarin frowned. No trinket could grant life, could it? Perhaps Artus was misdirecting him.

But whatever the amulet was for, it couldn't be good, since Artus wanted it. Jarin stayed far away from magic, if he could help it. Which, of course, he couldn't. He carried magic around in his veins, against his will.

"Alright," he replied. "I hope it's worth having the royal fleet after us. We'll have to set sail for the open waters right away."

"Gods, you're a sour one. Even more than usual." He fixed Jarin with a shrewd eye. "What's gotten into you? I'm sending Terrick and Lovel to scuttle the ship, along with everyone on board. No one left to tell the tale. It'll be presumed lost at sea —a tragic accident. Happens all the time, ya know."

"How many are still alive?" asked Jarin.

Artus waved his hand. "Dozen or so. Terrick and Lovel are keen to take care of 'em, don't you worry."

Terrick and Lovel were selecting weapons from a chest with open excitement, arming themselves for the foul assignment. Blood-thirsty hounds. Anyone still alive on that royal ship would soon wish they weren't, once that pair were set loose on them. The commander had to make sure that didn't happen, and he'd have to be subtle about it, or Artus would become paranoid about Jarin undermining him again.

The captain had forbidden his crew from torturing and raping, but only in words. In truth, he turned a blind eye. He enjoyed the added fear that the exploits of scum like Lovel and Terrick evoked in people.

When Jarin overthrew Artus, Terrick and Lovel would be among the first to walk the plank. Or be thrown overboard—Jarin wasn't picky about the details. May the weight of their sins drag them to the bottom of the ocean.

The Clan had once adhered to codes, and valued honor. But, it seemed the only men who survived the war with the sirens had been the most vicious. Half the crew were now little more than butchers. At the heart of the blackness was Artus himself. He needed to be rooted out and disposed of.

"I'll take Drue to scuttle the ship," said Jarin. "Be good for him to get his first blood."

Artus shrugged and waved his hand. "Go ahead. Do it near Skull Cave and take the rowboat to Klatos. Meet us at the docks. We'll set sail this evening."

"You don't still mean to go to Klatos?"

"Lad, what did I just say? No one'll have realized the ship's missing yet. It's the best time to dock."

Jarin thought of his deal with the siren. Would she keep her word and kill the captain? Nothing stopped her from making a deal with Artus, instead.

The commander couldn't go back on his decision to take Drue to scuttle the ship, though. Artus had a shark's nose for blood, and he'd realize Jarin was up to something. He'd have to be careful.

When he spoke, he tried to keep his voice casual. "There's a siren in the brig. Quite a sight."

Artus snorted. "How so?"

"Go see for yourself."

The captain smoothed the ratty lapels on his jacket. "I might. Now get going. I've a thirst for the many delights of Klatos."

Praying it was the last time he'd see Artus alive, Jarin rowed to the royal ship with Drue and Berolt.

They set sail for Skull Cave, adjusting the rigging as they stepped over dead bodies. Once they'd started the ship moving, Drue helped Jarin haul the bodies overboard. The cabin boy retched several times, but didn't beg out of his duties.

He was a stocky lad who'd stowed away on the Pandora at Port Hyacinth in the wintertime. The deep bruising on his face hinted why he'd left his home, and he'd proven himself a diligent enough worker to earn a place on the crew. He reminded Jarin of himself and his own beginnings. He knew what it meant to have no one to turn to and nowhere to go.

"Are we going to kill the folk down below?" asked Drue after they'd dispensed with the bodies.

He gazed at the blood-stained deck, as if hypnotized.

"Do you want to?" replied the commander.

The boy shook his head, brushing his messy black hair from his eyes.

"Good. Stay up here with Berolt. We'll leave the ship at Skull Cave and go ashore in the rowboats."

The commander went below deck to see how many crew members Artus had left alive. As he descended the stairs, he tore off his shirt and tied it around the bottom of his face.

Since he was not going to slaughter these people, he needed to conceal his identity.

Jarin already had enough blood on his hands. More blood than could ever come off. All Dark Tide Clan pirates did, except maybe Drue.

More than a dozen men and youths were beaten and gagged in the brig. Their eyes widened in fury and fear when he entered, cutlass on his belt. The cell was locked with a padlock, the key left on a shelf near the stairs. He turned the key over in his hand, deciding how to manage the situation. Although he meant to let the crew live, he also needed to prevent them from reaching Klatos before the Pandora set sail later that evening.

In the end, he replaced the padlock with ropes tied in hundreds of complicated knots. He used mostly constrictor and bowline knots, pulling them tight with each loop. By the time he'd finished, even the most experienced sailor would take a day and night to unravel the entire mess.

"You." He pointed at the smallest youth. "Over here, now."

The kid obeyed, shuffling to the iron bars.

"Give me your hands."

Jarin cut the bindings around the youth's wrists, noting the weak-looking nature of his hands. He wasn't a sailor. The kid would be lucky to set the crew free before tomorrow, by which time the Pandora would be long gone.

The boy dolefully began picking at the knots, frowning in confusion.

"Have fun with that, kid," said Jarin with a laugh.

Back on deck, the dark and jagged silhouette of Skull Cave appeared in the distance. The cave was deadly to sailors because of the unseen rocks beneath the water at its mouth. None but the most skilled sailors could navigate them, and every crew except the Dark Tide Clan steered well clear of the area.

The clan kept rowboats and supplies hidden inside, and the water-filled caves led to the outskirts of Klatos. It was the ideal place to enter the city by stealth. They'd row through the caves to a desolate beach and scale the city's walls. But a strong swimmer could dive through the underwater caverns that ran from Skull Cave to Klatos and arrive in the middle of the merchant district.

"What're you looking forward to doing in Klatos?" asked Jarin, as Berolt and Drue fed the anchor overboard at the mouth of the cave.

He'd said it to lighten the mood, after the gruesome task of disposing of the bodies, but the boy's answer made Jarin's stomach drop like the anchor.

"Ah, while you and Berolt were busy rigging up the royal ship, Artus pulled me aside and said he wanted to take me to Madame Quaan's." He frowned, scratching his head. "To celebrate my first blood. Said he's taking the siren, because Lovel told him what she's got between her legs. Said a rare ocean jewel like that will be worth a pot of gold."

"Rare ocean jewel?" he repeated.

Gods. He'd been wrong about Ferrante's prediction. Had the old man been referring to the bloody siren, not the Amulet of Delphine?

If the siren obeyed Jarin's command and killed Artus, she'd be safe from the captain's scheming. But would a siren obey Jarin? Especially if Artus went down there with the intent to take her ashore.

Jarin shared a grave look with Berolt.

They should've known Lovel would go straight to the captain to stir trouble and curry favor. Perhaps Artus had even let Jarin do the scuttle just to get rid of him. There was something bigger going on than Jarin understood. He wished for the hundredth time that the damn Seer would be specific, for once. Jarin swore the old man got off on causing confusion and mayhem.

Berolt rubbed his calloused hands together. "What do you want to do, boss?"

The blue and white water surged within the mouth of the cave, stalactites hanging from the roof like teeth. Swimming the underwater caverns would be the fastest way to get to her. His mother always warned him to never dispel the murmurings of a Seer, no matter how infuriating. And his mother, for all her faults, was seldom wrong about the mystical arts. Jarin needed that damn siren back. Or at least, to keep her out of Artus's hands.

He gave orders to Berolt. "Take Drue in the rowboat, like we planned. I'll meet you at the docks with the siren after I find her. Ferrante said she'll decide the destiny of the clan, so I want her with us, not Artus. Nor in Madame Quaan's seedy den, because who knows where she'd end up. In the meantime, get ready. If Artus survives the day, we mutiny tonight."

The commander climbed onto the bow of the ship and dove headfirst into the churning water.

CHAPTER 7

Riella stepped onto the gangway of the Pandora, blinking in the bright sunshine. Ships lined the bustling docks as far as the eye could see in both directions.

Beyond the docks loomed Klatos. She'd seen the hilly capital of Zermes kingdom from a distance, of course, where it appeared otherworldly and enchanting. Up close, the cityscape was imposing. The sheer density of the buildings was difficult for Riella to comprehend. How was it possible for humans to live all stacked on top of each other?

"Welcome to Klatos," said Artus, behind her. "Let's get a move on. I've got a lot to do before we set sail again."

Riella walked the gangway, holding the railing for support. The dock was crowded with sailors, merchants, and people in raggedy clothing begging for coin. Seagulls flocked to the area, diving for scraps of food. The scent of grilled squid mingling with the fresh smell of the ocean made Riella want to gag.

A general hush went over the dock when Artus and Riella stepped off the Pandora. The stares of so many humans made her want to turn and dive straight into the water. If only she could have done it and not drowned.

"Dark Tide Clan," someone murmured as they passed.

The captain ignored the attention, walking ahead of Riella toward the city fringe. Fletch stayed behind her, lumbering along in silence. The docks opened onto a street paved with alarmingly uneven cobblestones. She hesitated, unsure if she was ready to negotiate such terrain.

Artus hooked his thumbs into his belt. "Fletch can carry you, if you like?" he suggested with a wink.

"No," she replied sharply. "I can walk."

"Suit yourself." The captain continued onto the road.

Riella was about to follow, afraid of getting lost in the crowd, when a very tall man stepped in front of her, blocking her path. He glared down at her with cold eyes and a set jaw. He had a shaved head and wore rags.

"Move," she said to him. "You're standing too close to me. I don't like it."

His only response was to take a step nearer. She sized him up. Even in her weakened form, she was strong enough to throw this man.

Noticing Riella was no longer behind him, Artus circled back. "Ah, this is Tregor. Old shipmate of mine. No longer sails though, does he?"

Tregor shifted his gaze to the captain and grunted.

Artus made some kind of signal with his hand, then addressed Riella in a cheery voice. "He's deaf, you see. Can't hear a thing you say. These days, he begs on the docks to get by." The captain's eyes flashed with mischief. "Veteran of war, he is."

She exhaled in realization. Tregor turned his cold focus back to her, his sun-scabbed hands balling into fists. He'd been deafened by Sirensong.

Artus reached into his pocket and pulled out a copper

coin. With his thumb, he flicked it at Tregor, who made no move to catch it. The coin clattered to the walkway, while the deaf man continued to glare at Riella.

"Siren, Fletch, let's go," said Artus over his shoulder, already climbing the cobblestoned hill.

Her heart thudding with a complicated mix of emotions, she sidestepped Tregor and followed the captain. It took a lot of concentration to keep up with him while navigating the cobblestones. Pausing at a rise, she looked back.

Tregor stooped to pick up the coin and then loped toward the street hawkers, most of whom sold food.

Facing a person who'd been hurt by sirens was a new experience for her. She told herself that he probably deserved his injuries. If humans didn't want to be maimed by sirens, they only had to stay out of the ocean.

She just wished didn't look so pitiful, collecting the solitary copper coin from the dirty ground. It gave her a feeling she did not enjoy. The fact that he waited until they left somehow made the feeling worse.

All in all, she disliked being on land so far.

The stones were searing, which made her walk faster. More and more, she understood the value of shoes, and she vowed to procure a pair for herself as soon as possible. The only people who seemed to be barefoot were vagrants, like Tregor. That must've been exactly what she looked like in her filthy oversized clothes.

Even away from the docks, people stared at Riella. A small boy ran right up to her and tugged at the sleeve of her shirt, trying to get her attention. She shook him off in what she believed was a gentle fashion.

The humans she usually handled were pirates—large men —not small children. With accidental force, she sent the boy sprawling onto the cobblestones. He promptly burst into tears.

Artus roared with laughter, throwing her an appreciative glance over his shoulder. "Can't blame the little fella for being curious, siren. But you'll need to be more accommodating than that where we're going."

A woman wearing an apron ran to the boy and consoled him. The woman cringed away from Riella and refused eye contact, as though she feared the siren. Then she realized, the woman *did* fear her.

Riella, who was duty-bound to protect innocents, felt like her entire world had been turned upside down. Which, in essence, it had been. None of this was right. She was not where she was supposed to be, nor doing what she was supposed to be doing. Being caught between two worlds had rendered her useful to no one, including herself.

Fletch ushered her along and she let him, wanting to leave the scene of the woman and her crying child.

By now, her siren friends would have well and truly realized she'd met with trouble. They would have searched for her, and probably still were, but they would've found nothing. With no trace of Riella, what else could the sirens do to help her? Very little. She was alone.

Worse than being alone, really, because she was tethered to Dark Tide Clan pirates, of all humans. As if that wasn't bad enough, she was also on the run from a lunatic sorcerer. His last words to her had been a warning about how she didn't know what she was doing. How awfully correct he had been.

But at least as long as she had legs, she could rescue Seraphine. And then kill him, so that he could never kidnap and torment anyone again. The siren promised the elf she would not die, and Riella meant to keep that promise.

"Halt!"

A pair of uniformed royal guards blocked Artus's path. They wore polished versions of the captain's blue and red jacket, with a crown insignia on the lapels that his lacked. Either he was a royal guard long ago, or he wore the jacket to mock them.

The guards wore silver helmets and carried swords in their belts.

"Who's this?" one demanded, lifting his chin at her.

Artus gave a laconic shrug. "A rare ocean jewel. We are en route to Madame Quaan's right now."

The guard's frown cleared, and he took a second look at Riella. "Is that right?" His voice was different now, having lost the clipped professionalism.

Artus offered his hand to the guard. After a moment's hesitation, he shook it. When the man withdrew his hand, gold flashed in his palm.

Bribery did not surprise Riella. But she was interested that Artus carried gold. If she could relieve him of it, she could buy her way to the Black Cliffs.

Who was this Madame Quaan? Perhaps she was a mage. Her name certainly sounded like it belonged to one. Riella decided to hold off on robbing him until she found out. There was no sense in sabotaging what might be a solution to her problems.

The glow of the royal palace became visible before the palace itself. The golden gleam warmed the façades of the buildings on the opposite side of the street. When Riella and her companions reached the top of a hill, the incredible structure came into view.

She stopped and stared in awe. Artus, who sweated in the heat, took the opportunity to remove his jacket and fold it over his arm with deliberate care. Fletch offered to take it, but the captain waved him away.

The palace seemed to touch the heavens, puffs of white cloud drifting around the highest steeples. Zermetic flags flew from the spires and the entire structure was made of pale golden stone, with gold accents and elaborate edging. Riella had never seen such human-made beauty. She had not known they were capable of it.

Sirens had castles and temples beneath the ocean—intricate structures carved out of stone. The buildings were deep and blue and cool and quiet. The exact opposite of the bright and hot airiness of this castle.

Land and sea truly were two different worlds, and almost never the twain met. Certainly, no human had ever swam to the depths of Zydenthis. Had any sea-dweller set eyes on the royal palace of Klatos before?

"And they call us criminals."

She broke from her reverie. It was Artus who'd spoken.

"What do you mean?" she asked.

He inclined his head at the palace and gave her a knowing look. "You think they built a monstrosity like that out of goodwill and fairy kisses? Royalty bleeds their subjects dry. Now, pirates? We're democratic. Aren't we, Fletch?" He did not even look at Fletch. "We vote for our leaders. And if we're bad leaders, we'll be ousted without ceremony. Not like these crooks. They prop up that sentient corpse, King Leonid, and expect the rest of us to kiss their feet."

"I'm sure it's no concern of mine," replied the siren.

"Ha. The goings-on of the palace have a way of affecting us all, sooner or later, whether we like it or not." He wiped his brow with the back of his massive arm. "Come on. Nearly there."

He pulled open the gate at an opulent house constructed on a city block of its own. Set well back from the street, the house had two levels. It was made of stone, and stained-glass windows glimmered purple and pink and orange in the afternoon sun. The yard was populated by olive trees and hedges. There was no signage.

"Who is Madame Quaan?" she asked Artus as he led her down the gravel path.

Fletch followed Riella more closely than ever, making her want to elbow him in the face.

"I told you," he replied with a shrug. "She'll help you out. Couldn't very well stay on the ship, could you? This is the best place for you."

His answer, as innocuous as it sounded, made her feel like a dark shadow had crossed over her, even though the sun still blazed.

The door opened as they approached, without needing to knock. An unsmiling man dressed in black robes held the doorknob. He surveyed the three with cool detachment, his gaze lingering on Riella.

"Welcome to Madame Quaan's," he said, stepping aside.

CHAPTER 8

The inside of the house was tranquil and cool, setting Riella at ease.

The robed man led them to a plush bar area, where three young and beautiful women sat at a table. The women stared at Riella and her companions, one of them even rising in her seat to get a better view. The siren automatically gravitated toward them. She yearned for female company after a long, hard day being around men.

Emerald and sapphire tones decorated the salon and a peculiar brass contraption played music from the corner. Small circular tables dotted the room and a demure young woman polished glasses behind the gilded bar.

"Do you seek an introduction?" asked the robed man of Artus.

"I do," he replied. "But first, I'll need an audience with Madame Quaan. In private."

The robed man nodded, glancing at Riella. "Follow me."

He disappeared down a hallway and the captain followed, along with Fletch.

Left alone at last, Riella approached the women. Their

faces were painted prettily and they wore elaborate hairstyles and luxurious dresses. She was relieved that none of them seemed to fear her, unlike the woman on the street.

"Look at you!" exclaimed a girl with golden-blonde curls. "Are you . . . a *siren*? You look like the ones I met on my sea voyage from Stathgate. You have the same otherworldly beauty. But how on *earth* do you have legs?"

She grasped Riella's hand and urged her to sit at the table. The siren shifted on the seat in an attempt to get comfortable. She'd never sat in one before and it was an odd sensation.

"I am a siren," she said in confirmation. "Or at least, I think I still am. It's a long story. But what is this place? Can anyone here perform magic?"

The women giggled.

"Oh, all of us can," said a woman with long red braids. "We're true magicians."

She winked at the siren.

Riella frowned, and took another look around the room, an awful suspicion dawning on her.

The woman with red hair touched Riella's elbow. "Listen, we'll take good care of you, okay? That's what we do at Madame Quaan's. We look out for each other. Life here isn't perfect, but if you're being brought in by the captain—" She inclined her head where Artus went with the robed man. The other women scowled at the mention of him. "—then I'm sure it'll be an improvement on whatever the pirates were doing to you. Are you injured?"

Riella tugged at the sleeve of her oversized shirt. "No, but I'm quite dirty. I was in a brig."

"We'll get you cleaned up," the woman continued. "We've got an hour or so before the first of them arrive. Apparently, we're getting a visitor from the palace today, which means lots of gold. So, your timing is sublime in that regard."

At the mention of coin, the siren perked up. "I need gold. I need to get to the Black Cliffs."

"We all need gold, darling. And to get far away from here." She put her slender hand on her prominent bust. "I'm Sehild. This is Odeya." The golden-blonde woman smiled and nodded. "And this is Yvette."

Sehild gestured to a tall, willowy woman with a mass of dark curls.

"I'm Riella," she replied. "But why did the captain bring me here?"

The women exchanged glances, their smiles fading.

"How long have you had legs?" asked Odeya in a gentle voice.

"Since yesterday."

Odeya winced and leaned back in her chair, picking at her varnished nails. The women paused and exchanged glances again, as if none of them wanted to be the one to speak.

"We are here for men to buy sex," said Yvette, apparently deciding it would be her to break the awkward silence. "Madame Quaan is our boss. Overlord, more like it. I believe the captain is in the back right now, negotiating his fee for bringing you here."

Riella's eyes narrowed, her suspicions confirmed. "He's *selling* me?"

Slavers often traversed the seas, and she knew this was the fate of many of the female captives. Never did she imagine she'd be among their number. She should've slaughtered Artus when she first laid eyes on him.

Jarin had been right about the captain—Artus deserved death.

"Yes, darling," said Sehild, in a far more soothing tone than Yvette's blunt declaration. "It could be worse, though. This is one of the better establishments in Klatos. We receive wealthy clientele, including men of the Court. Madame Quaan runs the place with an iron fist, but as long as you don't get on her bad side, you'll not see the end of her cane."

"Why don't you overthrow her?" asked Riella. "It sounds like she has plenty of gold for the taking. Slavers always do."

"She has Gerret," explained Yvette. "And friends in high places."

"Gerret? The man in the black robe?"

Yvette nodded. "He's vicious."

"I see."

Sirens killed slavers as a matter of principle. But when she and her friends intercepted slave ships, the captors on board were always male. Could she kill a woman, even if that woman was a slaver? She had no frame of reference for such a dilemma.

Life on land became more complicated by the minute, and she'd only been part of their mad world for less than a day.

Voices carried from the hallway, including a familiar male baritone. Artus was returning and she needed to decide how to proceed. It was best if he believed the transaction had gone seamlessly, to get rid of him.

Then, she'd find a way to deal with Madame Quaan and her black-robed man-servant. Jarin could deal with Artus. Helping these women was more important than a feud between pirates.

"Where does she keep her coin?" she hissed at Sehild, before the captain returned.

Sehild chewed her lip, concern darkening her pretty features. "In her study, downstairs at the end of the hallway. But it's protected by steel and magic, and all the exits from the building are locked."

Fletch and Artus walked back into the bar. This time, a tall and sinewy woman with severe features accompanied them. Her steel-gray hair was pulled into a tight bun and her black dress covered her entire body. On her hands, she wore black gloves.

At once, her eagle-like gaze focused on Riella. After inspecting the siren, she turned to Artus. When she addressed him, she did not bother lowering her voice.

"All seems fine. As a bonus, I would like to offer you some entertainment before you leave. What say you?"

A cretinous smile spread across the captain's face. "Wouldn't say no, Madame. We've the time."

Madame Quaan clapped her hands once. "Yvette. Sehild."

As obediently as puppets on strings, the women stood. They smoothed their voluminous skirts and went to Artus and Fletch. Without a backward glance, they led the two men into the shadowy depths of the hallway.

Riella dug her talons into her palms to stop herself from going after both men and tearing them to shreds. Gerret still lurked somewhere unseen, and she could not risk the other women getting hurt. She would have to be wise about her movements.

Madame Quaan waved her hand in Odeya's general direction. "Take her to the washroom. Get her ready. She'll meet the Count when he arrives."

"Yes, Madame," said Odeya, rising dutifully to her feet and indicating for Riella to follow her. "Right away."

The washroom was behind one of many doors lining the hallway. Riella noted the dark recess at the end of the corridor leading to Madame Quaan's study.

"I'll run a bath for you," said Odeya, closing the door behind them. As soon as they were alone, the golden-haired woman noticeably relaxed. "We'll wash that lovely hair of yours, and we have plenty of dresses to choose from."

The washroom was windowless, and constructed of white marble with dark veins running through it. A bathtub sat against one wall, next to a bench crammed with various bottles and jars of cosmetic potions. Garments bulged from a rack on hangers, in tulle and lace and silk of all colors.

There were also several full-length mirrors in the room, some facing each other. Riella stood in front of one, noting she could see every angle of herself.

"To make sure we look good from the front and back," said Odeya, rotating the tap handles over the bath.

Riella frowned, turning this way and that. She was familiar with her own reflection, of course, but standing in front of the mirrors showed more detail than she'd ever seen before. The longer she looked, the less she liked what she saw. How did that work?

As the water rose in the tub, it drew the siren. Suddenly, she couldn't bear to be out of the water for a moment longer. She stripped the smelly pirate garments from her body and stepped into the bath.

The water was hotter than she was used to, and devoid of salt, but the sensation was divine nonetheless. Her skin felt as though it was coming to life. With a contented sigh, she lay back and submerged herself fully in the water. The familiar silence and weightlessness made her heart sing.

But after some time, she began to choke. In her excitement, she had forgotten she needed to hold her breath underwater now, and inhaled a gulp of liquid. She sat up, coughing.

Odeya was staring at her in wonder. "How did this happen to you? I've never seen anything like it."

"A mage," said Riella with a splutter, as she regained her breath.

"And how do you feel about it?" She tilted her head. "I can hardly imagine what it'd be like to wake up with a tail, and live in the ocean. To have the opposite happen must be very peculiar."

"Feel?" repeated Riella.

Sirens weren't encouraged to feel, much less talk about their feelings. But since Polinth had changed her, she couldn't deny that her emotions had been stronger than usual. And more complicated.

She frowned, trying to find the right words.

"It feels lonely," she said, surprising herself. "I feel a bit sad. And angry. And afraid. And . . . something else."

"Excited?" suggested Odeya.

"Yes, actually. How did you know?"

The blonde woman smiled. "The way you look at everything around you. You're fascinated. But that's normal, don't worry. Even scary things can be exciting."

"Normal." She kicked her legs in the water. "What a strange thing to be."

Odeya washed the siren's hair with suds smelling of flowers. When Riella was clean and the water began to cool, she reluctantly stepped from the tub and dried off.

The more Riella used her legs, the stronger she realized they were. If she could master how to operate them to their full potential, she could do a lot of damage. They were certainly no tail, but she could adapt.

"Where will you go when we escape this place?" asked Riella as the other woman selected undergarments and a dress for her, laying them over a chair.

"I dare not say, unless I know it'll truly happen. I don't want to get my hopes up."

The siren furrowed her brow. "Of course it will happen."

Odeya just smiled sadly.

She helped Riella into an overly complicated array of sheer, frilly undergarments. The clips and straps made no sense, and Riella was already resigned to the fact that she'd have to simply rip them off when the time came to remove them.

Odeya helped her into a simple blue dress, cinched at the waist and sheer at the bust.

"Blue to match your eyes," said Odeya as she tightened the bustier. She fluffed Riella's hair, arranging it in waves around her face and shoulders. "Count Zemora is an odd man. He'll adore you, but don't let him push you too far. He will, if you let him. They're all like that."

Riella sat on the chair while Odeya helped her put on silk slippers. Like all of the clothes, wearing the shoes made her feel oddly constricted.

But, here on the land, it seemed that body parts needed the protection of garments—for more than one reason. Jarin had been right about that, too.

There was a light rapping on the door, in a distinct rhythm.

"Come in," called Odeya.

Yvette and Sehild were in states of semi-undress, their hair and makeup messy.

"Done," said Yvette, heaving a sigh and flopping down on the chair. "Until the next one."

"That captain is a vile man." Sehild wriggled out of her dress with Odeya's help. "Thank the heavens he's gone."

"Get anything good from him?" asked Odeya.

Yvette unlaced a hidden section of her bustier and two gold coins fell into her waiting palm.

"Madame gave him a hefty bag of gold for you, alright," she said to Riella.

"You stole that from Artus?" asked the siren.

"Yes." Yvette gave her a wary look. "What's it to you?"

"Nothing. I'm glad."

Yvette's face relaxed. From the hidden compartment, she also withdrew a battered piece of folded parchment. She opened it and frowned at the contents.

"What's that?" asked Sehild, lowering herself into the

bathtub naked, having arranged her red braids on top of her head to stay dry.

"I thought it might be a title or deed." Yvette shrugged. "But it's just some nonsense."

She tossed it onto the cosmetics bench and began raking her fingers through her thick, unruly curls.

Out of pure curiosity, Riella picked it up. The parchment was indeed covered in nonsense markings and symbols. Except . . . some of them weren't nonsense to her.

"It's Shirranis," she said in wonder. "The ancient language of Shirrani mystics. We studied it during our language lessons with the elders, but we didn't learn in detail, because it's too rare. I recognize this symbol, though." She tapped the parchment. "It means sacrifice. What would Artus be doing with this?"

"Knowing Artus, something bad," said Yvette with disinterest, scrubbing her face with a dampened washcloth. "You can have it, if you like. I've certainly no use for it."

Riella wasn't sure she did either, but decided she may as well keep it, if for no other reason than Artus wanted it, and she liked the idea of depriving him of something he wanted.

She'd just stuffed the parchment down the front of her dress when the door banged open without warning. In the threshold stood Madame Quaan, surveying the women with blatant contempt.

"Siren." She pointed her gloved finger at Riella. "Your turn."

CHAPTER 9

The house had become crowded while Riella was in the washroom.

Prettily-painted women populated the hallway, chatting and laughing softly to each other. They filed downstairs from the second floor, where they resided. The bawdy laughter of men traveled into the hallway from the other direction, at the bar.

"Our guests are important people," said Madame Quaan as she walked. "You'll treat them with the respect they deserve."

"Oh, I will," replied Riella.

Madame Quaan halted abruptly, turning to glare into the siren's face, as if trying to detect insubordination.

The madame's eyes were sharp and hard, like flint. Riella realized Madame Quaan was trying to intimidate her, which made her want to cackle. She could've thrown Madame Quaan through the ceiling if she felt so inclined.

But her mirth quickly subsided when she remembered that humans had more ways to hurt and coerce people than sheer force. The women of the house surely feared Madame

Quaan for good reason. Riella would need to keep her wits about her and take nothing for granted.

The other women in the hallway averted their eyes as Riella and Madame Quaan came near, as if not wanting to draw the attention and seemingly inevitable ire of their boss.

"Do you know how to please a man?" demanded Madame Quaan in an imperious tone.

"It's a man," blurted out Riella. "How difficult can it be?"

Annoyance soured the madame's features, but only for a second, after which she sniffed in a manner that could almost be mistaken for amusement.

"Be warned, siren, that if you fail to entertain Count Zemora to his satisfaction, I'll send in Odeya and Sehild, both of whom are far more delicate in disposition than you are, and therefore less suited to his particular proclivities."

Riella's stomach clenched. What did the Count expect of her, exactly? Whatever ghastly perversion he enjoyed, she vowed to protect her new friends from him.

Before she could demand elaboration from the older woman, Madame Quaan stopped at a door and tapped on it. A pair of bodyguards in nondescript brown clothing stood at attention on either side of the door, swords on their hips. They were immobile except for their eyes feasting on the bodies of every woman who passed.

"Yes!" called a man from inside the room.

Madame Quaan stepped back and jerked her head at Riella, indicating she should enter.

For some reason, the siren had not reckoned on going in alone. She thought Madame Quaan would introduce her to the Count. Apparently, she was on her own already.

Bracing herself for strangeness or violence or some ugly combination of both, she stepped inside, closing the door behind her.

Count Zemora was younger and better-looking than she had expected.

He posed by the vanity, a crystal glass full of amber liquid in his hand and his nose in the air. Dressed in luxurious maroon brocade trousers and jacket, with a white ruffle at the chest, he resembled an exotic, slightly ridiculous bird.

His brown hair was meticulously styled and his pale face was freshly shaven. A rather beaky nose complemented his large brown eyes and prominent cheekbones. He wore heavy gold jewelry beset with gems.

At the sight of Riella, he gasped, his eyes widening and traveling the length of her body. "My dear, I am afraid Madame Quaan lied to me." He placed his drink on the vanity and moved toward her, slowly and at an angle. "When she said she had a siren for me, I was delighted and intrigued. She declared you pleasing to the eye. But you are, in fact, far more glorious than she led me to believe."

As he came within striking distance of her, she fought the desire to, in fact, strike him.

Instead, she swept the room with her eyes, trying to formulate a plan. There were no windows, and candles in sconces lit the room. The only furniture was a four-poster bed in pale wood with black silk linens. A flat pewter box sat on the vanity, piquing her interest. The Count was clearly wealthy—he would definitely have coin with him. Was it in the box? His pockets? With his guards?

"What's your name, my dear?" asked the Count, reaching to touch her hair, which was like spun silk after being washed in fresh water.

Without thinking, she smacked his hand before his fingertips could reach her.

He stared at her in shock, his mouth a perfectly round 'O'. Riella winced inwardly. The Count was a member of the Royal Court. He'd expect deference and licentiousness from everyone he came into contact with—especially someone he was paying for. It'd taken her exactly fifteen seconds to land herself in trouble.

Would he call for his bodyguards, or Madame Quaan? Riella knew she should apologize, and try to smooth things over. While she was prepared to punch and kick her way out of here, it'd be better to rob the Count and Madame Quaan with relative stealth. Less dangerous for her friends, too, who might get caught up in the violence.

And yet, she couldn't bring herself to say sorry. The words refused to leave her mouth. To give an unwarranted apology was too much of a betrayal of herself.

A siren could only take so much. Which was very little at all, it turned out.

Well, he wanted a siren. Everyone knew they were vicious and unforgiving. What had he expected?

Zemora blinked several times, before spluttering in delight.

"Oh, you are lovely. You are too perfect." He clapped his hands. "Now what?" he asked, looking at her keenly.

Riella blinked in confusion. Was he serious? What now, indeed.

Since he didn't seem to be upset by her rebuff, she led by instinct. "I want you to get away from me. Now. Stand in the corner, while I search you."

He almost fell over himself hurrying to the corner of the room, where he stood with his head bowed and his arms at his side. Riella could sense his whole body quivering. What in all the seven seas was going on?

He seemed to enjoy being pushed around by her. Would it truly be as simple as barking orders at him to get what she wanted? It couldn't be that easy—she had to be missing something.

Of course, he could yell for help at any moment and she'd

be set upon by his bodyguards, and possibly Gerret. Despite the Count's apparent harmlessness, she was still in a precarious situation.

Keeping a wary eye on him, she moved to the wooden box on the vanity, dragging her fingertips across the top of the lid. The Count whimpered pathetically.

The box held an array of polished silver weapons, and coils of black rope. She snorted. It was like Zemora and Quaan were daring her to rob him.

"I know," he said with a moan, catching the expression on her face. "I am disgusting. You would be right to deride me. I deserve it."

She exhaled, making up her mind. If she was to save Seraphine, she needed coin. Despite the risk of robbing a Count, the opportunity was too good to pass up. So, in the end, she withdrew the coils of rope.

"Stand by the post of the bed." She spoke as evenly as possible, because every time she injected feeling into her voice, he enjoyed it. "Put your arms around it."

He obeyed. She tied his wrists around the wooden post, binding them tightly, followed by his ankles. The whole time, he gave little yelps and sighs.

"Ah!" He grimaced. "That's tight. I can not escape you, siren."

"That's the idea."

The last thing she did was gag him, using rope. It wasn't until she started methodically rifling through his pockets that she sensed some reservation in him. He frowned, trying to speak in muffled grunts.

"Too late," she said as her fingers closed around a small yet pleasingly heavy velvet pouch. "Found what I wanted."

The pouch was filled with dozens of gold coins. She smiled in relief. Next, she removed all of his rings. The

Count curled his fingers in protest, trying to stop her, but her strength far outstripped his own.

Soon, she'd liberated all of his weighty rings and bracelets, adding them to the velvet pouch with satisfaction.

On impulse, she tore off one of his shirt ruffles and blindfolded him, too. The less aware he was of his surroundings, the longer she'd have to escape. As she put her ear to the door to listen, she stuffed the pouch down the front of her dress alongside the parchment.

"You'll be pleased to know this coin is going to an excellent cause," she said to the Count. "I'm going to rescue an elf."

The Count struggled harder, his face turning red.

Steeling herself with a deep breath, Riella opened the door and slipped into the hallway. Before she could close it again, the bodyguards sprang to attention. One threw his arm across her path and the other stuck his foot out to prevent the door from shutting.

"And where do you think you're going?" asked the guard who'd thrust out his arm, which she was trying very hard to not break in half.

For the second time in one day, she found herself in a serious enough situation to deploy her siren charm.

Riella gazed deeply into the guard's eyes, lowering her voice and smiling impishly. His eyes hazed over and his jaw dropped open. As much as she liked fighting, she had to admit that crippling men with a mere smile was satisfying, too.

Women had the same skill, of course, although they often didn't use these powers to their full extent. Probably because women had to live among their male counterparts. Sirens, on the other hand, could escape to the ocean after provoking men.

"The Count requested another girl to help me entertain

him," she whispered, so that he had to lean closer. "I'll be right back."

The other guard, who wasn't under her spell, squinted through the cracked door before she could leave. Riella tensed. The moment he saw his boss trussed up like a trout, the fight would be on.

And he definitely saw. But apparently Zemora being tied to a post was a routine occurrence, because the guard simply gave a quick, embarrassed nod of comprehension. He closed the door and waved his hand at Riella to go about her business.

Flushed with success, she hurried down the crowded hallway toward the stairs leading to Madame Quaan's study.

Halfway there, she realized she was being followed. The guard she'd hypnotized was trailing her like a suckerfish, slack-jawed and cloudy-eyed. His colleague frowned after him in bewilderment.

She clapped her hands in front of the guard's face. "Go back to the door."

He nodded dutifully and turned to leave.

"Wait," she said with a sudden stroke of inspiration. "I want you to keep the black-robed man and Madame Quaan away from me, alright?"

He nodded again with a dopey smile.

"Now go!"

She shooed him away, not wanting to loiter in the hallway. Madame Quaan and Gerret were around somewhere. To her intense relief, the guard did as she commanded.

Keeping her head bowed, she continued toward the study. She was paces from the top of the stairs when a huge hand clamped down on her shoulder and spun her around. The man who'd grabbed her was familiar, but also, she would've never expected to see him at that moment.

"I vow to kill you!" she hissed at him. "Artus sold me for coin, like I'm a curio!"

Jarin towered over her, his eyes serious. "You can kill me later. But right now, a patrol of royal guards are about to raid this establishment, by order of the Countess Zemora."

CHAPTER 10

"What are you talking about?" asked Riella. "Why are you here?"

The huge, tanned pirate looked incredibly out of place in the luxe surroundings. His white shirt was damp and clung to his broad chest, dark curls of hair between his tattooed pectorals visible through the fabric. Dainty women shrank from him as they passed, while eyeing him shyly. It was attention that he did not return, continuing to glare at Riella instead.

"I only discovered Artus was bringing you here when I got to Skull Cave," he said, glancing over his shoulder. "I swam here."

She raised her eyebrows, sizing him up. "You can swim?"

He scoffed. "Of course, I can swim. I'm a bloody pirate."

"I bet you look like you're drowning."

He grabbed her elbow and leaned down. "Hey, I came here to rescue you," he said with a snarl. "Should I not have bothered?"

Riella wrenched her arm from him, and shoved him for

good measure. It was like pushing an enormous boulder. She could do it, but it was harder than expected.

"Do I look like I need rescuing?" she demanded.

"Can you fight off twenty guards? Because an aristocrat's wife has ordered a raid on this place. Zemora. He's a regular here, apparently."

Riella hesitated. Out of all the men she'd met, Jarin seemed the most trustworthy. Certainly, she should've listened to him about Artus.

"Yes, he is," she said, adjusting her tone to be less combative. "I've met the Count."

Jarin's dark brows furrowed. "You don't mean—"

"He didn't touch me." She pointed up the hall, where the Count's bodyguards stood watch. "I bound and gagged him. I told his bodyguards I'm getting another girl."

Jarin snorted with laughter. "You bound and gagged a member of the Court? They'll hang you for treason."

"Not if they don't catch me." Riella placed her hand over her chest, where the Count's gold and jewelry were tucked away. How would she avoid the royal patrol *and* burgle Madame Quaan *and* help her friends escape with the gold she'd promised them?

"I also may've robbed him," she added. "I should probably hide."

"Not as much fun as fighting, but alright."

Before she could protest, he entered a room at random and pulled her inside by the wrist, closing the door behind them. The room was unoccupied, the bed neatly made up with navy blue and gold linens. A chandelier hung from the ceiling, casting a glittering glow. Like every other room in the house, it had no windows.

A disturbance came from outside in the hallway. There was banging and shouting and a few frightened squeals from the women. The house was indeed being raided.

"Quaan would usually pay a bribe to get rid of them," said Jarin. "But if she knows a siren robbed one of her clients, she'll let the guards do her dirty work and capture you." He surveyed the strangely featureless room. The only door was the one they'd entered through. "Do you know any other exits from the building? I did a quick sweep, but my priority was finding you, so I didn't get a good look."

She narrowed her eyes. "Why would you want to save me?"

"I need you to kill Artus. And you owe me, for stabbing me in the heart."

"Are you still on about that?"

"Still? It happened this morning!"

Guards pounded on hallway doors, and the thumps were getting closer.

"What now?" she asked. "As soon as they get to our door, we're caught."

He rubbed his stubbled jaw, considering her. "Do you trust me?"

"I don't know."

How would she be able to tell, beyond any doubt? Perhaps that wasn't possible. Trusting someone meant taking a leap of faith.

"Why?" she asked, folding her arms. "What do you propose?"

Royal guards were in a shouting match with the Count's henchmen out in the hall. Riella likely had moments before Zemora was found gagged and bound, by her doing.

"They won't dare interrupt a Dark Tide pirate with a maiden," said Jarin. "Get on the bed."

"*Excuse* me?" Riella's heart rate increased, and it had nothing to do with the guards bashing down doors. "I don't think—"

"Relax, I won't plough you for real. We'll pretend. But it'll work, I promise." He paused, leveling his gaze at her. "And listen, I didn't know Artus was bringing you here. I never would've let him do that to any woman. Or any siren," he added.

Riella gave a curt nod. "Very well."

This man was her sworn enemy and was helping her because he wanted her to kill his captain. And yet, she innately believed his words. She only hoped he wouldn't prove her foolish for it.

"Even if she did stab me," he said with a wicked grin that made her racing heart skip a beat.

Jarin then tore off his shirt, exposing his muscular shoulders and sharply defined abdominals. The dark tuft of hair on his chest ran a line through the middle of his stomach, past the prominent v-shape of his groin, disappearing into the top of his trousers. His torso was covered in tattoos, including an anchor, a rose, a ship and, biggest of all, a siren, her tail wrapping around his taut waist. The inked siren had a serene smile on her face and guileless eyes.

"That's not a very accurate depiction," said Riella.

Her voice came out higher than usual, and she couldn't decide where to look. Looking directly at him seemed somehow perverse, but averting her eyes might suggest she was rattled by him.

For a siren to be rattled by a man was unthinkable.

But, in truth, she was a little. With a thrill of disbelief, she understood that she was *attracted* to this pirate's body. This was her first time on the other end of such a dynamic. It was *attraction* causing her racing heart and frozen thoughts and higher-than-usual voice.

She thought of the fishermen on their broken ship, gawping at her with mouths ajar. Now, she was no better than they were. She surreptitiously touched the bottom of her chin, to ensure her mouth wasn't hanging open.

"An artist in Port Hyacinth tattooed it," said Jarin. Unlike her, he did not seem rattled at all, as if he undressed in front of sirens all of the time. He didn't, of course, but he probably bedded human women with the usual cretinous frequency pirates were known for. "You'll have to take it up with him."

He unbuckled his belt, casting off his cutlass. When he undid the top button of his pants, Riella hastened to speak.

"That's enough," she said. "Surely."

"As you wish."

He took a single long stride toward her, bringing him close enough to catch his scent of perspiration and leather. The guards continued their barrage, barking orders and demanding names. A scuffle seemed to have broken out as patience wore thin.

Jarin lifted Riella from the ground with his arm around her waist.

"Wrap your legs around me," he commanded.

She did as he said, the many layers of her skirt being pushed to her thighs, revealing the fastenings and sheer lace of her underthings. To stop herself from falling, she was forced to grab hold of the back of his neck. His body felt not unlike the hot rocks of the shoals she sunned herself on during winter, when the water was particularly cold.

He lowered her onto the bed, him on top of her. He held his weight with his elbows, her legs falling apart to accommodate his large body. Although several layers of fabric separated her sex from his, those layers now felt very thin indeed.

"If they're looking for a siren, we better hide your hair," he murmured into her ear, sending shivers across her skin. "Your hair shimmers like moonlight."

She writhed with discomfort, only to knock against his unrelenting body. The discomfort was not with his body, but rather, her own body's reaction to being near him. How did humans get anything done, feeling attraction like this? No wonder they acted so deranged.

Jarin slid his fingers up the sides of her neck and into her scalp. With gentle tugs from the base of her skull, he pulled her hair until most was hidden, her head cradled in his large hands. In this position, with his face and body bearing down on her, she had no choice but to look into his eyes.

For the first time, she noticed the tiny bronze flecks in his irises, and his thick, jet-black eyelashes. The gold pendant on the chain around his neck rested heavy and cold on her bare, flaming sternum.

"By the way," he said. "What's your name? You still haven't told me."

"Riella."

"Riella," he repeated softly. "You know I vowed to kill you, Riella?"

She rolled her eyes. "So you keep saying. I think you're all talk and no action."

"That right?"

As his gaze drifted from her eyes to her mouth and back again, he absentmindedly licked his bottom lip. Her breathing became shallow and she lost purchase of her thoughts. She found herself running her hands over his smooth shoulders, the muscles bulging from holding his own weight.

His breath was on her neck, steady and warm. Never had Riella felt so vulnerable. And yet, it didn't feel *bad*. How was that possible? She'd grown up being taught that vulnerability was always bad. Sirens were to avoid it at all costs.

"We better make it realistic, don't you think?" he asked, his eyes penetrating hers deeply.

She exhaled. "Sure. Fine. I don't care."

"Good. Because if we were doing this for real, I'd be

making you sing for me, siren. And not in the way you're used to."

"I doubt you could elicit such a response from me," she said, praying her words sounded convincing.

Then, he started moving his body, rocking forward and back to mimic thrusting. To her horror, she let out a husky moan. The next time he pushed forward, his groin made brief but firm contact with hers. She felt the hot rigidity of his very large and very human cock.

The effect it had on her was quite out of her control, sending a frisson of heat directly into her core.

"Go on," he muttered into her ear. "Lie to me. Tell me you don't like it."

She should've told him to stop. She should have fought the entire royal patrol before allowing herself to be rubbed against by a Dark Tide pirate. But she still didn't say a word, because she was experiencing the most incredible sensation when his groin touched hers.

He moved in again, pressing his bulge into her sex for longer. Her body responded in kind, apparently *wanting* to be pressed into. The fact that it was wrong somehow only made it feel better.

An intoxicating warmth spread from her stomach and flooded into the mysterious new region between her legs. The almost uncontrollable urge to move her hips against the rhythm of his thrusting came over her. It felt instinctual, as natural as beating her tail when swimming.

The flash of a smile crossed Jarin's handsome face, which incensed her. He thought he was the one in control. He thought he was getting to her.

To prove him wrong, she pulled him forward by his neck and ran her tongue over his parted lips, from bottom to top, lingering in the wetted middle. The spikiness of his stubble was a pleasurable contrast to the surprising softness of his mouth.

This time it was Jarin who gave an involuntary moan.

"You taste like the ocean," she whispered, licking her lips and detecting salt.

He gazed down at her with a drugged look, his fingers tightening around the base of her skull, jerking her head back with a firm tug of her hair. "I bet you do, too."

A pounding on the door jolted Riella out of her trance. She'd almost forgotten she was supposed to be evading a royal patrol. Moments later, the door opened.

Jarin's body blocked her view of the guards, but she heard them begin to bark orders.

"Royal guard, searching—"

He half turned around, scowling over his shoulder. "Get out. Now."

"Oh! Yes. Right you are, sir," said one of them. "Apologies."

"Carry on," said another.

The footsteps quickly receded and the door closed.

Riella was glad for the interruption, because now she could break whatever spell she'd unwittingly allowed to be cast between them. What would Mareen and Galeil say if they knew she'd been consorting with a male human? Touching him, lying with him, desiring him?

"Alright, they're gone," she said in the most no-nonsense voice she could muster. "Get off me."

She shoved him away and stood. What was the matter with her? Being struck by the compulsion to lick a man's lips was not right, let alone giving in to it. Sirens were legendarily reckless, but not about *that*. Their brazenness was intended to defend innocents and the ocean and themselves.

But what she hated most of all, was that she hadn't hated it...

Jarin was slower to stand. He moved to the end of the bed and sat for a while, taking deep, slow breaths. Facing away from her, the tattoo on his back was now visible. The image was the Dark Tide Clan emblem—a giant pair of crossed cutlasses.

Jarin had rightly predicted that the guards would make a fast exit once they knew who he was. The tattoo would've been the first thing they saw when they opened the door. Nobody except sirens were dauntless enough to purposely invoke the wrath of a member of the infamous pirate clan.

On this occasion, it seemed she'd been right to trust him.

Riella pressed her ear to the door, trying to pinpoint the guards' location. The commotion could work in her favor, if Madame Quaan and Gerret were distracted for long enough. She hoped none of her friends were hurt in the chaos.

Meanwhile, Jarin pulled his shirt on. When he finally stood, he had to adjust his bulge rather extensively to buckle up his pants. Riella determinedly looked anywhere except at him.

"What now?" he asked.

"I need to get to the study at the end of the hallway. Break into the stronghold and steal the gold."

A gleeful smile lit Jarin's face. "Now you're speaking my language."

CHAPTER 11

Riella cracked the door and peeked into the hallway.

Guards pushed and shoved their way through the mayhem of outraged men and women in varying states of undress. Most were expelled from their rooms during the search. Madame Quaan and Gerret were nowhere to be seen, nor was the Count.

Yvette leaned against the wall nearby, her dark curls loose, smoking a cigar with a bored expression.

Riella waved to get her attention. "Where are Madame Quaan and Gerret?"

She crossed the hallway, dodging a gray-haired man frantically trying to button his shirt. "In the Count's room. Trying to keep the guards out long enough to untie him." Yvette snickered and angled her head to blow a trio of smoke rings. "Quaan's out for your blood. She told them you're violent and wanted for robbery."

"We need to get into her study, and best we do it now, while she's waylaid with the Count."

Yvette's eyes widened in delight. "Do you really mean to rob her?" she whispered. "How can I help?"

Riella frowned, thinking. "Do you know anything about the magic guarding her riches?"

The siren could handle steel and padlocks, but magic was a different and potentially far trickier challenge.

"Only that no one can open it except for her," replied Yvette. "When we first moved to this house, she had a mage enchant the stronghold for her. I couldn't get close enough to find out any particulars, though."

"Alright, that's still helpful. You've been here a long time, then?"

Yvette's face shuttered. She glanced over her shoulder, feigning distraction. With a stab of shame, Riella realized she'd asked a rude question. The complexities of the human world seemed never-ending.

"I'll find Odeya and Sehild," said Yvette when she'd gathered herself, turning back to Riella. "We'll delay Madame Quaan and Gerret for as long as possible." She tugged a lace shawl from around her shoulders and pressed it into Riella's hands. "I'd cover my hair, if I were you. Madame Quaan described you to the guards."

"Thank you." Riella put the shawl over her head and tied it under her chin. "Jarin said something similar about my hair."

Yvette had been about to leave, but halted at this information, arching her brow. "Who's Jarin?"

"Oh." The siren opened the door wider to reveal the pirate adjusting his belt. "I'm working with him. Don't ask why."

Yvette snickered. "I don't need you to tell me why. Just look at him. Go ahead, then. And good luck."

The dark-haired woman gave an ironic salute, then wove

down the hallway through the melee toward the Count's room.

Riella and Jarin emerged and hastened in the opposite direction. He shoved his way through the royal guards, who took one look at him and turned their gazes, allowing him and Riella to reach the stairs quickly and without incident.

The first real obstacle lay at the bottom of the stairs, where the door was locked with three deadbolts. Riella could break them easily enough, but smashing the metal from the doorframe would create a tremendous noise.

The guards may've overlooked Jarin when they believed he was a customer at this establishment, but if he started actively robbing the place, they'd have to intervene.

"I need you to cause a diversion up in the hallway," she said to him. "Something loud."

She had expected him to be confused, or argue, or ask how. But he nodded without saying a word and ascended the stairs, as if he did this all the time. Which, she reflected, he probably did.

Moments later, a crash came from the hallway, followed by cursing and screams, then more crashing. Riella couldn't see the mayhem from the bottom of the stairs, but she felt sure it was Jarin's doing, and took it as her cue.

She drove her fist into the biggest of the metal locks. The door cracked, along with most of the frame, but the locks held. The hidden mechanisms were sturdier than she'd thought. Undeterred, she punched it again, making it loosen further. If Madame Quaan took such great lengths to secure her office, there was sure to be something of value inside.

The noise upstairs began subsiding. Jarin would only be able to cause so much chaos without risking arrest. There was no time to waste. Her next strike would need to break the door down.

A wild idea occurred to her as she drew her fist back

again. What if she *kicked* the door instead? Would that work better?

Dubious, she braced herself by pressing her hands against either side of the narrow entryway. After awkwardly drawing back one leg, she drove the sole of her foot into the main lock. The entire door flew into the study, the locks demolishing most of the frame as well, leaving behind a giant hole.

Laughing in delight, and with a newfound respect for her legs, she stepped into the study. Jarin joined her moments later, nodding in admiration at the damage she'd caused.

"The guards have the Count," he said. "He's trying to bribe them, but he's got no gold on him. Very sad."

"Did you see Madame Quaan and Gerret?"

"She's trying to argue the Count's case, but I don't think it's doing much good. I guess the Countess pays better."

Riella nodded, surveying the study. "We don't have much time, then."

The room was small, stuffy, and almost entirely decorated with gray. Gray tiled floor, gray wallpaper, and a wide marble desk with a neat stack of parchment on top. There was nothing personal about the study—no art or trinkets or even books. Nothing that suggested any kind of heart.

The stronghold was built into the wall behind the desk. Its door was round and made of steel, like Yvette said, with two arms attached to the front, running in opposite directions. There was no sign of magic, but enchantments were not often visible to the naked eye.

Riella went to grab the metal arms.

"Don't!" Jarin strode to her. "You don't know what'll happen."

The siren sighed, stopping just short of grasping them. "Then what do you suggest? We're getting into this stronghold. I made promises."

He tried to nudge her out of the way. "Let me do it."

She shoved him back, because his proximity annoyed her, on multiple fronts. First, he was in her way. Second, he was trying to stop her from doing as she pleased. And third, she caught his scent whenever he got close, and that scent made her stomach do backward somersaults.

"Why?" she demanded. "The magic won't care which one of us does it."

"I'm trying to be chivalrous." The pirate sighed, shaking his head. "You are maddening."

"I am not!"

"*You* don't get to decide if I find you maddening."

"We're wasting time. And I don't need your protection."

Before he could stop her, Riella gripped the arms and pulled with all her strength. The metal groaned, then clanked, but the door did not budge. The metal arms broke off in her hands, leaving behind a featureless round metal surface.

She raised her brows at Jarin. "See? It didn't hurt me."

"You were lucky."

She ran her hand around the circular door, looking for a crack or seam large enough to slide her talons into. "What's the magic of it, then?"

Jarin frowned, putting his hands on the door, too. Riella took hers away. The way his veins popped in his wrists and hands against his tanned skin was strangely indecent.

"The door sits perfectly flush with the wall," he said.

"So, we have to open it by force?"

He stood back, next to her. "That can't be right. The whole point of magic is to circumvent force."

Riella shrugged. "In my experience, anything can be broken with enough force."

To demonstrate, she kicked the metal door. Upon connection, a blinding pain surged up her leg, sending her sprawling backward. She cried out and Jarin caught her before she hit the floor.

"The harder you strike the door, the more pain it delivers to you," came a cold, clear voice from the doorway. "It'll never open for you, siren, no matter how much you try."

Madame Quaan stood in the remains of the office doorway, with Gerret.

Riella snarled. "I will kill you both. Slavers."

She got to her feet, her injured leg still smarting.

"I doubt it," replied the Madame. She crossed the room to Riella, Gerret on her heels like a ghastly shadow. "Sirens can't hurt women. It goes against your rules."

"I can make an exception," said Riella.

But even as she said the threat, her words rang false. The rule may not have been set in stone, but harming any woman went against the very fiber of a siren's heart and soul. In a way —perhaps the truest way—that was stronger than any rule.

Madame Quaan seemed to sense Riella's uncertainty, because she laughed. "You may have physical strength, but you have little else going for you."

Yvette rushed into the room, her dress torn and her dark hair askew.

"I'm sorry," she said to Riella. "I tried to delay her as much as I could. The guards are taking the Count."

Madame Quaan's expression changed in an instant, from mirth to cold fury. She rounded on Yvette, her tone becoming venomous.

"*This* is why you were pestering me?" she spat at her subordinate. "You colluded against me in my own house?"

Yvette's face drained of color and she cringed, like an abused animal who'd been long beaten into submission.

Her fear only seemed to incense the madame further.

"After all I have done for you!" she went on. "You worthless, ungrateful traitor! You will never be good for *anything* except for lying on your back and—"

Riella sunk her talons into Madame Quaan's shoulder blades and flung her against the wall, where she crumpled to the floor.

Gerret lunged at the siren, his black robes whipping the air with his speed, but Jarin intercepted. He punched Gerret in the face repeatedly with great force, making bones crack and blood fly, until the man's eyes rolled back in his head. Jarin let him collapse on the tiles and stepped away from the body, massaging his bloodied fists.

Covering her mouth with her hand, Yvette gazed at Madame Quaan slumped on the ground. The madame stirred, raising her head. Riella lifted her with one hand and pinned her against the wall by her throat.

"If you say one more word to her," said the siren through gritted teeth. "I will disembowel you with my bare hands. And this time, I do mean it."

Madame Quaan hesitated, searching the siren's face. She must've discerned that Riella was telling the truth, because she visibly quailed, swallowing hard under Riella's hand.

"Now, open the stronghold," said Riella.

"I can't." Her voice wavered slightly, but her eyes were as icy as ever. "Only my blood will open it, but the blood has to be willingly given. And I don't give it to you willingly. I will never, no matter what you do, because nothing in this world means anything to me, except what's in that stronghold. I'll gladly die before I relinquish all I have worked for. Especially to a mutant half-breed like you, or a common criminal like him."

Her eyes slid in Jarin's direction. With a triumphant smirk, she removed one of her gloves and held up her hand. Cuts and scars crisscrossed her palm many times over. Some marks were old and silvery, while others were fresh and pink.

Riella's heart sank. Naturally, a person this shrewd and heartless would protect her riches with her very love for those riches. It was brilliant, if not highly inconvenient for Riella and her cause.

"Let's try anyway." Jarin scowled, reaching for the handle of his cutlass. "We'll try until she bleeds out."

"No!" said Yvette, stepping forward.

Madame Quaan blinked at her, as if she'd forgotten the younger woman was even there.

Yvette's face was still pale, but her chin now had a determined jut. "Don't bother."

Taking a discreet, bone-handled dagger from the sleeve of her dress, she crossed the room.

In front of the stronghold, she touched the short blade to the palm of her hand. Madame Quaan's expression morphed from confusion to horror, her mouth falling open in realization. Riella shared a puzzled glance with Jarin.

"I'm not completely ungrateful, mother," said Yvette to Madame Quaan. "I am very grateful for your arrogance. You constantly overestimate yourself, and underestimate every person around you. Most of all, me."

Madame Quaan struggled against Riella's steely grip, gasping and spitting in panic. The older woman could do nothing except watch as Yvette cut her hand and pressed her bleeding palm to the metal door.

CHAPTER 12

Riella held her breath while Yvette took her hand from the door.

The metal came alive, the surface writhing and shifting like a hurricane sky. Then, just as suddenly, the surface froze. The door sprang open, which elicited a choked groan from Madame Quaan.

The stronghold's interior was far larger than appeared possible from the outside. It was low-ceilinged and dark with shadows, brightened only by columns of solid silver and gold coins, and piles of jewelry and trinkets.

After Riella's astonishment wore off, she was overcome by disgust. Not only had Madame Quaan sold her own daughter, she'd hoarded more wealth than she could ever spend in her lifetime.

Yvette's eyes bulged at the riches, before profound sorrow washed over her beautiful features. Then, she glared at Madame Quaan with such resentment that a chill shot down Riella's spine for being in the same line of sight. But the older woman showed no remorse, seething under Riella's grip, albeit silently.

"Not a bad haul," said Jarin in approval.

He stood over Gerret's inert body, his arms folded.

"It's not ours," said Riella.

"I know that." There was an indignant note to his voice.

"Right. Sorry."

Riella reminded herself to stop assuming the worst of him. He hadn't really done anything to deserve her scorn, except exist, and blackmail her into murder.

But she *did* stab him in the heart, so perhaps she ought to let the blackmail slide.

Sehild and Odeya entered through the demolished doorway, their wary expressions turning to amazement when they saw the stronghold.

"Oh, gods," said Odeya to Madame Quaan. "I knew you were swindling us, but this is beyond imagining."

"The guards are gone," said Sehild to Riella. "And most of the clientele. Some are still dressing."

She peered nervously at Madame Quaan, and quickly looked away again. The hold the older woman had on them was severe. Even while under Riella's control, the madame scared Sehild.

"Go upstairs and make sure the patrons leave," said Riella to Jarin. "Guard the front door and forbid anyone from entering. This establishment is no more."

He nodded and went upstairs.

Now, she addressed Odeya. "Bring all the other women down here. Tell them to bring a bag each."

Madame Quaan grizzled, but still did not dare speak.

The women of the house filed down. They were astounded by the contents of the stronghold, and equally surprised they could take their share of the riches. Yvette oversaw the process with grim satisfaction.

Riella tossed the pouch she stole from the Count to

Yvette, to add to the loot. Now that Jarin was here, he could take her to the Black Cliffs. She didn't need the gold.

As the riches were removed from the stronghold, Madame Quaan seemed to shrivel and shrink. By the time the last of the precious metals was divided among the women, her face was pale and her eyes were fathomless with rage.

The women native to Klatos offered to find lodging for those from other towns and kingdoms. After exchanging hugs and well wishes, the women gradually departed in small groups without ceremony.

Riella remained in the study with Yvette, Madame Quaan, and Gerret's unconscious body.

"What are you going to do to me?" asked Madame Quaan through a clenched jaw. "Whatever it is, get it over with. I have nothing left."

The siren frowned, trying to decide.

There was not a repentant bone in this woman's body. If Riella released her, there was every chance she'd restart her vile business of slavery, either here in Klatos or elsewhere. That was an unacceptable risk.

But executing her in cold blood was extreme. While Riella felt confident in her jurisdiction in the ocean, she did not belong here on land. Did she have the right to judge this woman unworthy of life?

In the end, she drew inspiration from the blood enchantment. Riella dragged Madame Quaan and Gerret into the dark depths of the stronghold, shoving the woman hard so that she wouldn't get up right away. Yvette stood back, watching impassively while holding her pouch of gold and silver to her chest.

"If you are deserving of life, your blood will grant it to you," said Riella before slamming the door closed.

At once, the door sealed itself. Madame Quaan's enraged

shouts and thumping became barely audible, even to the siren's highly attuned hearing.

When Riella looked up, she was alone in the room. Yvette had already left. Perhaps she'd return to save the madame and Gerret, having had a change of heart, but Riella suspected not.

Indeed, she found Yvette in the bar area, chatting animatedly with Sehild and Odeya. Their demeanor was completely different from just an hour ago. Their eyes were bright and they couldn't stop laughing.

Yvette ran at Riella and hugged her tightly. "Thank you."

The siren smiled into Yvette's dark curls. "I wish only that you lead happy lives."

Sehild and Odeya exchanged cheek kisses with Riella. Sirens did not practice this custom and the gesture spread a pleasant warmth through her chest. A siren would die for another siren in a heartbeat, but showing each other physical affection was unheard of.

Riella marveled at how the vitality and tenderness of human women were almost supernatural powers in themselves. In a horrid and twisted way, she saw why human men tried to capture it for themselves. Elves possessed similarly healing natures, and Seraphine was forced to confer her beautiful power to that ghoul, Polinth.

Eager to begin her journey to help the elf, Riella bid her new friends farewell and met Jarin by the front gate.

"Thank you," she said to him. "For helping."

"It was a tough job, hiding you from the guards, siren." A devilish smile lit his face, his teeth white in the hazy copper afternoon light. "But I'd do it again."

She balled her fist and punched his bicep, which only made his smile wider.

"Hey," he said. "It worked, didn't it? You achieved your ends."

"I did," replied Riella thoughtfully, watching a trio of women from Madame Quaan's disappear down the street together.

She put her hand to her chest. "Odeya said it's normal to feel many things at once, but it doesn't feel normal. It feels overwhelming."

"You're feeling things because you helped others. It's good."

"I did what anyone would do."

Jarin scoffed. "That's not true. Most people ignore the suffering of others."

"But how? How do you bear it?"

His face became serious, and his eyes remote. "Not well, much of the time, to be honest. It's why the world is the way it is. So many of us can't bear the pain of being human."

"How awful."

He cuffed her on the shoulder, then directed her toward the bustling cobblestone street. "It's not all bad. The good moments make all the pain worth it. Or, so I've heard."

Riella fell into step beside him while thinking of Seraphine, Tregor, the boy cringing from her on the street, and the women enslaved by Madame Quaan. "I don't know if I can imagine anything feeling good enough to offset the pain."

"Maybe one day you'll find out."

She sighed. "I'll be happy if I can get to the Black Cliffs. You said you'd take me there."

"And you said you'd kill Artus. I'm leading a mutiny tonight, and you can kill him then. But only if we make it back to the Pandora before dusk. Once the ship is mine, I'll take you to the cliffs."

She raised her brows at him. "Promise?"

"I promise."

"A mutiny does sound like fun."

"I'm not doing it for fun. I'm doing it because Artus flogs and kills his own men, and I have to stop him before his strength grows. Even if I'm outnumbered."

The streets became more crowded the farther downhill they walked, toward the docks. Seagulls floated overhead and the taverns steadily filled, rowdy with rosy-faced sailors and local folk. The scent of smoky cooked food reached Riella's nostrils. She had never consumed human dishes, and yet her stomach growled. She'd not eaten since the day before.

"Well, I deeply enjoy fighting pirates, so it'd be no burden for me," said Riella.

Jarin glanced sideways at her. Everyone on the street automatically gave him a wide berth, parting like tidal water as he approached. "You would fight alongside me?"

"If it means you'll take me to the cliffs, then yes. I'd far prefer to travel by sea to land. I feel very much like I don't belong here."

"I know what you mean," he said half to himself, staring around at the people laughing and chatting.

"Being a pirate is not the same as being a siren."

"And yet, the people in this city would sooner welcome you into their company than me. You know nothing about me, except that I'm a pirate."

"What else is there?"

He cleared his throat. "I come from questionable stock, let's put it that way."

"Your father was a mountain troll?" She raked her eyes over his body. "That would explain your gigantic, lumbering structure."

She'd been joking, but Jarin's expression darkened and he refused to meet her gaze. "My father wasn't a troll. He was a great warrior."

"Oh. I'm sorry. I shouldn't have said that. What of your mother?"

"Tell me what's at the Black Cliffs, really?"

Riella noted that he yet again had changed the subject, but she answered anyway. If she was more open with him, perhaps he would respond in kind.

"An elf named Seraphine. Polinth holds her captive. She sacrificed her freedom so that I could escape."

"Brave elf," commented Jarin. "They aren't known for being fighters."

"Which makes it all the more terrible." Guilt splintered Riella's heart. "Because sirens are. And I left her there."

"Knowing Polinth, you didn't get much choice. He's a gifted sorcerer. A degenerate, but gifted." Jarin paused. "Try not to dwell on the bad feelings. That doesn't do you any good, tempting though it may be."

"Guilt is a particularly heavy feeling."

"Aye, that it is. But it also does nothing to help your elven friend." He pointed at the food stalls lining the side of the cramped street. "You should eat something now. The food here is leagues better than anything you'll be fed on the ship, believe me."

"Is there any kelp?" she asked, peering doubtfully at the stalls.

Jarin barked with laughter. "*Kelp*. Let me get you some real food."

He carved a line through the throng of people toward a food cart. An elderly man cooked something in a pot of oil, chopped and served in a cup fashioned from parchment.

While she waited, Riella wondered what was so questionable about Jarin's stock, if his father had been a great warrior. Obviously, it was a sore subject.

The pirate gave a few coins to the elderly man and brought the food to Riella.

"It's not fish, is it?" she asked, taking the little parcel from him and sniffing it. "I will never eat fish."

"It's a vegetable. I promise you'll like it."

She picked up a piece and touched the tip of her tongue to it. Her eyebrows flew up in delight. "Ooh! Salty."

Jarin grinned. She hated how handsome that made him look, and covered her discomfort by cramming the food into her mouth. At first, she wasn't sure if she liked it. But then she chewed, and a pleasant greasy explosion happened in her mouth.

"It's potato, salted and fried." Jarin guided her farther down the street. "And one other thing. I don't *lumber*."

She ate as they walked, demolishing the food in less than a minute and disposing of the parchment cup.

He was right about the lumbering, although she'd never give him the satisfaction of acknowledging it. For his size, he was remarkably agile. A result of residing on a ship, she supposed. Walking on land must've seemed far easier when you spent most of your time rocking back and forth on the ocean.

"Need anything else before we set sail?" he asked. "You need to be fit for combat."

"Well, I might need—"

Riella stumbled on the cobblestones, forcing her to grab Jarin's steel-threaded arm to right herself. She removed her hand at once. Against her will, she was reminded of his body's heat as he'd cradled her head and pressed his groin into hers.

"What do you need?" A smirk danced on his lips, as if reading her thoughts.

Had she really licked those lips? Voluntarily? What had she been thinking?

She *didn't* think, that was the problem. She'd given in to her instincts, and those instincts seemed drawn to Jarin.

As a siren, she was taught to trust her instincts implicitly. They kept her safe. Did the same hold true now that she had legs? Could she trust her instincts, even if they put her in a position of feeling vulnerable?

"Shoes," she said, stepping back from him. "I need shoes more suited to fighting."

The ornate silk slippers Odeya had given her were beautiful, but highly impractical.

"That I can do," he said. "Mind if I—"

He kneeled in the middle of the street, forcing everyone to move around them, and reached for her foot. She bit her bottom lip as he held her ankle and eased off the shoe. Balancing on a single foot made her wobble, and she steadied herself by grasping his broad shoulders.

He stood, tapping the shoe in his hand. "So I know which size to get. Stay here."

Strangely breathless, she leaned against a lamppost while Jarin disappeared into a nearby shopfront. The window displayed saddlery and belts and rather more sensible-looking shoes than the ones she'd been wearing. He returned minutes later with a pair of brown leather boots in her size.

Holding Jarin's arm for support, she changed into the boots. She tested them out, pacing up and down, amazed at the difference. The grips on the flat soles made walking far easier.

"Good?" he asked.

"Good," she confirmed.

"Let's go start a mutiny, then," he said, handing her silk slippers to a grubby-faced girl on the side of the street.

Dusk drew nearer, the docks striped with long shadows as Riella and Jarin descended the street.

"Is Artus invulnerable, like you?" she asked. "If I'm to fight him, I ought to know."

"No, he's not. I believe he's trying to be, though. It's why he attacked a royal ship carrying artifacts, and why I need to move against him. He's always hated my invulnerability—

secretly though, so he can keep me close. I helped him take the Pandora from the last captain. But he's always known I'd be his biggest threat, one day."

Riella thought of Yvette's toxic bondage to Madame Quaan. "*He's* not your father, is he?"

"No. But he saved me when I was younger, which is why it's taken me so long to overthrow him. When I lost my parents, I stowed away on a pirate ship. Artus was the gunner and he took me under his wing. Best and worst thing that could happen to an angry young man."

"What were you angry about?" she asked, trying to fill in the gaps in his cryptic story. "Were your parents killed, then?"

"My father was killed, yes. My mother . . ." He squinted at the crimson horizon. ". . . is complicated."

"Was she invulnerable too?"

"No. She's not. But she made me so."

The siren's mind brimmed with questions, but she and Jarin were fast approaching the docks, so she asked the most pressing one. "What are Artus's weaknesses?"

"He takes advantage of any kindness," answered Jarin without hesitation. "Show him none."

A horn blared long and loud, penetrating the late afternoon din of the city. The sound echoed through the streets and sent chills through Riella.

"The Pandora's horn," said Jarin, quickening his pace.

"What does it mean?" she asked.

"I don't know. But we don't sound the horn at port unless there's dire trouble." He turned to Riella. "Whatever it is, I can't leave my men to fend for themselves. If you want to part ways, now's the time."

"You'll still take me to the Black Cliffs?"

"I will."

"Then, let's go."

CHAPTER 13

Jarin was grateful that Artus could no longer access Ferrante and his prophetic words. The captain hadn't yet realized that Riella was valuable on a grander level. He was too focused on finding the amulet, and had only wanted to earn a pouch of gold from selling her.

If the siren fought on Jarin's side during the mutiny, that might tip the scales of victory in his favor, thus altering the destiny of the clan like Ferrante said she would. All in all, Jarin felt sure he'd decoded the Seer's prediction correctly, and could use it to his advantage. Artus would fall, that very night.

The docks were as crowded as ever, but as dusk approached, the mood changed. Everyone was in a rush to either set sail or finish unloading cargo. The stallholders packed up, and the beggars migrated uphill to the tavern district. No one was more generous than a drunken sailor stopped at port for the night.

At first, he could see no reason for the horn. Against the scarlet late afternoon sky, his crew mates hauled the anchor and climbed the rigging, preparing to set sail. But when he looked closer, he realized there were fewer crew members than usual, and the men were in a great rush.

Riella stopped dead, pointing at the ship.

"What's wrong with that boy?" she asked in an uncertain voice.

Drue was hobbling along the gangway, holding his ribcage.

"That's the cabin boy," replied Jarin, a sense of doom descending on him like a dark cloud. "He's on my side."

The commander ran to meet Drue at the end of the gangway, where the boy sagged against the railing. Up close, his face was stained with tears and blood. The back of his grubby shirt was shredded and streaked red. He'd been flogged.

"Artus knows," said Drue, fresh tears springing to his brown eyes. "I'm sorry. He made me tell him everything. About the mutiny, the royal ship at Skull Cave. I tried to hold out, but then he let Terrick—"

Jarin held up his hand for silence, anger flaming in his gut. "He was about to find out, anyway."

"It's Berolt sounding the horn," said Drue. "We hoped you'd get back before Artus left."

"Left?" repeated Jarin. "What do you mean?"

Before Drue could answer, a short, sharp whistle rang out, cutting through the ceaseless ghostly drone of the horn. Two ships down, Artus waved from the deck of a merchant schooner, grinning like a jester. Terrick and Lovel and at least ten other crew mates were pulling the anchor and setting sail.

One of them hoisted a dark flag up the mast. Only then, Jarin realized the Dark Tide Clan flag was missing from the Pandora. They'd stolen another ship.

Artus cupped his hands around his mouth, amplifying his

gleeful voice. "You wanted to be captain of the Pandora? It's all yours!"

He dropped his hands and roared with laughter, his crew joining in.

Jarin gritted his teeth. This was so much worse than Artus discovering the mutiny. The captain loved the Pandora—he'd only abandon the ship if it was severely compromised.

Riella tapped her talons on his arm. "Uh, why's that patrol coming down here?"

Sure enough, a cavalcade of royal soldiers rode on horseback toward the docks, from farther up the hill. Either Artus leaked the scuttling of the royal ship, or that soft-handed kid in the brig was faster at untying knots than Jarin had reckoned. He and his men and the siren were about to be ambushed.

"Artus tortured and killed many on the royal ship," said Drue, his face turning from white to gray. "If the patrol catches us, we'll hang."

With a snarl, Jarin watched Artus depart in his schooner. The captain gave a mock salute as the vessel picked up speed on the glossy blue water, gliding to the safety of the open sea.

"We ought to set sail, no?" asked Riella mildly, still eyeing the incoming cavalcade of soldiers. "The mutiny was a success, strictly speaking, so you must take me to the Black Cliffs."

"Oh, must I? Now is not—"

Drue coughed. "There's one other thing. Lovel put an axe through the hull before they took off. Ulyss is down there trying to patch it up."

Repressing the urge to roar in frustration, Jarin hooked Drue under one arm while Riella took the other side. Together, they hauled the bleeding cabin boy on board and Jarin dragged the gangway in behind them.

"To Hieros Isle!" he hollered at his crew. "Fast as you can, lads!"

Then, he addressed Riella. "We'll take Drue to the infirmary."

The boy was losing blood and badly needed patching up.

Below deck, a single porthole lit the barebones infirmary. The only supplies were a box of tattered bandages and ancient ointments, but that'd have to do until they could get Drue ashore. Riella helped the cabin boy remove what was left of his shirt.

"I can do this," she said without looking up. "Go."

Relieved that Drue was in good hands, maybe, Jarin hurtled upstairs. The boy's injuries wouldn't matter if the whole bloody ship went down. The vessel, which had begun to pick up pace, gave a sudden creaking lurch as he reached the deck.

The shore rapidly disappeared in the bronze dusk.

The royal cavalcade was on the docks, a few of the horsemen dismounting where the Pandora had been just minutes ago. A solider watched the ship through a spyglass, while the others argued between themselves. Jarin wagered they were deciding whether or not to commandeer a vessel and give chase.

The royal guardsmen would surely realize they were no match for Dark Tide pirates when it came to sailing. Night would soon fall, and finding a ship in the dark was a fool's errand.

But then, the Pandora also had a damaged hull, which made her an easier quarry. Did the royal patrol know about the damage? Jarin prayed they did not.

The deck lurched again, more violently. Jarin and the crew braced against the rocking with instinctive ease. Sometimes he thought traversing the deck of a ship was easier than walking on land—in more ways than one. On the water, he felt like he belonged. Not in the way of a siren, of course, but in the way of an outsider.

Once he was satisfied the soldiers wouldn't pursue, he went below deck. Ulyss, the boatswain, was in the bilge with Berolt, a lantern swinging wildly from a nail on the wall. The two men frantically hammered boards over a splintered hole in the hull, through which seawater gushed. Left unattended, the hole was large enough to sink them within the hour.

"Evening, Captain," said Berolt with a grin when he caught sight of Jarin. He was drenched from head to toe. "Fancy a bath?"

"Think we caught it in time," said Ulyss, puffing. "The Pandora's tough."

"Aye," said Jarin. "We aren't drowning tonight."

He worked alongside his men, sloshing through the bilge with boards and hammers and nails. They reinforced the hull until the leaking had slowed to a trickle.

Ulyss sat back, wiping his forehead with the back of his arm. The dreadlocked, dark-skinned boatswain had once been a master shipbuilder in the kingdom of Hatara. He left his homeland after he was caught pilfering a sapphire necklace from a noblewoman.

Artus discovered him in Port Hyacinth, where he'd been trading his ship-building skills for food and lodging, and promptly inducted him into the Dark Tide Clan.

"We'll be out of action for a while," he said to Jarin with a grimace. "She'll need some major repairs. Where're we headed now?"

"Hieros Isle."

The boatswain nodded. "That'll work. Plenty of space there."

"How long will repairs take, do you reckon?"

"A week, maybe more."

So much for getting Riella to the Black Cliffs anytime

soon. Whether she liked it or not, she was about to be stranded on a desert island along with the rest of the crew.

Jarin sighed, rubbing his face. "Probably for the best, with the royal guard after us. We could stand to lie low. Let Artus cause mayhem with his new vessel, as he's sure to do, and draw their ire."

"Aye."

Night had fallen when Jarin returned to the deck. He inhaled deeply, the fresh salty air clearing his lungs. A million diamonds sparkled in the sky. The slender crescent moon spilled silvery light across the ocean.

The crew were at ease, drinking and eating and joking around. Once the danger passed, a celebration was always called for—usually in the form of rum and tall tales. Their raucous conversations were punctuated by the great sails flapping rhythmically, like the wings of a giant bird.

Jarin considered the new reality. The Dark Tide Clan dividing meant the end of an era, and hopefully the beginning of a better one.

But Artus would want him dead, there was no question. Jarin, of course, could not be so easily killed. The older man would be even more singleminded in getting his hands on that blasted amulet now.

Jarin found Riella at the bow, her forearms resting on the railing and her face turned to the sky. Her platinum hair streamed behind her in the wind current, almost making it appear like she was underwater. She leveled her blue gaze at him, making his heart double its pace.

Had she bewitched him with siren charm? Sure felt like it. Back at Madame Quaan's, when they were hiding from the guards, he'd never desired anyone so much in his life.

Why'd she have to run her tongue over his mouth? The last thing he needed right now was to be lusting after a bloody siren, to whom he owed death for stabbing him in the heart.

But then, he wasn't exactly innocent. He'd gotten her on the bed in the first place. And he'd do it again, who was he kidding?

"If you've cast some siren witchcraft on me," he said in a gruff voice, by way of greeting. "You need to stop it."

"I haven't done anything to you. Do you think I'd waste the energy?"

He scratched his stubbled cheek. "Right. Well."

"The cabin boy sleeps," she said, arching her brow at him. "His wounds will heal."

Shame dumped over Jarin. The poor kid had been flogged to shreds, and all Jarin could think about was Riella's soft pink tongue sliding over his lips. He was a scoundrel.

"Thank you." He leaned on the rail next to her.

"I've never tended to a male human before," she said thoughtfully. "The compassion I felt for him surprised me."

"Why'd it surprise you?"

She shrugged. "I guess I never thought about men feeling vulnerable before. It didn't occur to me. Although, you don't, of course," she added. "You're invulnerable."

"Just because I can't die doesn't mean I can't be destroyed," he murmured, thinking of his mother and her fate. Though she lived, she was destroyed beyond recognition, and by her own hand, too. "Sometimes, death can be a mercy."

Riella's voice softened. "Do you wish you could die? Would you give the protection up, if you could?"

"It's not as simple as wishing I could die. I wish I had something I'd give my life for."

"Everyone wishes that, don't they?"

"Not everyone. But the ones worth knowing do."

They were quiet for some time, the bow slicing through

the dark water. It was incredible to think that Riella lived down there, just days ago. If he was honest with himself, he held a private, selfish desire that she'd not regain her tail anytime soon. He wasn't ready to let her go yet.

Then, he remembered his conversation with Ulyss. "I've got some bad news for you. We'll be stuck on an island while the crew fixes the hull. A week, give or take."

Riella's face fell. "A week? But Seraphine could be dead by then!"

"I'm sorry. Nothing about today went to plan."

She sighed. "I suppose Polinth needs her alive. That might tip the odds in my favor."

Jarin's so-called invulnerable heart flared with warmth for the siren. She was so determined that he almost wished he could make her a Dark Tide pirate. If only the rest of the crew wouldn't mutiny if he tried.

He nudged her. "From what I saw today, my money's on you."

She smiled sadly and looked to the horizon, where the obsidian-dark silhouette of Hieros Isle loomed against the twinkling navy sky.

CHAPTER 14

Riella awoke to jungle sounds and dazzling yellow sunshine.

A breeze from the open treehouse window slid over her bare legs. Sitting up in bed, she wriggled her toes and sighed. Unfortunately, she had not magically reverted to her full siren form during the night.

Jarin had brought her to the treehouse after they disembarked the Pandora in the dead of the night. Hieros Isle was one of dozens of Dark Tide hideouts on remote islands dotted throughout the ocean. Sentinels had immediately been posted all around the perimeter of the isle, to provide warning should Artus and his crew attack.

She thought glumly of Seraphine, and willed the elf to hold on for another week. What if Polinth drained her of life completely during that time? And Riella was stuck here on an island with a bunch of stinky pirates.

The day was already hot. She still wore the dress from Madame Quaan's, the layered skirts tangled in the white linens of her brass-framed bed. Tearing the fabric, she shortened the dress to above her knees and removed the sleeves. Her boots lay on the floor where she'd kicked them off last night. For now, she left them there, wandering around the treehouse barefoot instead.

The floorboards were smooth, and the rooms were furnished simply in brass fittings and cane, with cream linen curtains billowing in the salt-scented breeze. Excited bird chatter was the only sound apart from the distant crash of waves on the beach.

Riella drank the pitcher of water on the small round table. Hunger prompted her to search the shelves and drawers for food, but there was nothing. Her stomach ached as she wistfully recalled the fried potatoes Jarin gave her in Klatos.

She decided to go and find him. He'd know what to eat, and if he couldn't help her, the ocean was right there. She could always dive for kelp.

As she stepped across the threshold of the front door, her head spun. The treehouse, connected to several others by a complex network of narrow wood-and-rope suspension bridges, was far higher off the ground than she thought. Last night, she arrived in the dark with Jarin leading her and hadn't realized.

She gripped the railings as she navigated the structure, trying to find a way to the ground that didn't involve falling to her death.

The treehouses were made of bamboo and wood, covered in snaking vines and surrounded by palm fronds. The jungle was dense on all sides and she seemed to be alone. She was struck by the horrible possibility that Jarin and the crew had abandoned her on this island. *Marooned*, pirates called it. What would she do?

Then, the bubbly sound of children's laughter came from

somewhere below. Riella followed it, eventually finding her way to the ground, touching down on the soft white sand with relief.

A path under the canopy led her to a clearing. In the middle of the clearing was a fire pit, ringed by overturned barrels and lean-to bamboo shelters.

Two children and an elderly woman sat under a shelter, playing and eating. The kids, a boy and a girl around eight years old, looked up as Riella approached. She smiled, raising her hand to wave.

Pure fear transformed the children's faces, and the little girl let out a high-pitched scream. The boy scrambled to his feet and dragged the shrieking girl into the tree line. They crouched among palm fronds, watching Riella, the girl falling into petrified silence.

The siren's heart sank. Why were they so afraid of her?

The woman, at least, seemed unbothered by Riella's presence. She had kind brown eyes and a heavily-lined face, and gave the siren a knowing look. Her hands were busy peeling fruit.

"They've been raised on horror stories about sirens." Her accent was lilting and melodic, and not one Riella had ever heard before. "Perhaps they even saw a few at sea, with Ulyss."

"These are Ulyss's children?"

"Aye. Their mother is in the Beyond." The woman made a fluid, ritualistic hand movement in front of her chest. "The way to deal with a child's shyness is to ignore it. Allow them to come to you, in their own time. Curiosity will triumph in the end." She patted the sandy spot on the ground beside her. "They are like cats in that way."

"I met a cat once, on a ship. It didn't like me, either." Riella sat down, needing several attempts to arrange her legs in a manner that did not feel too strange. She settled for extending the limbs in front of her and crossing the ankles. "My name's Riella."

"I'm Kohara. The boy is Ruslo and the girl is Nuri." She offered a plate of fruit to Riella. "You must try the mango."

Riella bit into the soft orange flesh and a flowery sweetness filled her mouth. "That's wonderful!"

Kohara smiled, showing several gaps in her teeth. "Eat as much as you will. The men work now on the Pandora, but they'll return soon for lunch. Excepting my husband, Ferrante." She jabbed her thumb over her shoulder, in the direction of the dense jungle. "He's been at the caves for many days and nights now."

"What's he doing there?"

"Thinking. Dreaming. Divining. Searching the stars and rocks and sand for truth."

"Really? Humans do that?" Riella slowed her chewing. "He sounds like the siren elders."

"Aye. Humans and sirens have more in common than anyone might suspect. Our elders, too, are founts of wisdom, after a life well-lived. Being young is for loving and fighting and stirring oneself. It is for mistakes and mishaps. Being old is for reflecting on the journey. Preparing to return home."

"To the Beyond," said Riella. "Sirens call it that, too."

Kohara nodded, slicing a pale yellow tubular fruit. "This lunar cycle brought a great change in energies. You can feel it in here." She tapped the center of her chest with her gnarled fingers. "The cycle isn't over yet, of course. It has just begun. More change is coming."

A tingle went through Riella's body. She knew of the lunar cycle, of course, because of her strength waxing and waning with it. And if anyone had changed during this lunar cycle, it was Riella.

"What kind of change?" she asked, hoping for some clarity.

But Kohara just shrugged. "Ferrante is trying to See. When he's ready, he'll impart what he finds."

The pirates began tramping through the jungle path to the clearing. Their faces were flushed and most had been working without shirts, their muscular torsos shining with sweat. All were tattooed, and several glared at Riella with unveiled revulsion. One bearded man spat on the ground as he held eye contact with her.

Rage flamed in her chest. If she'd not been so outnumbered, she'd maul him. And to think, these men were the better Dark Tide Clan pirates. The worst of the lot had gone with Artus.

Berolt, his face as red as coral, walked straight to a bucket of water and dunked his whole head in. At the sight of their father, Ruslo and Nuri ran from the tree line, launching themselves at Ulyss. They climbed his limbs like rigging, while loudly whispering about the sudden terrifying appearance of the siren-who-walks.

Jarin was one of the last to arrive. He locked eyes on Riella as soon as he entered the clearing and strode toward her. His shirt was translucent from perspiration and his trousers were rolled to show his tanned calves, covered in tattoos. Like everyone else, he was barefoot.

He sat near Riella in the blue shade, his eyes dragging over her body. "Still got legs."

"I do."

"Good," he replied with a straight face.

She narrowed her eyes at him, trying to discern if he was making a joke at her expense.

Everyone helped themselves to the food Kohara had prepared, on plates made of large flat leaves. As well as the fruits, she removed the woven straw covers from clay bowls of cooked grains and bread and charcoal fish. Jarin sat next to Riella on the sand while they ate.

"How's Drue?" she asked. "I haven't seen him."

"Better." Jarin tore at a piece of bread with his teeth. "He's resting in his hut. Kohara made a tincture for his wounds and it seems to be helping."

"And the ship?"

He grimaced. "Lots of work to be done."

"I'll help."

"Really?"

"Of course. So that we might leave the island faster." She gestured around at the pirates. "And I'm stronger than any of them."

She said the last part louder than necessary, and was gratified when several men scowled at her.

Jarin shook his head ruefully. "Sure, you can help. But if you end up rolled in a sail again, on your own head be it. Pirates don't take kindly to insult. Especially from sirens."

He flashed a quick smile and winked at her, causing her stomach to flutter.

"Come on, break's over." He stood, pitching his leaf-plate into the scrub. "Let's put you to work."

Jarin led the way down to the beach, Riella trailing him while gazing around.

The plant life was enthralling to the siren, and she stopped every few paces to inspect the ferns and flowers and tiny creatures on leaves. The tapestry of green had a distinctly calming effect on her. It was a similar feeling to swimming through the coral reefs.

Once the fresh ocean breeze reached her, Riella broke into a run, the pristine white sand squeaking underfoot. The crystal blue sea called to her. No matter how beautiful the land was, the ocean was her home. More than her home—it *was* her. She was part of it. Or at least, she had been.

She stood in the water up to her waist, sighing at the cool relief of the water. The Pandora sat on the beach, supported by wooden beams driven into the sand.

At night, when the tide came in, the water would tug at the vessel, tempting it to ruin in the oceanic depths. She smiled at the thought, despite needing the ship very much. It was heartening that not all of her siren inclinations were gone.

The pirates swarmed over the ship like fish at feeding time, hauling ruined soaked wood from below deck, while others sawed and hammered new, dry wood farther up the sand under palm trees. Jarin waved his arm at her from one of the palms.

With a certain amount of reluctance, not wanting to leave the water, she went to him.

"You'll work up here with me," he said, tilting his head toward the Pandora. "So I can keep an eye on you. Don't want you tearing my crew to shreds."

"Fine by me."

Jarin took up a saw and buried the serrated edge into a thick plank of wood, pumping his arm back and forth. The veins on his muscular, tensed arm became even more prominent, and the sweltering mid-summer sun imparted a lustrous golden sheen to his skin. Appalled at herself for noticing, Riella snatched up a saw and began working on another plank, facing away from him.

The scent of the cut wood filled the air, mixing with the salty tang of the ocean. Although she wasn't afraid of the pirates, she was glad the nearest ones were out of earshot. It was impossible to be at ease when surrounded by your natural enemy.

"Tell me why you can't die," she said.

"Jeez. Right into it, huh?"

"Tell me."

"I'm just lucky, I guess."

"No. You said your mother made you that way. How?"

He merely grunted, tossing a piece of cut wood on a pile.

"Tell me," she repeated. "Please?"

A muscle in his jaw ticked. "She cast a spell on me, alright? Because she thought the palace would come after me on account of her crimes."

Riella immediately stopped sawing, fascinated. "What crimes?"

Jarin straightened up, his face guarded. "And she was right. The palace did pursue me. It's how I came to be a stowaway."

"What crimes?" pressed Riella.

He hesitated again, the blade of his saw suspended over the wood. "I suppose you're going to find out anyway. Everyone knows about it. I'd rather you hear it from me, while I'm armed with a saw."

She raised her eyebrows, her curiosity reaching fever pitch. "What?"

"Did you know of Queen Petra Nikolaou of Zermes?"

Riella nodded. "She was a great friend to the sirens. We gifted her a Sirenstone for helping us during the war. I was quite young then, but we were enraged and devastated when we heard she'd been—" Her eyes narrowed in comprehension. "Queen Petra was murdered by a mad sorceress. You don't mean to tell me that—"

Jarin heaved a sigh. "Yes. My mother was Levissina. *Is* Levissina. She lives still, in Velandia, being a scourge upon Petra's son, Davron. I don't condone what she—"

Anger stirred Riella's blood. "How dare she!"

"Petra's husband, the king, had my father murdered, that's how," retorted the pirate. "My mother loved my father beyond reason, and yes, madness took hold. But her actions weren't unprovoked."

"I don't understand humans," said Riella, her fury fading as quickly as it appeared. She never realized the sorceress's mate was slain by the king. "You kill each other over feelings."

The pirate scoffed. "And sirens don't? Rage is a feeling too, you know."

She resumed sawing. "Our fury is righteous."

"Everyone thinks their fury is righteous."

Riella recalled Kohara saying that humans and sirens were more alike than many thought. Certainly, since being given legs and other human attributes, Riella was experiencing unprecedented levels of emotion. She shivered as she tried to imagine the rage that would take hold of her if she loved someone, and that someone was murdered.

The siren had never been in love, of course. The notion had never interested her. But now, as feelings filled her like floodwater, she wondered if she might ever experience it. Did she even want to, given the atrocities humans were prone to committing when it was taken from them? How was love worth the risk of such destruction and pain? It must've been, though, for humans to continue seeking it out.

Another thought occurred to her. "The spell of invulnerability your mother cast, why does Polinth not perform it on himself?"

"Because he can't. No one can." Jarin made a derisive noise in his throat. "She was more gifted than any of them, the High Magus included. No one will ever admit that, of course, after what she did."

When he continued, Riella detected an odd blend of bitterness and sadness in his voice. "But to answer your question. My mother cursed the Nikolaou family for killing my father, right? Such a curse takes an enormous amount of energy. Spell-work that potent would be too unstable to last beyond a few moments, had she not figured out a way to balance the energies. She extended the spell to me, except I got the backward end. The light to the dark, or the dark to the light—not sure which you'd call it. But the ongoing counter-energy from the curse preserves my life. She felt guilty for choosing vengeance over her only child, so she solved the problem the same way she solved every problem. With magic. As long as the curse is in place, I can't die."

"Can you not break it yourself?" asked Riella. "If the magic was cast on you, too?"

"No, she would never make it that easy." He shook his head. "Every now and then, I hear news of Prince Davron from other sailors. He's been alone in his Velandian castle for a decade. Given up hope, probably. Not that you could blame him."

Riella nodded slowly. "You said Artus wants the same thing that you have. But if a mage can't give it to him, how would he do it?"

"Not by a curse, but a trinket called the Amulet of Delphine. It's why the royal patrol came after us at the docks. He sank a ship in pursuit of it. It'll give him life, apparently. I'm sure he believes it will allow him to surpass me, and all others."

A cold shiver ran through Riella. "The Amulet of Delphine. Polinth wants it, too."

She tilted her head, trying to remember what he'd said, exactly. She'd been shackled and incandescent with rage at the time, so it was hard to recall. "He draws life from Seraphine, but sooner or later that will kill her. The amulet would restore him in full, he believes. Ever since I was young, I've heard stories about the Sea Witch and the amulet she created. Strange to think it might be real. The idea of a vile human stealing it infuriates me, though. Stories say the Sea Witch gave her mortal life to create something beautiful and everlasting."

Jarin grunted. "Artus reckons he has the map to find it."

"He has the *what*?"

Riella burst into unhinged laughter, which made Jarin frown in bemusement. He watched as she put her hand down the front of her dress. A moment later, she retrieved a crumpled piece of parchment.

"Do you mean this map?"

CHAPTER 15

Riella smoothed out the parchment with excitement. It was damp and grubby, but the symbols were still legible.

Jarin took it from her in disbelief. "Where did you get this? Are you sure it's the map?" He squinted. "I can't understand these symbols."

"Nor can I. Or at least, not many of them. But Yvette stole it from the pocket of Artus's jacket yesterday. The language is Shirranis."

The pirate laughed uproariously, causing red and green parrots to fly from a nearby tree.

"Artus would've lost his mind when he realized. This is fantastic." Then, he sobered. "Lucky Yvette and the rest of them are gone from Madame Quaan's. He'll surely return there looking for it."

"And all he'll find is an empty house, save for perhaps Quaan shouting from within the walls of the study. But this is fortunate, isn't it? He has little chance of finding the amulet without the map. And we'll certainly not give it to him."

"You're right." He returned the parchment to Riella. "We must keep it a secret, though. Pirates have big mouths. Ferrante will be able to decipher the map for us, I believe."

"And when will that be?"

"When he's ready."

Riella sighed. "That's what Kohara said."

"What are Polinth's chances of finding the amulet, do you think? He's incredibly resourceful."

The siren exhaled hard through her nose. "*Resourceful* is a nice way of putting it. The man is a parasite. He thinks my Voice will help him claim the amulet."

"Then, we better find the amulet first. We have the map and soon, the Pandora will sail. I must deprive Artus of the power it would give him."

"And Polinth." Riella had a hopeful realization. "If we find the amulet, I could use it on Seraphine, to restore her." She sighed, looking out to sea. "I wish I could talk to my friends. If the amulet is real, someone among the sirens must know more about it. Are you sure we can't hurry Ferrante along?"

The pirate chuckled. "Have you ever tried to hurry along a mystic?"

"Fine." She pushed her hair off her forehead in the blazing sun. "Let's mend the ship, at least, so we're ready to sail at the earliest opportunity."

˗ˏˋ ✦ ˎˊ˗

DAYS PASSED with Riella working on the ship alongside the pirates, and with no news from the Seer.

The crew did not warm to her, so she worked with Jarin. Now and then, he would hack green coconuts open on the beach with a machete and offer one to her.

The progress of the Pandora's reparations improved Riella's mood. While she thought about Seraphine often, she was glad that each day brought her closer to rescuing the elf.

To pass the time, she talked to Jarin, peppering him with questions about humans, and life on the land, and feelings. He stayed by her side nearly always, reasoning that she'd need protection from the rest of the pirates. She'd scoff, but not send him away.

Near dusk, they'd put down their tools and make their way into the jungle. The trees came alive with evening creatures, darting and rustling unseen. The palms stood tall against the infinite amethyst sky, the pastel sand retaining the heat of the day.

Ulyss and his children built a bonfire each night in the clearing at camp. Riella sat on the sand, inspecting her sunburnt arms and shoulders in dismay. Her skin was a bright, angry pink.

"Here," said Jarin, bringing over a wooden bowl with clear liquid inside. "Coconut oil. For your sunburn."

His tawny skin had only become more tanned from being in the constant sun.

The oil did help, melting into her raw flesh as she massaged. The pirates seemed to have resolved to ignore her, keeping their distance while talking and laughing among themselves. Kohara sat with the children, preparing food.

Night settled over the island. The only light was the yellow bonfire, leaping and dancing in the air like a living thing. Riella stared into the flames, mesmerized. The heat warmed the oil on her skin, scenting the air with the sweet earthiness of coconut.

She was so entranced that she didn't notice Jarin had returned with food for her until he put a leaf plate near her knee.

"The fire is lovely to behold," she said, picking up the plate.

"Aye."

Jarin stabbed a piece of charcoal fish with a fork and crammed it into his mouth.

"How can you eat flesh?" asked Riella in disgust. "It turns my stomach to see you eat it night after night."

He'd loaded her plate with her preferred fruits, vegetables, and grains.

"It's not *flesh*. It's fish," he said, swallowing. "It's different."

"Different to what? I swim with fish. I'm from the ocean. Would you eat me?"

"You've no idea."

Inexplicably, Jarin chuckled to himself, looking into the fire.

After the meal, handed her a green coconut, into which he poured a measure from a rum flagon.

"Here," he said. "Try this."

She sipped the drink, amazed at its burning nature. Why would anyone drink such a thing? But within minutes, she understood. Her limbs grew pleasantly relaxed and when she looked around, everything had a new soft, warm glow.

"How is it?" asked Jarin.

"Good." She reached for the coconut. "I want more."

"Go slow, eh? I don't know what rum does to a siren's system."

She shrugged and took another sip.

A pirate brought out a fiddle and started playing while others sang a bawdy sailor's tune.

Riella sat back, watching them. She contemplated how everything about her life on land was different. Where the ocean had been cool and dark and serene and feminine, the land was bright and hot and loud and masculine. And yet, it was oddly *compelling*. She had to admit that she wasn't having an awful time, Polinth and Artus and Seraphine notwithstanding.

"What do sirens do for fun?" asked Jarin as they lounged by the fire, the pirates becoming increasingly rowdy and inebriated.

"Fun," repeated Riella, thinking. "Well, we swim, of course. We explore, we learn. We sing. And when we get the chance, we teach lessons to humans." She smiled.

"What do you miss the most?"

She shifted on the spot, the sand chafing the backs of her legs. "Feeling perfectly clean all the time. Underwater, you never get dirty." Riella adjusted the torn remains of her dress around her thighs. "I have sand everywhere."

"Because you've only been bathing in the ocean." He stood, motioning for her to follow. "You need a freshwater shower. I'll take you there."

"Where's *there*?"

"Just come on."

He walked through the music-filled clearing, the firelight making the tattoos on his back dance in time to the flames. She followed him, not wanting to be left with the other pirates.

The jungle seemed impenetrable in the velvety night, lit only by the moon, but Jarin knew the path well. They walked until the din at the bonfire subsided, replaced by the chattering of insects in the trees. Branches hung across the path and Jarin moved them aside for her.

When a ceaseless thundering became audible, the siren understood. He was taking her to a waterfall. Sure enough, he led her over expansive black rocks to an echoing cavern.

A waterfall flew over the cliff, hammering the pool of dark water below. The walls of the cavern surrounded the pool, arching to a high natural roof. Scant moonlight bounced off the water, making patterns on the stone.

Jarin hopped over the rocks around the pool's edge. Without a backward glance at Riella, he tore off his trousers

—the only clothes he wore—and tossed them on the dry rocks. In the low light, his muscular body almost blended into the water-beaten rock around him.

She couldn't help noticing his sculpted buttocks and substantial thighs. The front of him was not visible to her, which somehow gave her a shot of both relief and disappointment. He stepped into a rock pool beneath the waterfall up to his knees, the crashing white water obscuring his form.

"Hurry up!" he shouted over the roar of the waterfall. "It feels fantastic."

She longed to cool and clean herself, as the sand and sunburn irritated her skin, despite the coconut oil. But she was nervous to be naked with him. Mostly because a big part of her *wanted* to be naked with him. She didn't know how to act in such a situation, which was ridiculous, given she never used to wear clothing at all.

The rum was definitely emboldening her, though.

After hopping over the rocks as Jarin had done, she wriggled out of her lacy underwear and her filthy dress, casting them near his trousers. While Jarin's back was turned, she lowered herself into the pool, the waterline coming to her waist. The skin that'd been covered by the dress was pale and clean compared to her sandy, dirty limbs.

Jarin seemed unfazed by her, holding his head under the waterfall and scrubbing at his hair and neck, his eyes squeezed closed against the torrent.

Keeping a deliberate distance, she walked under the waterfall too, laughing in delight as the cool, fresh water soaked her hair and body. The sand on her arms and legs was washed away, soothing her sunburn.

"Good, right?" came Jarin's voice from behind her.

She turned around to face him. How long had he been standing there?

Droplets clung to his eyelashes and his hair was slicked

back, rivulets of water traveling the planes of his muscular body. The hair in the middle of his tattooed chest was onyx-black with wetness, trailing down to a dark mound in his groin. His cock swayed before her, impossibly massive and veined, like his wrists and hands.

"I'll go away if you'd rather be alone," he said over the thundering water.

"No, I don't want you to go away."

He nodded. "Hey, can I ask you something?"

"I suppose."

"What's it like to have a tail?"

She giggled. "It's wonderful." Riella swished her hands through the cool water. "Far simpler. Freeing."

"That makes sense. And what's it like having legs?"

She shrugged, glancing down at him. "You would know, wouldn't you?"

"I think it's different for men."

Her face grew warm. "Honestly? It's distracting at times."

"Oh, yeah?" A smile danced at the corner of his mouth. "What times?"

She splashed water at him. "Nothing to do with you."

To hide the blatant lie she'd just told, she dove under the waterfall, surfacing in the pool on the other side. Jarin followed her. They swam to the center, where the water was calm, and floated on their backs. Patterns of light shifted on the rock walls, like shadow puppets.

With her ears submerged, Riella couldn't converse with Jarin. But she stayed close to him. Now and then, almost as if by accident, their fingers grazed.

After this happened a few times, Jarin took her hand, threading his fingers through hers and holding it tight.

Riella smiled to the dark cavern, the feeling in her chest expanding and flowing through her like warm honey.

CHAPTER 16

The waterfall made rainbows in the sunny mist. Riella awoke on a rock while Jarin still slumbered, his arm under her neck like a pillow. After bathing and dressing last night, they'd talked until falling asleep in the early hours.

He awoke when she tapped her talons on his shoulder, sitting up and squinting against the brightness of the day.

"Good morning," he grumbled, scratching his stubbled cheek. "We fell asleep."

Riella felt strangely shy, even though nothing happened between them. Nothing except holding hands and sleeping side by side and talking, at least. But those things weren't as monumental as sex, were they?

She stood. "We should return to camp and work on the ship. They've probably started without us already."

After gazing up at her for several moments, he hauled his long body from the rock. "You're right. We should go back."

Once they left the cavern and filed through the vibrant green path back to camp, the night they spent in the rock pools seemed almost like a dream. Jarin walked in silence, and Riella did not speak either, unsure what to say. What did last night mean, if anything?

She'd liked it, she knew that much. She liked talking to Jarin, and being near him. But growing close to a pirate was not her mission. Her mission was to fulfill her promise to Seraphine.

Back at camp, Kohara braided straw with the children, the pirates already at the beach. The older woman looked up as Riella and Jarin approached. If Kohara had any thoughts about them disappearing all night, she let nothing show on her lovely, lined face.

She smiled. "A good day to both of you. And some fine news. My husband's ready to speak with you."

"At the cave?" asked Jarin, his face brightening.

Kohara nodded.

The children peered at Riella nervously, though they did not hide. After a breakfast of mango and banana and chunks of coconut, she and Jarin set down a different path, headed farther inland through the jungle, so that the crashing waves faded altogether. The only sounds were the buzzing of insects and the odd birdcall.

This path was wider, allowing them to walk side by side, and rusted ship parts marked the route to the cave. Jarin appeared deep in thought, the gold pendant around his neck glinting in the sun.

"Where did you get the pendant?" she asked.

"It was my mother's," he replied without looking down at it. "It's the Starlight Gardens symbol."

"Of course, I remember now. I saw that same symbol at Polinth's workshop."

"The High Magus gifted it to her, for her excellence in magic. She gave it to me because she had a silver and garnet necklace that she preferred. It belonged to her grandmother, I believe."

"Oh. A grandmother. What's it like to have family?"

He glanced over at her, his brow creasing. "What do you mean? Don't you have family?"

"Not really. Another siren would've birthed me, but I don't know who, nor have I really cared. A siren can only become pregnant on the eve of the dark moon, and only if she chooses. It's all very straightforward. What difference does it make who birthed me, anyway? We are all one."

"Well, it makes a difference to humans. Who we are and where we come from means a lot. Sometimes, it feels like it means everything."

Riella waved an insect from her face. "Yes, you do get very attached to other humans. But also, you are very cruel to one another. That's what I don't understand."

"We don't understand it either, truth be told. It's a constant source of anguish. Ferrante says that attachment is the root of all pain, and I can't say I disagree with him there."

"What are you attached to?"

"Nothing, if I can help it."

"Then, what's the point of being a human if you aren't going to get attached to anything?"

"Good question." He shook his head. "Wish I knew the answer. Maybe Ferrante can tell me."

"How long has he been here on Hieros Isle?"

"He was marooned over a year ago now, for giving Artus a prediction he strongly disliked. Neither of them would tell me what it was. I reckon that Ferrante predicted his downfall. It'd be the only explanation for his reaction." Jarin gestured at the lush green flora. "I think Ferrante likes it better here anyway. He says that Artus leaving him here was fate."

"Fate," repeated Riella. "Do you believe in it?"

"Me? I'm just a simple pirate. I believe in rum and salt water and a favorable wind."

She clicked her tongue. "Tell me, really."

He was silent for a long time.

"I know my father believed in it," he said eventually. "Seers in his own village, back in Hatara, told him that he'd meet my mother. They said she would lead him to his death. He still sought her out, and married her, because he believed there was a reason for everything. He would gladly fight anyone and anything, but not fate."

Riella pondered this. "Sounds like he was brave, and wise."

"He was." Jarin pointed to a sandstone overhang ahead. "Those are the caves. We're nearly there."

At his instruction, Riella dove from a sandstone bank through turquoise freshwater, which tunneled under a natural wall. She emerged on the other side to a temple-like interior. The floor was red sand and the smooth golden sandstone arced high to form the cave. Sunlight filtered through natural circular holes in the walls.

A small man with leathery skin sat crosslegged on the sandy floor. He was very thin and wore a loose white cotton outfit, his bare feet black on the bottom. Intricate patterns were traced into the sand in front of him.

Seeming to hear them arrive, he opened his eyes as they approached.

"Ah—" he said, smiling up at Jarin. "My boy, you are here."

"Hello, Ferrante. But of course, you knew I was coming."

"Sit, sit, please," he replied.

Only when Riella sat did she notice that his eyes were milky white and blind.

He bowed his head. "Welcome. I am Ferrante."

"I'm Riella."

"I have been expecting to meet you," he said, resting his hands in his lap. "The dark moon whispered your imminent arrival, nights ago. I am glad you found your way here."

"I didn't find my way," said Riella uncertainly. "Jarin brought me."

The old man continued to smile serenely.

"We found a map," said Jarin. "Artus was sure he'd find the Amulet of Delphine with it. Can you read it? It's in Shirranis."

"Shirranis? Then, I will need to view it on another plane. Lay it on the sand."

Jarin nudged Riella. She withdrew the parchment and put it down, taking care to avoid the patterns the Seer had drawn. Ferrante stared straight ahead without blinking.

When he spoke again, he traced his fingertip through the sand. "This lunar cycle heralds enormous shifts, in this realm and others. You are part of that shift. Both of you. The end of the cycle will mean the end of your fate."

Riella's heart thudded. What in the seven seas did that mean?

The Seer continued. "The key to victory lies in sacrifice. The siren-who-walks is written in this parchment. You are meant to be here. You are meant to walk. Never doubt that, or your power."

The old man stopped moving his finger in the sand. "Do you want to know more?"

"Yes," said Riella. "Of course."

But he simply sat there, staring straight ahead as if in a trance. Riella raised her brows at Jarin. The pirate held up his hand for her to wait.

Pools of sunshine moved across the sandy floor as the sun traversed the sky.

While they waited, Jarin picked up handfuls of sand and let them fall into little mounds, grain by grain, like sand through an hourglass. Eventually, a beam of sunlight touched the parchment. The sun progressed until the entire surface of the parchment was illuminated.

Riella looked up into Ferrante's eyes. At once, the rest of the cave fell away, leaving only his two white irises. Then, she experienced the strangest sensation, as if being pulled into the ocean by a strong current.

Ferrante's eyes now looked healthy and blue, with black pupils, and the cave was replaced with endless cobalt depths. She and the Seer were somehow in the ocean, or a realm very much like it. Dark blue streaks, like liquid smoke, swirled around her and the old man. Riella longed to tear her gaze from his eyes to investigate her surroundings, but found herself unable.

Ferrante's voice appeared in her head, although his mouth did not move. He was Sending.

"Only a siren's Voice may open the chest where the Amulet of Delphine lies. The amulet will be found, and an adversary will be defeated. But a dusk must follow every dawn. A loss for every gift. On the next full moon, the siren-who-walks will be reunited with her Voice, only to—"

Abruptly, he withdrew from her head, like water sucked out to sea during low tide. The dark blue streaks also receded, until they faded to nothing. Ferrante's eyes returned to white, and the sunny, sandy cave materialized around her.

Riella blinked, trying to reorient herself.

Ferrante leaned forward to pick up the parchment. The mystical symbols were gone, replaced by the lines and markings of a proper map.

"What was that?" asked Riella. "Where did we go?"

"To the home of the Sea Witch, of course. She does not dwell on the flesh-and-blood plane. With her blessing, I offer you the map."

Riella took the parchment and inspected it, letting out a small laugh of victory. The marked undersea caves were familiar to her. But then, she remembered that she could no longer swim to those depths. On the bright side, nor could any human.

"Thank you," said Riella to Ferrante. "But was there anything else? I believe I was severed from your voice midway through a sentence."

The old man heaved a sigh. "Some things are best not to know."

A violent sense of premonition washed over her. At that moment, she knew that she was existing in the time before some great and awful truth. And when that moment passed, she'd be living in the after.

"Tell me," she said, gripping the map.

He bowed his head and spoke the same sentence aloud, this time to completion.

"On the next full moon, the siren-who-walks will be reunited with her Voice, only to perish at dawn and be washed away with the tide."

CHAPTER 17

Riella felt impossibly calm in the face of Ferrante's prediction.

She stood, returning the map to her bustier. "Well, thank you. I am glad to be forewarned."

Ferrante gave her a solemn nod.

She hastened to the turquoise water, Jarin closely following.

"Riella—" he started, reaching for her elbow.

But she did not wish for more words—especially not from a human. The siren dove under the crystalline water and swam to the other side. Those peaceful few moments underwater were a respite from reality.

Then, she surfaced, and her situation hit her in the face like the harsh sun.

Riella would die at the next full moon, less than two weeks away. The fate foretold was hers, no doubt. She was the only siren-who-walked.

And someone would wield the amulet. But who? Since Ferrante did not specify, perhaps that part of the prophecy was not set in stone. She could find the amulet, and use it to defeat Polinth. That could be her fate.

Feeling strangely numb, she climbed from the water and sat on the edge of the sandstone bank while Jarin swam after her.

If she was to die, all she could do was make her final days count for as much as possible. Find the amulet. Save the elf. Kill Polinth.

Jarin surfaced, flicking his wet hair from his eyes, and looked for her.

"I didn't realize that would be the message," he said, swimming over to the siren.

"Of course, you didn't," she replied stiffly, her legs in the water. "How could you?"

He shook his head, his handsome face aggrieved. "Perhaps he's wrong."

"Is he often wrong?"

Jarin clenched his jaw, saying nothing.

The siren squeezed the water from her hair. "I only care about saving Seraphine now. And that's fine, because what kind of life would I have had with legs, anyway? I'm a mutant."

"You can't—" He faltered.

She narrowed her eyes at him. "I can't what?"

"You mustn't give up on yourself. On your life."

"I'm not! I didn't ask for this."

Before he could reply, she stood and went down the path toward the camp.

As she walked, Riella became hyperaware of everything. The way the fern leaves tickled her ankles as she brushed past them, the sun making dappled patterns on the jungle floor, the birdcall comprised of the same three notes over and over again. It suddenly all seemed painfully perfect and precious.

In a matter of days and nights, she would cease to be here, or anywhere. *Washed away with the tide*, Ferrante said. It would almost be as if she never existed at all.

Jarin jogged from behind her, falling into step with her. "But why can't we use the amulet to save your life? Perhaps that's why the Sea Witch revealed the map to you."

"And go against the prophecy? I doubt the Sea Witch would allow it, or why would there be a prophecy at all?" Riella pushed a branch aside. "If I find the amulet, it'll be to restore Seraphine. That's my fate."

The pirate sighed heavily. "There would be other ways to restore her. Polinth is not the only mage in the land. But you can't save anyone if you're dead."

"And I will surely *try* not to die. But everyone does, sooner or later. I'm not exempt." She shielded her eyes from the sun with her hand. "You want to help? Get the Pandora seaworthy. Allow me to fulfill my mission.'

"I will," he replied quietly. "I'll do more than that. I'll help you to fulfill it. I owe you, for waylaying you on this island in the first place."

"I thought you owed me death?"

"Turns out I needn't have bothered. Fate has it in for you, big time."

He gave her a sidelong look, which she returned.

She shook her head. "You're not funny."

"Do you want to talk about—"

"No."

Riella feared that if she let down the barrier around her feelings, she'd never be able to put it back up. Jarin would see her at her most vulnerable, and she couldn't allow that. She didn't have time for feelings. She certainly didn't have time to fall apart.

So, she swallowed hard, willing the gigantic, scary tidal wave of emotion building in her chest to dissolve.

"I must find a way to contact my friends," she said, chewing her lip. "I'll need their help to retrieve the amulet, because the undersea caves are too deep for us to reach alone."

"How're you going to contact them?"

"Sirens can Send to each other underwater. Talk through our minds. Over a long distance, we can Send only a general distress signal. That's what I'll have to try, because I don't know where my friends are right now."

Jarin spluttered. "You can read each other's minds? Gods. That explains a lot."

"Only underwater," she clarified. "And the greater the distance, the more difficult it is. Near an island as big as this one, it'll be hard for the Sending to travel through the water undisturbed."

"We'll head out to sea on a rowboat, then. Tomorrow?"

She nodded her assent.

The sun was low and red in the sky when they reached the camp. A resigned melancholy settled over Riella as the initial shock of Ferrante's revelation wore off. The melancholy was hardly an improvement, though, because she didn't wish to spend her remaining time alive feeling miserable, either.

Kohara and the children arranged kindling in the fire pit. The old woman's smile quickly faded as she registered Riella and Jarin's stoic expressions. Ruslo and Nuri had evidently decided the siren was unlikely to maul them, because they circled Riella as she walked over.

"We're making a fire." Ruslo's cheek was smudged with ash and his dark hair was askew. "Would you like to help?"

"Yes, I would," she replied, glad for the distraction. "I've never made a fire before."

Jarin hung back. "Will you be alright if I look in on Drue?"

"Of course. Tell Drue I wish him well."

Nuri and Ruslo demonstrated how to make fire by striking flint with a blade. Golden sparks flew from the flint into the mound of dried coconut husks, transforming the pile into flames.

Fire lighting was far more difficult than it looked, and she had to try several times to get the spark to jump correctly. But eventually, the fire caught, and yellow flames danced high and bright.

Riella felt Kohara's thoughtful gaze on her the whole time, but the older woman didn't try to discuss Ferrante or the cave, for which she was grateful.

As night fell, stars decorated the lilac sky and the crescent moon rose. Riella usually adored staring at the moon. But this evening, she kept her eyes firmly at ground level, knowing the waxing moon was now counting down to her death.

Jarin returned from visiting Drue as the crew came up from the beach.

The men guzzled water before progressing to flagons of mead and bottles of rum. They sat on the stumps around the fire, or sprawled out on the sandy ground. Crickets chirruped behind the tree line and bats swooped silently overhead like ghosts.

"How's Drue?" she asked Jarin as he brought food to her.

She picked at the fruit, which seemed to have lost all flavor.

"He improves."

The siren nodded. She gazed into the hypnotic flames, the weight in her chest too heavy for her to bear carrying on a conversation. Jarin sat by in pensive silence.

It was harsh and unusual to know *when* she was going to die, but not *how*. Everyone knew they'd die one day, of course. But it was something else entirely to have a countdown, and to be unable to stop it.

After all, who was she to go against fate? Jarin's father hadn't been able to stop it. In fact, he'd walked right into it, head held high. Perhaps that was the strongest thing to do.

As she watched the fire, she wondered if she would've lived differently, if she had known she'd die so soon. Would she have made different choices?

But, if she had made different choices, she'd not be in this mess to begin with. Galeil and Mareen wisely avoided humans, and they still had their tails and Singing voices to show for it. They were free. And what could be more wonderful than freedom?

"Dance with us," said Ruslo, offering his hand to Riella.

Snapping out of her trance-like state, she agreed. While Berolt played a fiddle, the children showed her a simple dance, repeating the steps for her until she could do them too. She twirled and spun around the clearing until her mind was blessedly free of thought. On the other side of the fire, Jarin eyed her through the flames, even when talking with his men.

This was a kind of freedom, she thought. Feeling giddy and joyful, dancing with children on the warm sand. She would die, like everyone would, but not yet. Until then, she could savor her remaining life.

She tried to convince herself to be alright with the situation. After all, had she not always been willing to die in battle, during the war? Was this so different?

The music grew louder as the rum flowed, and more pirates joined the dancing. Riella eventually ran out of breath, her hair sticking to her hot face, and she wandered from the fire pit to breathe the cool night air.

The shadows greeted her like an old friend. Away from the music, the jungle was alive with night noises. She let her feet guide her toward the distant crashing of the ocean, alone.

As she climbed the silver dunes, sea grass bowing in the stiff breeze, she felt lost and bereft. The wine-dark sea was no longer her home. If she tried to return to it, the ocean would kill her as if she were human. She dwelled on land now, and yet she didn't belong here, either.

But even when she'd lived in the sea, she'd never completely fit in with her friends. She'd always felt different. Like there was no place for her.

Perhaps it did not matter anymore that she didn't belong. Perhaps that was the point the whole time—she wasn't meant to. Her life was not about belonging.

It was about fulfilling a prophecy, and then dying.

In the middle of the expansive beach, there was no hiding from the moon. It bathed her in pearly light, making her skin glow. The thundering waves were so loud that she didn't hear Jarin until he was very close.

He stood before her without saying a word, blocking her view of the ferocious sea. He covered her shoulders with his large hands, and she let him. She took a deep breath and looked up into his serious eyes.

When she opened her mouth to speak, she tasted salt. Tears were streaming down her cheeks. How long had she been crying?

It was too late to hide her vulnerability from Jarin. He'd already seen, and nothing bad happened. Perhaps she ought to let the tidal wave rise inside of her and flow outward.

"I don't want to die," she said, her voice breaking. "I'm scared."

Jarin wrapped his arms around her and hugged her against his chest. From one ear, she could hear the pounding of the waves. From the other, the strong and steady beat of his heart. She felt warm, and safe, in a way she never had before. She wanted more of that feeling. It was incredibly appealing, especially in the face of death. There was no reason for her to deny her attraction to him anymore. No reason at all.

She tilted her head back to meet his penetrating gaze.

"Will you kiss me?" she asked, her voice husky from crying.

Without a moment's hesitation, as if he'd been just waiting for her to ask, he cupped her face and leaned down, pressing his lips to hers.

The warmth of his mouth felt intimate and comforting, even as it felt foreign. She liked how he tasted, and that kissing him meant they breathed the same air. He parted her lips with a gently probing tongue, his lips sliding against her teeth, and her tears finally stopped.

She returned the kiss—slowly at first, while she got used to the rhythm of the movements. Then, with the urgency of someone whose very days were numbered.

CHAPTER 18

❧

Jarin watched over Riella while she slept.

He'd taken her to a treehouse in a secluded part of the tree-borne labyrinth, the thatched roof blending almost seamlessly with the surrounding palm fronds. Torches in brackets cast light over the doorway as he guided her inside. It'd been difficult to get any words out of her after those sad, terrible sentences she uttered on the beach amidst flowing tears.

I don't want to die. I'm scared.

What could he say to that? What could he do? He couldn't look her in the face and tell her that fate was *incorrect*. Jarin didn't pretend to know more than Ferrante. So far, everything the old Seer said had come true. Riella was indeed the rare ocean jewel he'd referred to. It was too late for Jarin to distance himself from the siren—her fate and the fate of the clan were already entwined.

In the treehouse, she'd taken him by the hand to the unmade bed. He removed his shirt while she curled up on the white sheets. When he lay beside her, she pulled his arm under her neck and rested her hand in the middle of his tattooed chest.

He'd expected her to lie awake for a long time, as he knew he would, but after a few minutes of fighting to keep her eyes open, she fell into a deep sleep.

Jarin was left with his churning thoughts and the conflicted burn in his chest. What if he'd ruined fate by bringing Riella aboard the Pandora when she needed to get to the Black Cliffs? His feud with Artus blinded him to the possibility that fate had bigger concerns than Jarin usurping his old mentor.

But the truly shameful thing? Jarin would use the amulet to save Riella's life, even against her wishes. He'd let the elf die a thousand deaths if it meant keeping the siren alive. It was not rational, but it was so.

Maybe he took after his mother more than he realized.

He'd always been afraid of his dark side veering too close to hers. Obsessive, deranged, intense-beyond-words. For that reason, he'd sworn to never let himself grow close to a woman, fearful of triggering the traits for which his mother was infamous.

But now, he cursed that he wasn't *more* like her. What he wouldn't give for her magic, her power. Although she'd done terrible things, at least she'd never had to feel helpless, the way he did now.

Jarin had never considered himself a good man. He'd never *been* a good man, and he'd never cared, because darkness was innate to him. But Riella deserved better than imminent death. She was remarkable and brave. One-of-a-kind, in every sense.

He stared at the shifting moonlit patterns on the walls and smiled faintly to himself. How ironic that he'd sworn to never let himself care about a woman. That was still true. He cared about a bloody siren instead—one who'd stabbed him in the heart, no less.

Maybe his true purpose was to assist the siren-who-walks during this fateful time. His whole life, he'd felt adrift and like he belonged nowhere. Was this why? If it wasn't, could he make it that way? Force himself into fate?

He and Riella would find the amulet, and they'd use it to save her. She wouldn't know that, of course. Riella was adamant the amulet wasn't meant for her.

There would no doubt be another way to save the elf. If being a pirate had taught him anything, it was that every impossible situation had a way out. There was always an escape hatch, a hidden weapon, a secret solution. It was just a matter of finding it. Or, failing that, inventing it.

He ran his fingertips through the spun silk that was Riella's hair. Her eyelids lightly fluttered as she slept, indicating she was dreaming. She appeared uncharacteristically sweet when she slept, her signature fierceness dormant.

Gods, he wanted her. It felt profane, to lust so intensely for a siren doomed to die. He had no business allowing his blood to be stirred. And yet, he was a man. He could not help his body's reaction to her.

"It seems like such a waste to sleep," came her breathy voice.

Jarin had been tracing the infinity symbol on her fabric-covered hip, over and over again. He hadn't noticed her eyes open.

But now, she gazed at him in the creamy moonlight, wide awake.

"Time goes too quickly in the land of dreams," she said. "That's not how I want to spend the nights I have left."

"You have to sleep sometime," he replied in a low voice.

"Sleep isn't what I want right now," she murmured, studying his face. "If I am to die, first I want to live."

She batted her long eyelashes at him and blood rushed to his groin. While holding eye contact, she picked up his wrist and placed his hand on her waist. His fingers dug gently into her soft flesh beneath the fabric of her dress.

"Are you sure?" he asked. "It might not be what you expect."

"That's the point. And yes, I'm sure."

Riella lifted her knees toward the ceiling as Jarin's pulse increased. He'd never wanted anything more than he wanted her in this moment. She let her knees fall open, revealing her translucent underwear, through which he could make out the delicate lines of her entrance. The material lying over her opening was dark with dampness, making him half-mad with desire.

Jarin pulled himself up to kneel between her legs, his hands resting on her slender calves. The sight before him made his erection harder than steel. She rested her arms above her head, her platinum hair splayed around her like a halo. In the pale moonlight, she glowed like the otherworldly being that she was.

Grasping one of her ankles, he lifted her leg to his mouth and kissed the inner line of her calf. His eyes were still on her face, and she smiled. As he kissed his way over her knee and to her thigh, he trailed his fingers up her other leg.

The intoxicating scent of her arousal reached his nostrils, making his blood surge. He put one large hand on her hip and with the other, traced small circles on the damp spot of her underwear, barely grazing the tender flesh beneath it. She squirmed with pleasure.

"I want more," she whispered.

You and me both, he thought.

Every muscle in his body was tense with the effort of preventing himself from taking down his trousers, tugging her sodden underwear to the side, and spearing himself into her sweet pinkness.

But he couldn't do that to her. Not tonight. Despite her insistence that she wanted to experience everything life had to offer, she didn't truly know what she was asking for. She couldn't comprehend how overwhelming his cock would feel if he unleashed himself on her, when she'd never had sex before. He would work up to it.

Licking his lips, he tore off her underwear and cast them aside. She was even more perfect without the constraints of the fabric. Her slick opening was flushed a delicate rose color, the paler outer edges merging with the pearly cast of the rest of her skin.

At the top of the folds was her shining, swollen little clit. With a groan of longing, he leaned forward and pressed his mouth firmly to her drenched folds. She exhaled sharply in surprise, then sucked in a long breath while writhing on the sheets.

Jarin ran his tongue from the very bottom of her slit, all the way up the center. He stopped on her clit and applied a pulsing pressure, which made Riella moan. Before she could get used to the sensation, he ran his tongue in random, ceaseless patterns across her wet folds. Whenever he reached her clit, he encircled it with his tongue and kissed it.

When he felt the telltale tensing of her body, he slid his tongue into her entrance, as far as he could go, moaning at the exquisite fragrance and tightness of her. He smiled to himself, because she really did taste like the ocean, only sweeter.

He worked his way back up to her clit, running his tongue across it in a steady, coaxing rhythm. Then he slid two fingers inside of her slick folds, the pressure of her muscles immediate and intense against his intrusion. But she drilled herself down on his fingers, moaning, and he drove a third inside.

He alternated smoothly between thrusting into her depths and hooking his fingers to touch the soft spot inside that turned her moaning into rapid pants. While sliding his fingers into her, he kept the relentless pressure on her swollen clit with his tongue.

When she reached the pinnacle of pleasure, he felt the waves moving through her body, from her core outward.

Yet, he did not let up. His face drenched with her desire, he continued until she crested another wave, and then another.

Only when she was weakened and breathless on the sheets did he finally release her from his mouth and hands.

When he moved to lie next to her, she buried her face in his neck. And it made his heavily guarded heart burst wide open.

CHAPTER 19

The next morning, Riella and Jarin set off into the ocean on a rowboat to contact her friends.

"Do you believe this will work?" asked Jarin, his body moving with the steady back and forth of his strokes.

He was much better at rowing than Riella, having the advantage of years of experience. The siren found handling the oars to be cumbersome and awkward. Hieros Isle out of sight, the glittering blue ocean extended in every direction.

"I can only hope," she replied, struggling to make the oar enter the water at the correct angle. "I haven't tried to Send since Polinth changed me. I'm not sure I can still do it."

"I suppose we'll find out."

The siren had awoken that morning in his arms. For a few blissful seconds, she'd forgotten everything bad about her past, present, and future. All she felt was the soft tickle of the morning breeze through the window and the lingering glow of the pleasure he'd given her in the early hours of the morning, when the moon still shone.

But the peace did not last, and cruel reality came flooding back. Ferrante's prophetic words repeated in her head. In her mind's eye, she saw the red flash of Polinth's spell as he caught Seraphine.

Riella was now in a race with him and Artus to find the Amulet of Delphine.

She and Jarin's one big advantage was the map, thanks to Yvette's light-fingered ways. If the siren could communicate with her friends and enlist their help, her advantage would be two-fold. The hard part would be getting the message to them.

Physical mass could interrupt a siren's telepathic waves. If an island or ship or even a giant squid was in the path of her signal, the Sending would scatter to pieces. And even if nothing was in the way, Sending over long distances was a shot in the dark. She'd have no way of knowing if the message reached a siren's mind at all.

Without her Voice, she couldn't Sing to other sirens, which would move through the water with greater force and durability than a Sending.

A terrible thought occurred to her. What if Polinth used her Voice to lure other sirens? Force them to do his bidding, and dive for the amulet? The prospect chilled her. With Polinth, she couldn't rule out anything. He was powerful and disturbed and, if he truly was dying, he had nothing to lose.

Well, the same could now be said of Riella, and she vowed to stop at nothing to defeat him. And Artus too, if she could help it. The man was a scourge. Now that she'd experienced sexual intimacy for herself, she understood the true seriousness of Artus selling her to Madame Quaan. She'd liked sharing her body with Jarin, very much, but the thought of being forced to do such a thing with any man who could pay was terrible.

More and more, she was glad to be with Jarin. Her life as a land-walker would've been so much harder without him. And she'd be facing death completely alone.

Although, when the actual time came, she would no doubt be alone. That was the nature of death. No one could go with you.

Riella sat at the boat's bow, trying to concentrate on her stroke, determined to master the rhythm. As they slowly progressed, she gazed straight down into the blue depths with longing. Swimming had been second nature to her—something she'd never had to consider. All her life, she'd taken her tail for granted. She'd taken her very life for granted.

"Do you know what it feels like to die?" asked Riella as an atoll came into view. "When I stabbed you in the heart, did you get a glimpse of death, I mean? Or do you feel nothing at all when wounded?"

The atoll—a small ring-shaped island—was lush and green with vegetation, edged by white beaches. An aqua-blue lagoon sparkled in the center. No manmade structures or signs of habitation were visible. Jarin had recommended the atoll, having passed it many times but never visited.

"I didn't feel a thing," replied Jarin. "The shard barely tickled."

"Really?" She raised her eyebrows.

He laughed. "No. It hurt like the seven hells. I'm not impervious to pain."

"Oh. You hid it very convincingly."

"Yeah, well. Pirates can't show pain. But no, I haven't experienced dying. I doubt death is painful, though. It's life that's bloody painful."

Waves surged the rowboat to shore. Riella and Jarin dragged the vessel up the smooth sandy beach, beyond the clutches of the coming tide.

The atoll was pristine. The sand was fine and white, like powdered diamonds. Seabirds nested in the trees and palms created shade at the tree line.

Riella looked around. "I suppose there's no reason to delay. What will you do while I'm gone?"

Jarin sat on the sand and kicked off his boots, gesturing at the narrow strip of jungle. "I'll go have a look around. Never know what you might find."

Her blood tingling with the anticipation of returning to the ocean, she stripped off her dress and underwear, throwing them on the sand. Jarin gazed at her with raw lust, the muscles in his arms and jaw flexing, as if physically restraining himself.

Riella allowed him a few more seconds to look, then she turned and sauntered toward the surf. Right as she got to the water's edge, she turned and smirked at him. Jarin beat the sand with his fists and roared with frustration.

"Get in the water right now, before I drag you back here and desecrate you!" he shouted.

Waist-deep in the water, waves breaking around her, Riella cackled. She took a breath and dove under the surface.

The cool serenity embraced her like she was having the sweetest dream. Sunlight danced on the sandy floor and the crystal-blue water curled overhead as it crested in waves.

Immediately, she forgot she no longer had a tail, and went to kick it. Her legs cut through the water instead, barely creating any movement. She swam as best she could with her arms and legs, remembering how she'd derided Jarin for the way humans swam. It really was very difficult without a tail.

Soon, she was in deeper water, gliding over a coral reef that shimmered with pinks and greens and purples. Schools of tiny fish angled around her, moving as one.

Once she'd traveled far enough to Send a signal, she required another breath. She kicked straight upward, her chest burning, and gasped for air the moment she broke the surface. Her inability to breathe underwater made her feel even less like a siren than losing her tail.

In the distance, Jarin was a small, anonymous figure on the white beach. She had swum farther than a human could've with one breath. But that wasn't saying much.

With another lungful of air, she dove underwater. She tried to access the pocket of her mind that could Send telepathically. To her immense relief, she found it thrumming and receptive. To experiment, she Sent a general probe, calling to any siren nearby.

It went unanswered, but she'd expected as much. Sirens had no cause to swim these waters, which were far from any of their settlements. The important thing was that she could Send the signal to begin with.

Concentrating hard, she summoned all her mental strength to Send into the blue aether as far as possible. The message she crafted was simple, and attuned to her pod. If any of them received the message, they'd recognize her as one of their own. Or at least they would've, before Polinth changed her. She prayed that was still the case.

"This is Riella," she Sent. "I need help. I'm at Hieros Isle. Approach with caution. Humans on shore."

She stopped short of mentioning Dark Tide Clan pirates, because her friends would assume she was abducted. The sirens would destroy the Pandora on sight, thus restarting the war.

Intuitively, she also said nothing about the amulet. She couldn't be sure where the message would end up, exactly. It was bad enough mentioning her location, lest Polinth somehow caught wind of it, but she could see no way around that part. If her friends were to find her, they'd need to know where she was. Right now, the sirens were Riella's only real hope of retrieving the amulet.

She pushed the message through the water until it disappeared from range. Now, she would wait. Even if the message found her pod, it could be hours or days before the sirens were able to reach Hieros Isle.

For pure pleasure, she stayed underwater a little longer. She did backward somersaults and visited coral and simply drifted along with the current, basking in the joy of the weightlessness and penetrating blue silence. Eventually though, she could ignore her burning lungs no longer, and she surfaced. The tide had taken her even farther out to sea. She could still discern Jarin on the beach, although something seemed amiss now.

He paced up and down the sand, waving his arms frantically, trying to get her attention.

CHAPTER 20

Riella's heart rate quickened.
She looked around for danger, but saw none. The ocean stretched uninterrupted on all sides, except for the atoll. Jarin put his hands around his mouth to project his voice as he shouted to her. But the wind must've snatched his words away, because she heard nothing except the lapping of the water and the screech of a seagull overhead.

Perhaps he'd seen a shark fin. Humans were extraordinarily and rather needlessly afraid of sharks. They wouldn't bite a human unless the human acted like prey.

Jarin was a pirate, though. He'd know a siren had no cause to fear a shark—sirens played with sharks the way humans played with dogs. There must've been some other danger.

With a deep breath, she dove underwater and swam for shore.

Jarin met her in the breaking waves when she emerged. The first thing she noticed was the rowboat missing. Had it washed out to sea? Were they stranded?

"What is it?" she asked while catching her breath.

"Hurry," he said, grabbing her hand and guiding her out of the water. He passed her dress to her and led her up the beach.

The alabaster sand was blinding after being in the cool haze of the blue water.

Jarin only spoke again when they reached the dark shade of the tree line. "Get dressed."

His eyes were not on her, but scanning the horizon to the east. All she could see was the green and white islet extending into the distance.

"I was exploring on the other side of the atoll," he said. "I saw Artus's schooner at sea. They're at cruising speed and closer to shore than they ought to be. That means they're searching. And they are surely searching for us. Specifically, the map."

The siren hissed in dismay, tugging her dress over her head. "Already? I thought we'd have longer before he came looking."

"He must've doubled right back to Klatos when he realized he didn't have the map on him. The royal patrol was looking for the Pandora, not him. He would've been free to dock."

"Won't he look for us at Hieros Isle?"

"He won't expect I've gone somewhere so exposed, and he hates the place because he considers Ferrante bad luck. Nothing is stronger than a sailor's superstitions. But sooner or later, yeah, he'll check Hieros Isle. He'll have to. We need to get the Pandora seaworthy, and leave."

Jarin had dragged the rowboat up the beach and concealed it in the trees, covering the vessel with palm fronds and snaking green vines. It would be enough to remain undetected, but only if Artus and his crew decided not to come ashore. If they did, Riella and Jarin would have few places to hide on the tiny islet.

"There!" said Jarin, pointing.

Sure enough, a schooner glided around the edge of the atoll, a dark blight on the pristine horizon. Together, she and Jarin retreated farther into the shadows, hidden by trees.

"He'll have a spyglass," explained Jarin, drawing her even lower to the ground. "He'll be able to see the shore in a fair amount of detail. Let's pray he doesn't notice the track from the rowboat running up the beach."

The schooner moved with painstaking slowness across the ocean. Was it slowing down, or was that just Riella's anxiety?

"What do we do if they come ashore?" asked Riella. "There are dozens of them."

"We have two choices. We can set off in the rowboat, hoping we make it beyond their reach before they can pursue us. Or, we stay and fight."

Riella knew the choice was only the illusion of one. Even with her and Jarin's combined strength, a rowboat would never outpace a schooner.

"We'll fight," she said decisively. "I won't paddle away in fear, only to be captured again when they give chase. I never want to be captured again in my life."

Jarin had his cutlass, and she could wield one or both oars. They would be at a hefty disadvantage, but that had never stopped a siren before.

But, in the end, a fight wasn't necessary, because the vessel continued without turning toward them. Eventually, it sailed from view altogether.

"Let's wait before leaving," said Jarin. "To make sure he's not coming back."

The pair tramped through the jungle to the other side, to ensure Artus had indeed passed by. When the horizon remained clear, Riella and Jarin pushed the rowboat to the water and began their long return journey.

"We got lucky," said Jarin as he heaved the oars. "But it's only a matter of time before he finds us."

Riella nodded. "Let's go straight to the ship and help with the repairs. The sooner we can leave, the better."

Upon their return, they steered the rowboat to the Pandora, climbing the ropes to board the great vessel. Ulyss and Berolt and the crew were hard at work repairing the hull, sweaty and red-faced in the afternoon sun. Anchored just offshore, the Pandora swayed gently with the nudge of the tide.

"He's on our tail," said Jarin to Berolt with a grimace. "Artus. He's scanning the seas for us."

Berolt put his hands on his hips, puffing. "Well, we'll be on our way soon. The hull is patched, we just need to reinforce it."

Itching to help, Riella carried planks of wood and tools down to the bilge. Seeing Artus's ship had reminded her that Polinth wasn't necessarily her most immediate threat.

On her way back upstairs, she ran into Drue.

The boy moved stiffly, but his face had more color than the last time she'd seen him.

"How are you doing?" she asked.

Drue shrugged. "Heaps better. I'm not good for hard labor, but I can prepare the rigging."

He patted the coil of rope he was carrying.

Riella brightened. "Can you show me?" She leaned in and lowered her voice. "I'd never say this to any other pirate, in case it made them feel good, but the way they climb the rigging is quite impressive. They remind me of land-crabs on webs. Now that I have legs, I want to learn how."

The cabin boy nodded along, frowning slightly. "Right. Webs. Do you mean spiders?"

"Yes! Land-crabs."

Drue chuckled. "Alright, sure. I can show you."

She took the rope and followed his instructions, which he issued with complete patience, even when she dropped the main sail from a great height and he had to dive out of the way, lest he was killed.

"Sorry!" she called down, gripping the main mast, which creaked in the salty breeze.

"It's alright."

He continued his instructions, except from several paces back.

The other pirates scowled at her as she worked, but Riella ignored them. She spent hours on the rigging, until she felt confident with the basic methods of sailing.

"How long have you been with the Dark Tide?" asked Riella when she was back on deck, helping Drue roll up a sail.

"Less than a year," he replied.

"Ah. So, after the war ended. That explains why you aren't wary of me, like the others."

"I'm not afraid of *you*, but I know well enough to be wary around other sirens. I may not have fought in the war, but I've heard stories aplenty from the crew."

He reached into his pocket and withdrew a small white ball.

"Candle wax," he said, squishing it slightly with his fingers. "We plug our ears with it when we suspect sirens are nearby."

Riella raised her brows, bemused the pirates had found a way around Sirensong. "Does it work?"

He shrugged. "I've never had cause to test it. Hopefully never will. Berolt reckons it stops the worst of the Song, but not all of it."

A pirate hauled a toolbox past at that moment, glowering at Riella. He paused to mutter something into Drue's ear before stomping down the stairs.

Drue returned the wax to his pocket, his face flushing. "He's angry I was telling you our secrets," he explained. "He thinks it's traitorous. The crew have been grumbling about you ever since we arrived on the isle."

Riella looked around uneasily. "But they will obey Jarin's orders, won't they? He's the captain now."

What if they refused to sail for the Black Cliffs to rescue Seraphine? The crew loathed having Riella on board, let alone sailing the Pandora at her behest. Jarin and Drue liking her obviously meant very little to the rest of them.

Sirens and pirates were still enemies, and they seemed committed to treating her like one. Jarin couldn't afford dissent in the ranks so soon after becoming captain. And without the Pandora, Riella had nothing. She'd be stuck.

And really, why should the pirates put their lives on the line for her? Naturally, they had no desire or cause to sail around finding magical amulets and rescuing elves. They wanted to plunder and loot and drink mead at port cities.

Riella was dragged from her thoughts by a pirate's panicked shouts. He stood at the bow, spyglass in hand, looking to sea. He hollered a warning over his shoulder, causing the ship to come alive with activity at once.

"Enemy! Enemy incoming!"

CHAPTER 21

"Sirens attacking! Arm yourselves, lads! Sirens incoming!"

Riella's stomach dropped. She threw down the sail she'd be working on and ran to the bow.

"No!" she said to the pirate. "They aren't attacking."

He pointed at three dark blue shadows hurtling through the water toward the Pandora. "Sure looks like they are."

Riella snatched the man's spyglass.

"I said they aren't attacking," she hissed. "You're going to get people killed."

He scowled at her and drew his cutlass from his belt. "*Sirens* killed, you mean."

Her temper flared, and for a moment she forgot about Jarin and Seraphine and the amulet. All she could focus on was the disgusting pirate snarling in her face about killing sirens.

"Not likely," she spat.

"Positions, lads!" he shouted.

Riella picked him up by the collar and threw him hard

against the railing. He howled in pain as he crumpled to the wooden boards.

Before she could slash his face with her talons, Jarin emerged from below deck and ran to the bow. He assessed the situation with a glance at Riella, whose chest heaved with fury, and a look at the fast-approaching blue shadows in the water.

"Stand down!" he shouted at the crew. He hauled the man Riella had thrown to his feet, giving him orders. "Get to the bilge. Finish work on the hull. Now."

The man glared at Riella, then stomped away.

Jarin turned to her, lowering his voice. "They aren't attacking, right? They're here to help you?"

"Yes," she said with more certainty than she felt. "But perhaps I better head them off before they reach the ship, all the same."

Although a truce existed between sirens and pirates, she didn't wish to test it. The pirates' tempers were nothing compared to her friends', especially Mareen. She took special pleasure in tormenting her prey before killing it.

If sirens attacked the pirates now, Riella could kiss the amulet and Seraphine goodbye. But how would her friends receive her? They likely didn't know she had legs now.

Jarin nodded. "Go."

She climbed onto the wooden railing of the bow and dove headfirst into the turquoise water. Right away, she heard her friends' thoughts.

"Stay there," she Sent to them. "I'm coming to you."

"Riella! What in the seven seas—"

"I'll explain. Just stop advancing. The pirates are getting ready to defend themselves."

"She's ordering us around. Unbelievable."

That was Mareen. Despite her nerves, Riella's heart lifted at the familiarity of her friend's haughtiness. Perhaps this meeting would go well. The sirens might even want to help her to defeat Polinth.

She swam through the blue depths as fast as she could, painfully aware of how much slower she was traveling than her friends.

"I can't see you," Sent Galeil.

"I'm coming. Right in front of you."

Mareen's vivid orange hair became visible first, then Galeil and Thera. Although the younger siren had just come of age, Thera looked every bit as fierce and beautiful as the other two, with her cloud of brown hair and powerful pink tail.

Riella's optimism vanished as she took in the majestic sight of her friends. Never had she missed her tail more than in that moment. She steeled herself for their reactions to her new body.

"Where have you—" started Mareen. Then, a moment later, she saw the rest of Riella. "Ugh! What happened to you?"

Mareen propelled herself forward to get a better look, then surged backward again in disgust. "Riella! You have *legs*. Is this some kind of trick?"

Riella was treading water to stop herself from sinking to the ocean floor. Her air would run out soon and she'd need to surface, but for now, she could communicate via Sending.

The three sirens circled her, their faces aghast.

"That day with the fishing boat," Sent Riella. "I was captured by a sorcerer. He experimented on me."

"But what *are* you now?" Sent Galeil in fascination and horror.

"I'm still me!" she replied desperately. "He just gave me legs. And stole my Singing voice."

Mareen swam right up to her, gazing into her eyes. "You seem so . . . fragile now."

She wrapped her hand around Riella's wrist and twisted her arm back. Riella gasped in pain and tried to shove her off, but Mareen easily overpowered her. Riella's physical strength used to outstrip Mareen's, before Polinth changed her.

"What are you doing on a Dark Tide Clan pirate ship?" Mareen seethed, releasing her wrist with a look of derision. "Traitor."

Riella rushed to explain, mindful that she'd need to surface shortly. Sirens were perfectly able to speak above water, as humans did, but she suspected her friends would further deride her for it. "I'm trying to save an elf named Seraphine. She's being held hostage by Polinth, the sorcerer who captured me. Seraphine helped me to escape him. But then I was dragged up by a Dark Tide Clan net. I need your help."

"Do you, though?" Sent Galeil. "It seems pirates are your friends now. *Land-walker*," she added.

Galeil swam to Riella with a single tail kick, glaring into her face as Mareen had. Thera circled ceaselessly and silently. For the first time, Riella glimpsed what it was like to face sirens as opponents, as humans did. It was utterly chilling.

As apex predators, the trio innately sensed Riella's fear, heightening their killer instincts. They circled her more closely, pressing in on all sides. She willed herself to focus on her reason for summoning them in the first place.

"The Amulet of Delphine is hidden in the caves of Neredes. Please, swim down there and find the amulet, before our enemies do."

"What do you mean by *our* enemies?" Sent Galeil. "Land-walkers are our enemies. Their petty squabbles aren't our concern."

Mareen stopped swimming, floating before Riella with

blazing eyes. "How would you know where to find the amulet?"

"The Sea Witch told me." Riella's chest was beginning to ache. She needed air. But this was a critical moment, and she didn't want to ruin it by acting human. "She told me via a Seer."

"The Sea Witch?" Mareen scoffed. "She would never appear to a land-walking Seer. You've been tricked." She shook her head, her hair flailing around her terrifying face. "The amulet has a greater purpose than land-walkers can comprehend. Typical human arrogance to suppose they might plunder the sea for such an artifact." She shrugged. "But, let them drown trying."

"I'm not human, though," Sent Riella.

But her timing was terrible. Her lungs burned beyond endurance, and she was forced to kick upward. As she broke the surface, she lost the telepathic connection with the sirens. They emerged a moment later, glaring at her in revulsion as she gulped air.

"There's much you are not telling us, and I don't appreciate the deception," said Mareen. Her eyes slid to the Pandora, where it bobbed in the shallows. "Who is that?"

Riella looked over her shoulder. Jarin stood at the bow, arms folded in front of his chest, watching her.

"Is that who you're wearing a *dress* for?" asked Galeil.

"He's a necessary evil. He agreed to help me rescue the elf."

"Ha!" said Mareen, as if catching Riella out. "So you *have* sided with the Dark Tide cretins."

Thera spoke for the first time. "Are we going to fight them or not?" she asked with a slight whine, eyeing the ship. "I've never fought a pirate before."

Despite herself, Riella recalled having the same bloodlust

when she was younger. In a siren, it never truly went away. She felt it still. Not that her friends would believe her.

"We've patrolled nonstop trying to find you, or any trace of you," said Galeil, a hint of reproach entering her voice. "You only Sent us a message when you wanted us to do your bidding."

"There's no bidding!" Riella felt like tearing her hair out. "I'm trying to keep the amulet out of the hands of bad people. Why can't you just do as I ask?"

As soon as the words left her mouth, she knew they were a mistake. The very last thing a siren appreciated was being bossed around. Perhaps her friends were right, and she'd become more human than she'd realized.

"Enjoy your new life," said Mareen coldly. "Do not call on us again. We don't exist to run errands for land-walkers."

Before Riella could reply, the red-haired siren dove, kicking a wave of water into Riella's face. Galeil followed. Thera alone stayed above the surface with Riella.

"Mareen searched harder for you than anyone," said Thera quietly. "She hasn't rested since you disappeared."

Then, Thera left too, diving after her friends, headed out to sea.

Riella swam straight to shore instead of the ship. Her heart was too heavy to be around humans, who hated her, for meeting with sirens, who also hated her.

Perhaps she was destined to die soon simply because she had no power, no friends, no plan, and no weapons. What if she declined to participate in the prophecy? Could she opt out of her fate by refusing to seek the amulet?

But, as she reached the shallows of the beach, Seraphine's haunted face appeared in her mind's eye. She couldn't abandon the elf after she'd sacrificed herself for Riella.

And Jarin?

He waited for her on the powdery sand. Her enemy, and yet the only one in her corner. How did that come to pass?

"Why were you watching like that from the ship?" she demanded, shaking her wet hair. "They scorned me for it."

"In case I needed to step in." He gestured at the sea. "What if they'd attacked you?"

"You would've restarted the war." She sighed. "But it doesn't matter anyway. They aren't going to help me with the amulet."

"I figured that, by the look on your face. Did you tell them about the prophecy?"

"They don't believe it. The more I tried to convince them, the more annoyed they became. I should've known they'd react like that."

Jarin rubbed his tattooed hands together. "It was worth a try. Come, let's return to camp."

They walked together in silence as the sun dipped lower in the sky, Riella trying in vain to ignore her broken heart. The sirens had dispensed with her. The rejection hurt in a very deep and essential way.

Jarin cleared his throat and spoke once they neared the camp. His words were the first good news she'd received that day.

CHAPTER 22

"The Pandora's ready to sail."

Riella's heart leaped. "We can go to the Black Cliffs?"

He nodded. "Tomorrow morning, we'll set off. We can't dock in the bay of the Black Cliffs, because it's far too shallow, but we'll get as close as we can and travel by horseback the rest of the way."

He and Riella sat on tree stumps on the edge of the clearing, their conversation masked by the crackling and spitting of the growing bonfire.

Inky darkness fell across the island like a cloak. Ulyss helped Kohara and the children prepare food, as the rest of the crew drank and talked and cast grudging looks at Riella.

"And your crew?" she asked doubtfully. "They're willing to assist a siren?"

"Once we dock, they're going to plunder the inland armory of a slaver, to fortify ourselves against Artus. A showdown with him is inevitable, and we need weapons. To the crew's knowledge, that is why we are sailing tomorrow.

Meanwhile, I'll go to the Black Cliffs with you. We'll be more stealthy with just the two of us."

Riella nodded, mulling this over. "Yes, that's wise. Polinth has an excellent vantage point from his workshop on the cliffs. And I'm sure he uses magic to defend his territory." The siren allowed herself a brief glimmer of hope. At least she'd have the chance to face the sorcerer. "I look forward to killing him."

"And I look forward to watching you do it."

They smiled at each other. Even if she had no chance of attaining the amulet, she could stop Polinth and Artus the old-fashioned way. She could disembowel them.

But right now, it was a balmy evening on a tropical island, and she had naught to do except wait until the morning.

The pirates became steadily drunk, their jibes and insults about Riella traveling across the fire to her ears. Perhaps she ought to get rotten drunk, too. That might dissolve some of her painful thoughts about her friends and Seraphine.

"Want to go see the best place on the island?" asked Jarin, eyeing her.

She nodded gratefully and stood. "Very much so."

He led her to a steep rock formation in a quiet pocket of the island. Vines covered the path and she had to walk with care to avoid tripping. The canopy blocked out the moon and the only light was the darting flame of the torch Jarin carried.

But once they climbed to the top of the formation, the canopy of the jungle spread at their feet like a green velvet carpet. The dark sea and distant horizon lay beyond. The surface at the summit was flat, and the stone was still warm from the now-absent sun. A light breeze teased at the hem of Riella's dress, which was now quite worn and ragged.

"This is where I sleep most of the time, when I don't have a siren to look after. No one else knows about this spot."

Riella tilted her head. "Look after me? Is that what you've been doing?"

Chuckling, he wedged the torch in a crevice and sat on the rock overlooking the emerald canopy. She sat next to him.

"Yes, looking after you. You've survived, haven't you?"

She made a noise in her throat. "For now."

He touched her arm. "It's not like a siren to give up."

"Well, lots of things about me are not like a siren anymore."

"Hey." He lay on the rock, putting his hands behind his head. "Lie back and get a load of the view."

She did as he said. The cloudless night sky filled her vision completely and took her breath away. Stars were packed densely into every bit of darkness, sparkling white and pink and blue and yellow. She'd gazed at the night sky before, of course, but never while lying high on a hilltop like this.

She ignored the waxing moon—the celestial time-keeper for Riella's mortality.

"I feel like I could stay up here forever," she said. "I wish I could."

"Some legends say that we end up among the stars when we die."

"Ours say that we dwell in the sea forevermore, floating on the currents."

He reached down and took her hand, holding it to his chest. The gesture made her feel strangely shy, and she was glad of the dark and that she faced the heavens. The heat from the rock seeped into her body, relaxing her muscles.

"If you knew your days were numbered, how would you prefer to spend your remaining time?" she asked in a pensive voice. "I mean, what would you like to do?"

"Honestly?"

"Yeah."

"This," he replied quietly. "I'd do this."

Riella's chest quaked. The sensation felt new but also achingly natural, and she didn't speak, because she worried that if she did, she would cry. Jarin held her hand tighter, rubbing his thumb back and forth on her palm.

All her life, Riella had only ever viewed humans from the outside. From her vantage point, they seemed like illogical and brash creatures. But she was learning more and more that a deep undercurrent of passion accounted for their perceived madness. Humans had different, more complicated bonds to navigate than sirens. Family and friends and lovers.

Jarin seemed to have a particularly complicated emotional tapestry, despite his insistence that he was just a simple pirate. He was an outcast, his mother was a murderer, and he fought to usurp his mentor, Artus. And now, he lay on a warm rock in the dark with a siren, his sworn enemy.

"Tell me a nice memory of your mother," said Riella after some time. "If you have them?"

"I do." He paused. "You know, I don't think anyone's ever asked me that before. Everyone assumes she's a demon. All bad, all the time. Sometimes I feel guilty for even thinking about good memories of her."

Jarin exhaled. "Well, she used to tell me stories about where she grew up, in Morktland. A place made of ice and snow. Of course, growing up in Zermes, I'd never seen proper snow, but it sounded magical and I really wanted to, especially during the festive season. One night, on the eve of Yule, my father woke me in the early hours and brought me outside. It was snowing, as if we were in another world. There were great snowy drifts on the ground and icicles on the trees and flurries dancing through the air. My mother had learned how to conjure snow from the sky. And in her typical excessive style, she did not just conjure it. She covered the whole land in it. The High Magus was furious and she was punished severely, but she didn't care. She said it was worth it to see the look on my face. She was brilliant, and unstoppable, like a wildfire." He swallowed. "Unstoppable by anything, except her own heart."

"What a tragedy. For one so talented to fall prey to madness."

"Can't have one side of the coin without the other, I suppose. Duality exists in all of nature. Land and sea, dark and light."

"Sirens and pirates," said Riella with a smile.

He squeezed her hand. "Aye. Sirens and pirates."

Her attraction to Jarin was peculiar, given their traditional hatred and distrust of one another. But their opposing natures seemed to stoke the passion between them, not lessen it. Was that why she craved him in a way she didn't quite understand? Was he the land to her sea?

The familiar recklessness of her nature stole over her. Riella pushed herself up and threw a leg over his body, lowering herself to straddle him. A slow smirk started on one side of his mouth, his white teeth gleaming. His hands found her hips, and his sex hardened beneath her as his blood flowed rapidly to his groin.

Trailing her fingertips over the fabric of his shirt, lightly grazing his skin, she admired him. His strong tanned arms, chiseled jaw dark with stubble, broad tattooed chest. Deep, intense gray-green eyes, like the ocean right before a storm.

Wanting to see more of him, she sank her talons into the fabric of his shirt. Once she'd hooked them in, she tore the shirt off, leaving the material in shreds on the stone beside him. She ran her hot palms over his muscular chest, feeling the thump of his heart under the tuft of dark hair. With her touch, she memorized his solid pectorals, strong shoulders, and prominent abdominal muscles. She traced the line of hair leading down the center of his stomach to the top of his trousers.

Holding his gaze, she removed her dress, slowly pulling it over her head. With a teasing smile, she let the dress dangle from her hand for a moment before dropping it on the remains of his shirt, then eased herself out of her underwear. Naked, she enjoyed the feel of the ocean breeze and Jarin's intense stare on her bare skin.

His engorged cock strained against the confines of his pants. Riella giggled, enjoying the power she had over him. Wriggling her hips, she ground her own throbbing sex against his, eliciting a moan from Jarin. Her blood tingled with desire, her skin ultra-sensitive to every sensation. Her pink nipples hardened in the night air and warmth poured through her core.

Unable to restrain himself any longer, Jarin dug his fingers into her hips, gripping her so hard that she gasped. He drove his bulge against her, lifting her off the ground. A small moan escaped her throat.

In response, she grabbed his wrists, yanked them off her hips and slammed them into the stone over his head. She leaned over him, her platinum hair tickling her breasts and falling over his face and chest. He ran his tongue across his bottom lip, his eyes hazy and half-mad with desire.

"Gods," he said huskily. "You really are perfect."

She climbed up farther, so that her knees pinned his wrists to the stone and she was kneeling upright over him. He gazed as if mesmerized at her pink slit directly over his face, his forearm muscles taut under her knees.

Riella tilted her head back, the stars sparkling like a million diamonds in the sky. She lowered her body onto his face, his eager mouth greeting her parted entrance with a guttural moan. Jarin swirled his tongue around her slick folds, then slid it back and forth over her pulsing clit. Her head still tilted back, she ran her fingertips over her erect nipples, amazed at how they seemed to be connected to her clit by currents of pleasure.

He dipped his tongue into her tight opening, making her rock suddenly forward with the shock of how good it felt. She grabbed his dark hair with both hands and rode his mouth, her juices of arousal spilling down her thighs and drenching his face. His fists clenched and unclenched the air, unable to move anything except his mouth and tongue.

Intense waves of pleasure inside of Riella grew, and she smiled at the sky in anticipation of climax. When the waves peaked, she cried out into the warm night. Jarin sank his tongue into her, eagerly tasting her waterfall. As staggering as the climax felt, it only made her want Jarin more intensely. She craved more than his mouth and tongue—she wanted all of him, inside of her.

"Take off your pants," she commanded as she released his wrists. "And then don't move."

She shifted to the side and watched as he ripped his pants off, kicking them indiscriminately out of the way. From between his muscular thighs, his cock extended thick and long from dark curls of hair. In wonder, she ran her fingers all the way up the veiny shaft, starting from the base.

A single clear drop beaded in the indent at the very end of the tip. She touched the bead and it turned to silky liquid, which she then used to make the head of his cock slippery as she rubbed it between her thumb and two fingers. Jarin gritted his teeth and slammed his head back on the rock.

"Riella—" he said, a growl of warning in his throat. "You're about two seconds away from finding out whether I really can overpower you."

With a soft, evil laugh, she straddled him again, hovering just above his gigantic cock. She guided his shaft vertically with one hand, positioning the silky tip against her throbbing opening. Jarin's eyes rolled back in his head and he grabbed her waist.

Riella pushed the tip of his cock into her aching slit, making the delicate opening part for him. She drove herself down on the head, his erection impaling her. She gasped at the wholly unfamiliar sensation of being penetrated. The burn was overwhelming and made her dizzy, yet she longed for more. The combined pain and pleasure brought tears to her eyes and made her pant with arousal. Using her strength, she plunged his cock all the way in, to the hilt.

There she sat, lightheaded and ecstatic, her inner muscles encasing his steel-hard cock in its entirety. Her walls pulsed with the overload of sensation, her entrance growing slicker to accommodate the invasion.

"Gods, your strength makes you so tight," said Jarin with a groan. "Your muscles are going to crush my cock."

Riella was disappointed. "Oh. Do you want me to stop?"

"No. Don't you dare stop. It's a good thing, believe me."

She looked down at Jarin to realize he was gazing at her face. The pirate snaked his hand around her neck and pulled her forward, kissing her hard on the mouth. She kissed him back with equal force, sliding her tongue into his mouth and eagerly accepting his into her own. The sudden change in her body's angle made his rod press into her core more firmly and she moaned into his mouth.

Her clit pressing flush against his groin sent another strong current into her depths. She ground her heat down into him, the head of his cock driven strongly into her core. The potent sensations quickly brought her to climax. She rode the wave, rocking back and forth on his groin, kissing him deeply.

Breathless, she leaned back, exposing her breasts to him. He kneaded them roughly, rubbing her erect pink nipples to make her gasp. While he watched, she lifted her hips higher off his body, his slick cock revealed incrementally as her entrance stretched around him. When she neared the tip, she drove herself back down on him, burying his length inside of her.

She gazed down at her pink clit, shining and swollen, and marveled that her body could accommodate his incredible girth and length. Not only that, but it felt heavenly—even better than she'd imagined. Just to see what would happen, she clenched her core muscles around his cock.

Jarin let out a guttural moan. "Riella. Don't. I'm moments away from flooding you. That feels too damn good."

She didn't know what he meant by *flooding* her, but she giggled and clenched again, enjoying the sensation of gripping his thick, unrelenting shaft.

He gave a husky laugh. "You know what, Riella? I was going to go easy on you, but if that's how you want to play, you got it."

With a grunt, Jarin lifted her with one arm and flipped her onto her back, his cock remaining inside of her. She wrapped her slender legs around his waist and anticipation curled in Riella's core. The pirate tensed his sculpted, muscle-bound physique and drove his cock into her depths with all his strength, making her cry out. He speared onward until his entire cock was buried inside of her, making her pearl sing with pleasure.

His chest glistened with perspiration as he pumped into her tight depths without pause. She felt every stroke in perfect detail.

The sensations weren't confined to her folds and pearl—they spread through her entire body. As Jarin rammed his shaft into her willing depths, a tidal wave built in her core with such intensity that she vowed to murder him if he stopped. She wrapped both legs around his svelte waist as he drilled into her.

Her talons pierced the skin of his muscle-bound shoulders, blood trickling from the wounds. Jarin seemed not to notice, thrusting into her with frantic speed and strength, his jaw clenched. Then, the tidal wave inside Riella broke, releasing an explosion of impossibly intense pleasure through her body, starting at her core and spreading through her chest and limbs.

The pirate did not relent, pumping her interior while another wave crashed through her body, then another. Her moans and cries filled the sky. Jarin looked down with a lustful, victorious smile as he continued driving into her.

"Told you I'd make you sing for me, siren," he said.

On the next out-thrust, he let his cock slide out of her. She cried out in annoyance, not wanting to stop yet. But neither did Jarin.

"Turn over," he said, kneeling over her, his veiny erect cock flushed and shining.

"What? Why?"

"Just do as I say."

Too aroused to argue, she rolled over on the rock. Jarin grasped her hips and yanked them upward, so that her knees propped her ass into the air and she leaned forward on her arms. He kneaded her cheeks, parting them to expose her aching sex fully.

Unable to see what he was doing, she cried out when his tongue swirled around her clit, then firmly lapped at her opening. But he didn't stop there. His hands held her steady while his tongue progressed to the tight pink rosebud between her cheeks, making her inhale. He teased the opening with feather-soft licks to gauge her reaction.

Her eyes slid unfocused and she rested the side of her face on the hot stone, arching her back further and sighing. Jarin encircled the rosebud with his tongue, while reaching his hand around to rub her clit with his fingertips. With Riella moaning in the warm night air, he coaxed another deep and reverberating climax from her.

She felt it on a different level this time, intensified by his attention to her forbidden back entrance. As she reached the peak, her body quivering, he maintained his fingers' steady rhythm on her clit and pushed his wet, smooth tongue into her tight rosebud, making her almost pass out from the sweetness of the sensation.

As the waves of pleasure moved through her core, he straightened up while she remained on all fours. He lined himself up and slammed the length of his cock into her swollen opening, amplifying the tail-end of her climax. Barely giving her a chance to breathe, he grasped her waist and pummeled her depths from behind. Each thrust sent a thrill of bliss into Riella, his cock causing new sensations by entering at the unfamiliar angle. She could do nothing except moan and hold onto the rock as he pounded her without pause.

His rod hardened and finally, he flooded her depths with his hot seed. He made a sound that was almost inhuman, groaning in ecstasy and digging his fingertips into her skin. Her muscles squeezed his shaft, compressing every last drop of the pulsations from him.

Her body hummed with the reverberations of pleasure, and her legs felt shaky. Jarin's must've too, because when he finally withdrew from her, he sagged next to her on the rock, panting while he pulled her close.

In the distance, waves crashed endlessly against the dark shore.

CHAPTER 23

The Pandora sailed at dawn, rays of sunshine making the sails glow yellow.

Riella busied herself with the rigging while Jarin steered from the helm. She was avoiding the rest of the crew, whose disgust toward her had only grown since Mareen, Galeil, and Thera visited. She had to swallow her rage whenever any of the pirates spat on the deck while glaring at her, because without a crew, the Pandora would not sail. And without the Pandora, she'd be marooned on Hieros Isle until the day of her death.

After tying off the last of the rigging, she hauled herself into the crow's nest. Standing at the top of the main sail felt akin to flying. The ship cut through the clear blue water at speed, buoying Riella's mood. Although she could not swim anymore, this was perhaps the next best thing.

She wore a loose white blouse and women's trews, given to her by Kohara, with her leather boots, and a knife strapped to her thigh. Kohara had also braided her hair in three sections and pinned the braids to her head. The new style was a revelation to Riella, whose long, fine strands kept getting tangled.

Her tender sex ached whenever she moved, and even sometimes when she was stationary. It was a sweet and spearing feeling, almost as though the phantom of Jarin's cock remained inside of her. Her entire being glowed from the intensity and pleasure of having sex with him.

As the Pandora progressed toward the Black Cliffs and the sun climbed higher in the sky, Riella couldn't help glancing down at Jarin periodically. Often, she'd feel him looking up at her, and they'd share a long gaze full of meaning. It was the strangest thing—the way he made her feel both excited and calm at the same time.

Her sense of calm would surely be short-lived. That night, she and Jarin planned to storm Polinth's workshop on the cliffs. She would kill the sorcerer and rescue Seraphine. Not an easy mission, but a simple one.

Land came into view, green and mountainous and wild, and Jarin steered the ship toward a secluded bay several leagues from the Black Cliffs. After dropping anchor, the pirates and Riella climbed ropes onto wooden boats and rowed ashore.

The bank was rocky, fronting a dense forest of pine trees. Riella and Jarin headed north through the trees, while the rest of the crew traveled southward along the rocky bank toward the slaver's stronghold. They were all to meet back at the Pandora the next morning to return to their island hideout. The pirates hoped to have a cache of weapons and gold with them, while Riella would return bearing Seraphine, and Polinth's blood under her talons.

At the edge of the forest, Jarin pointed to a farm across the dirt road. "We'll take a horse to ride the rest of the way."

Riella narrowed her eyes. "Take? You mean steal?"

"Do you object?" He raised his dark brows at her. "Should

a horse really be locked up in a paddock like that, anyway? Don't they deserve to run free, with us?"

"You're making fun of me."

"You stole from the Count."

"Well, he was a man."

Jarin laughed. "The farmer's probably a man, if that makes you feel any better. Look, we can return the horse in the morning on our way back through, alright? So it's not really stealing at all. We're borrowing." He shook his head. "Gods, Riella, the things you have me doing. Who ever heard of a pirate *borrowing*?"

He climbed the low fence into the field, while Riella kept lookout on the road. Minutes later, he returned with a huge black horse, urging the equine to jump the fence with ease. Jarin pulled the horse to a stop in front of her and she fought to appear unfazed. She'd never seen a horse up close before, and the idea of riding the beast was daunting.

"I couldn't find a saddle, only reins and a bridle," said Jarin, the leather straps wound around one hand. "But with two of us, a saddle would've been uncomfortable anyway."

She hung back, unsure. "Well, I do sometimes ride with whales. But if you lose your hold in the water, all that happens is that you float away. If I fall off the horse, I'll break my neck."

Jarin leaned down, offering his hand to her. "I won't let you fall. I promise."

With a steadying breath, she took his hand and let him haul her onto the horse's back, awkwardly swinging her leg over. Jarin sat flush behind her, for which she was grateful, because he provided a reassuring stability. And also because his hard, hot body felt very nice against hers.

"Now, press your knees into his flank," he said, adjusting her leg to show her. "Do it firmly, but not too tight. And give him a pat on the neck, so he knows you're a friend."

Riella followed his instructions. But then, she glanced down at the pebbly road, which made her stomach swoop. The distance seemed far greater now than from her vantage point on the ground.

"Ready?" asked Jarin.

She nodded, not really feeling ready at all, but knowing she likely never would.

Jarin twitched his heels and the horse lurched forward. Riella swallowed the urge to yelp, threading her fingers through the horse's tufty mane to have something to hold onto.

"Don't worry," murmured Jarin into her ear. "I've got you." He wrapped one strong arm around her waist. "This is called trotting, but to get there faster, we'll need to canter, alright? The gait is quicker, but smoother, too."

"Fine," said Riella in a tight voice. "It's all terrifying. Just get us there, please."

Jarin twitched his heels again, and the pace increased.

"Don't fight the movement," he said. "Try to feel the rhythm. And stop looking at the ground."

She exhaled, lifting her chin to look straight ahead. At first, it was even scarier, to see the green and brown woods flying past. But soon, her body instinctively moved with the flow of the horse. It was not unlike the undulations of a siren's tail when swimming.

After some time, when they'd passed a handful of small settlements, she even began to enjoy the ride. If Jarin removed his arm from around her waist, she still would've shrieked, but it was a little bit fun. And, true to his word, he didn't let her fall.

The Black Cliffs came into view when the sun shone directly overhead. To reach Polinth's workshop, they'd need to climb the mountainous ridge leading to the cliffs. A thrill of anticipation rippled through Riella. She was close to the sorcerer, she could feel it.

Jarin tugged the reins as they approached the next settlement, which was little more than a tavern and stables and a few cottages.

"We should dismount now that we're close to the base of the mountain," said Jarin as the horse slowed to a walk. "Our friend here will need a break, and we should lie low until the sun begins to set."

Riella was all too pleased with this plan, because her legs and core ached from the ride.

Jarin directed the horse to the stables. A ruddy-faced young man wearing overalls was sticking hay with a pitchfork out the front. The stables were modest, with room to house a handful of horses. Most of the stalls were occupied, the horses poking their heads out to look at Jarin and Riella and their steed.

"Afternoon," said Jarin to the young man.

The stablehand rested his pitchfork on the side of a stall and eyed the pirate in silence, taking in Jarin's tattoos, cutlass, and formidable build. While voices were audible from within the tavern, the stablehand was the only person outside.

"Can you feed and water our horse?" Jarin dismounted while keeping one hand on Riella. "Swing your leg up high," he said as she tried to mimic his movement. "Higher than you think you'll need to."

Even heeding his words, she barely cleared the stallion's rump. She landed on the ground lightly with Jarin's help, but staggered from the stiffness in her legs. Seeming to anticipate this, he held her arm until she regained her balance.

"Walk around a little," he said. "It's the best thing to get the feeling back."

Wincing, she took a few tentative steps while Jarin

handed the reins to the stablehand, along with a solid gold coin. The boy, who'd been solemn and nervy before, suddenly relaxed.

"I'll take good care of him," he said with a nod at Jarin.

He led the horse to the water trough and Jarin turned to Riella.

"You did great." He drew her into a hug, kissing the top of her head. "Come, let's walk in the forest until you have feeling back in your legs. Then we'll go to the tavern and coax whatever information we can from the local folk about the defenses of Polinth's workshop."

She took his hand and followed him past the tree line. The forest was verdant, with velvety moss growing on damp boulders and tree trunks. "By coax, do you mean torture?"

"Ha. Gold and mead are usually encouragement enough, I find."

They walked until the blood flow returned to Riella's legs and she ceased hobbling.

"How on earth do people ride horses all the time?" she asked. "It's unnatural."

"You get used to it."

She stopped under a huge fir tree, gazing up at the branches. "The land really is more varied and lovely than I'd supposed."

"No doubt the same is true of the ocean. I've mostly only seen the surface. What lies beneath is always far more interesting."

As he spoke, he traced one fingertip over her cheek, then he leaned in to kiss her on the lips. Riella smiled and kissed him back. His fingertips progressed down the side of her neck, over her clothed breasts and stomach, coming to a rest on the tender, flaming spot between her legs. At his touch, desire ignited in her stomach.

"Turn around, my siren," he murmured. "I'm going to make you feel better."

Heart thudding, she faced the tree trunk. She placed her palms on its rough bark to steady herself while he tugged down her trews. He knelt and placed his huge hands on her bare cheeks, easing them apart to expose her raw pinkness from behind.

He ran his tongue from her pearl, over her flushed folds, and dipped it into her aching slit, which was swollen and tight from Jarin pounding it the night before. Riella inhaled sharply, her spine tingling. The sensation of his smooth, insistent tongue against her inner walls made her feel better indeed.

Her hands gripped the tree bark. The pressure inside her core grew, begging for release. Jarin stood up, towering over her from behind. He undid his pants and she felt his rock-hard shaft spring against her back.

Sighing in anticipation, she let him position the head of his cock against her slick opening. He wrapped one arm around her waist and the other across the front of her shoulders, her head falling gently back onto his muscle-bound chest. He jerked his hips to snatch her off the ground and plunge himself into her tight depths, clamping his hand over her mouth to stifle the cry she let out.

He held her in place with his steel-threaded arms as he thrust himself in and out of her with relentless strength, her feet dangling in midair. His strokes were frantic and fast and Riella could hardly catch her breath, moaning into the palm of his hand and gripping his wrist with both hands as she bounced up and down on his cock. As he pumped against her taut interior, he snaked his fingers down to caress her aching clit.

His direct touch pushed her over the edge. Her body shuddered on his cock as she climaxed, more powerfully than she had before. A moment later, the pirate groaned as he filled her core with his hot surges, holding her upright with only his massive erection and his arms.

As the final waves moved through their bodies, he leaned in and pressed his lips to her neck. She tilted her head to the side, wanting his tongue in her mouth.

He obliged, and they kissed feverishly while the trees of the forest whispered around them.

CHAPTER 24

Every person in the tavern looked up when Riella and Jarin walked in.

She supposed they mustn't see strangers often, living in such a remote hamlet. As the patrons and elderly bartender peered from the shadowy interior, it occurred to her that Polinth might have spies among the local populace. If anyone left in a hurry, she and Jarin would have to follow them.

Riella sat at a long wooden communal table while Jarin went to the bar. She shifted on her stool, unsettled by the curious gazes of the other patrons. To distract herself, she looked around. Candles lit the tavern and the floor was packed with earth.

Most patrons drank from flagons, but a few had steaming plates of food and the scents caused to Riella's stomach to rumble. The horse riding and the forest sex had made her particularly hungry. Jarin's seed trickled hotly from her throbbing entrance even as she sat with a carefully impassive expression.

But she did not wish to dwell on Jarin either, because feelings would only muddy the waters. She needed to focus on her mission—not the way his deep voice was like a caress down her spine. Or the way his smile made her pulse quicken. Or that she now craved his touch every second she did not have it, and even when she did, it never seemed like enough.

Such yearning had to be why sirens lacked the drive to mate. It would compromise their ability to fulfill their purposes. Although they possessed seductiveness and beauty, these qualities were only ever meant to ensnare men, not themselves. And Riella felt dangerously close to being captured by Jarin. Not in a net, or a brig, but in a different way altogether.

She looked at his tall form leaning on the bar as he spoke quietly with the bartender. Her growing feelings didn't matter, really. After all, she'd be gone soon. Jarin would remain, and she'd be just a memory to him. The thought made her heart ache, but what could she do?

He carried flagons of mead to the table and sat opposite her. She sipped the foamy liquid. It was somehow sweet and bitter at the same time.

"We're in luck," said the pirate in a low voice. "The local people loathe Polinth. All manner of children, women, and animals have gone missing since he set up his workshop on the cliffs. They blame him for the disappearances, though they have no proof."

Riella's hand tightened around the flagon. "I'm sure their assumptions are correct. Any word on how we might access his caves?"

"No one's been up there, save those who don't return."

"I know there's a narrow path of stairs next to the cave. That must lead down the mountainside, surely."

"Sounds promising." Jarin shrugged. "And if there isn't a way, we'll make one."

The bartender carried a heaving tray to the table, setting

down plates and bowls in front of the siren and pirate. Riella sniffed dubiously at the plate of food, sided with bread.

"Roasted vegetable stew with rosemary bread," said Jarin, pointing at the plate, then at the bowl. "And peach pie with cream for dessert. You'll like it, I promise."

She cocked her eyebrow. "You promised I'd like riding the horse."

"No," he corrected. "I promised I wouldn't let you fall."

"Oh. That's true."

He picked up his spoon and started on the stew. Riella was unsure how it could possibly taste nice, when it looked like sludge. The steam curling from the plate smelled enticing though, so she put a spoonful in her mouth.

The stew was earthy and savory, and she liked it. Not as much as she'd liked the fried potatoes in Klatos, but she couldn't imagine ever liking a food as much as that. She dipped a chunk of bread into the stew, as Jarin did, which improved the whole experience. In the end, she finished the stew before he did, and promptly pulled a dessert bowl to her.

Riella was not prepared for the pie. Her eyes rolled back in her head when the spoonful of fruity, creamy dessert melted into her tongue.

Jarin chuckled into his mead. "Better than kelp, no?"

By the time Riella finished her meal, the patrons had stopped staring at her and Jarin. Their attention had turned to the contents of a news bulletin. A few stools down from Riella, a man laid the parchment before him and read aloud to the table in general.

"Join all the kingdom in celebration of King Leonid's wedding. The festivities will take place in Klatos, under the joyous light of the coming full moon. The High Magus of Starlight Gardens will be an honored guest."

"That's next week. Are we going, Papa?" asked one little girl of the man.

"We'll see," he replied. "Might be hard to find a place to lie our heads, with everyone piling into the city like that."

At the mention of the full moon and Starlight Gardens, the contents of Riella's stomach curdled. The night Polinth captured her, he'd ranted about wanting the amulet to bring Starlight Gardens to heel. He had a vendetta against them.

"Can't believe they're propping up King Leonid for a wedding to a Garstang bride," said a dark-haired woman. "Rumor is, he's got one foot in the grave already."

"And the wedding's so sudden, too. But that's the Garstang family for you. The slimy bunch are trying to sink their teeth into the palace all the way from Morktland kingdom," said another man. "You hear the other rumor, about Prince Davron being alive in Velandia? They reckon he even has a lady now. He commanded her to his castle. Can you imagine? Poor lass. He's supposed to be monstrous."

Jarin flinched, knocking his empty flagon over. He refused to meet Riella's gaze as he righted it, but his brow was deeply furrowed.

"What is it?" she whispered to him.

"Nothing."

Then, she remembered what he'd told her about the royal family. He probably felt guilt on behalf of his mother's murderous actions, which would be triggered by mention of the prince, naturally.

The dark-haired woman's face lit up with intrigue. "I heard the Garstangs sent an assassin after him."

"Ah, who knows?" replied the man. "The corrupt Court in Klatos will be panicking though, if he's alive. That'll be why there're sudden nuptials. They're installing their own queen before the prince can return. Leonid will croak any day now, and it'd be war with Morktland if Davron tried to take the throne from a Garstang."

Jarin cleared his throat.

"Let's get out of here," he said to Riella.

He seemed restless, suddenly unable to sit still. She didn't particularly enjoy being idle either, so she stood at once. After placing a small stack of coins on the table, he followed her outside to the late afternoon sunshine.

"Are you worried the prince might return?" asked Riella as they started walking up the dirt road that snaked through the forest toward the mountain. "Do you believe he'll hunt you down?"

"What?" Jarin seemed genuinely nonplussed, looking at her in surprise. "No. If he'd wanted to do that, I believe he would've tried long ago. He was always an honorable man. It was the Court who pursued me, back when it all happened."

"They said he commanded a woman to his castle. That does not sound very honorable to me."

Jarin kicked a rock with his boot. It skittered over the road, disappearing into dense green bushes. "I'll not cast judgment on a man's character based on rumors overheard in a tavern."

"Well, I will."

He gave her a sidelong glance. "You can't save every woman in the world, you know."

"I didn't say I was going to save her." She paused. "But if I had longer to live, I might bid you sail for Velandia, in case he really is holding her captive."

"Dammit, Riella!" Jarin stopped in the middle of the road.

She halted, confused. "What?"

He closed his eyes, exhaling hard through his nose. "You're not going to die."

"But Ferrante—"

"Forget Ferrante. Forget fate." He opened his eyes, and

she took an involuntary step backward at the ferocity in his stare. "You aren't going to die."

She gaped at him, lost for words. What was wrong with him? It wasn't as though she *wanted* to die.

He kneaded his hands together, cracking his knuckles, his face a mask of darkness. She'd never seen him this agitated before, not even when Artus taunted him on the docks of Klatos.

"Are you losing your mind?" she asked.

While she knew this probably wasn't the most tactful question, she was completely lost. She didn't even know what to ask him. Was he experiencing some mysterious human emotion to which she was ignorant?

The pirate glared at her for several moments, while she grew increasingly bewildered.

"Yes," he replied finally, in a dull tone. "Perhaps I am losing my mind."

Then, without waiting for a response, he continued up the road. She hastened after him, her mind whirling with everything he'd said. Every few paces, Jarin would look down at his hands, flexing them and turning them over.

Ahead, the mountainside grew closer, blotting out the last dying light of the day.

CHAPTER 25

For the past decade, Jarin had wished for his mother's curse to break.

He wanted freedom from it, and he wanted Prince Davron liberated, too. The magic coursed through Jarin's veins ceaselessly, like a dark pulse. When he was threatened, the pulse grew stronger. In a decade, it'd never not been there.

And it was there still. But for how much longer, if the rumors about the prince were true? Curses were made to be broken, and his mother's was no different, strong though it was.

If a woman fell in love with Davron, the curse would end. And along with it, the protection given to Jarin by his mother. That had never bothered him before—he'd wanted it.

But now? Riella needed him, and Artus was wreaking havoc. It would be the worst possible time for the curse to break.

Saving Riella's life would be a difficult enough task on its own, let alone without his invulnerability as a shield against the likes of Polinth and Artus.

Jarin never wanted to become attached to anyone. How could he, when he saw the devastation that passion wrought upon the people around him? Love and grief turned people into monsters.

To avoid such loss, he became a pirate, married only to the seas. That he'd grown attached to a violent siren was proof of fate's humor. That she was doomed to die, and soon, was proof of fate's cruelty.

Jarin could not let Riella die. He knew that as surely as he knew his own name. If he lost her, he would spend the rest of his life looking for her ghost, and counting the minutes until he could reunite with her in the Beyond. He truly believed now that it was his fate to meet her, and protect her.

His whole life, he'd felt rudderless. He'd been forgotten by the powers that governed the universe—as if he was a spare part, an unimportant cast-off. A consequence of a far grander story. A mistake, even.

Since growing close to Riella, he no longer believed that.

He hoped the elf could be rescued without complication, so that Polinth would have no hostage to hide behind. Jarin and Riella could bring him to justice, and move on with finding the amulet, to save her.

All he had to do was bend fate to his will, and stop at nothing to do it.

But for now, he needed to keep her in the dark about his true intentions.

"Sorry about that," he said to Riella as they neared the mountainside. The road became steeper and more narrow, and birdcalls ceased. The only sound was leaves clattering in a stiff, cool breeze uncharacteristic of summer. "I didn't mean to scare you."

Her face relaxed into an easy smile, and he fought the

urge to take her in his arms and run away with her, far from danger.

"It's alright," she said with a shrug. Her braided hair only emphasized her beauty, because it showed more of her face. He could stare at her endlessly. "And besides, you didn't scare me. I just want to know what occupies your mind so fiercely."

Jarin shoved his hands in his pockets, his cutlass bumping against his thigh. If she knew the precise contents of his mind, she might indeed become scared.

Mostly, he tried to repress his dark side, believing it to be shameful. But it was useful on occasion, like when he was fighting for something he wanted. And he definitely wanted something now. He wanted to save her.

"I was thinking about the curse," he said truthfully. "Hearing about Davron is always jarring. In a twisted way, he's my counterpart. My mirror image. Our fates are bound."

"I daresay you got the better end of the deal."

"No doubt. Although, it might be dangerous to assume that fate has no tricks up its sleeve."

She gestured to the summit overshadowing them. "I'm sure Polinth does, too. And yet, that doesn't mean we won't defeat him."

They reached the base of the mountain as the sun slid past the horizon. The shadows deepened, the trees turning a uniform gray.

Jarin scanned the trees and rocky ground constantly as they climbed the steep ridge. Aside from their boots snapping twigs and disturbing leaves, nothing moved or made a sound. Nevertheless, his senses tingled with a sick premonition. The feeling only grew as they traveled higher, but no traps appeared.

Night fell in earnest. The scant light of the moon and

stars offered little visibility, but Jarin hadn't dared to bring a lantern, lest the glow alert Polinth of their presence.

Riella tripped, her boot stuck on something.

Jarin caught her before she fell into the leaf litter. "Are you alright?"

"Fine." She regained her footing and peered at the ground. "I stood on a stick that wouldn't give way."

He crouched in the spot where she'd tripped. The dead leaves were crunchy and piled high, and he swept them away. Then, in the dim light, a stark white ribcage stood out against the murky brown ground.

Riella gripped his shoulder. "What is that? Some kind of animal?"

It looked small, like a dog or a hare. His heart thudding, he uncovered more of the bones. The distinct skull of a tiny human child stared blankly up at him.

Riella hissed. He stood and turned around to hold her, expecting her to be distraught. Instead, her face twisted with rage.

"You see?" she asked. "You see why we must kill him? He is putrid."

Without waiting for Jarin's input, she stepped around him and stomped onward.

As much as he supported her homicidal tendencies, he was concerned that her brashness would lead her right into a trap. She saw the world in black-and-white and, for better or worse, she still didn't fathom the extent to which humans were capable of foulness and deceit. And Polinth was surely among the worst of all humans.

But Riella would not be slowed.

"We're too close," she said, pushing past him when he tried to make her stop. "I came here to retrieve Seraphine and kill Polinth, and that's exactly what I'm going to do."

The siren reverberated with fury—it poured off her in

waves. Despite knowing she wasn't his combatant at this moment, the Dark Tide pirate in him instinctively reacted to proximity to an enraged siren. His pulse raced and his senses became hyper-sharp, as if preparing him for a fight. He was glad that, for once, he wouldn't be on the receiving end of such potent ire.

Three more skeletons lay in their path to the summit—two humans and one delicate skull of an elf. The skull was too weathered to be Seraphine, but the carnage did make Jarin wonder how many other bodies were hidden on the mountain.

The most powerful energy source to a mage was living beings, his mother once told him. Tapping the life force of a person or creature or even a tree was not particularly difficult for a sorcerer, but it was considered abhorrent and crude. Like a vampire or parasite.

From what Riella said, Polinth leached the elf's life force. He hadn't stopped there, though. He'd harvested Riella's gifts, too. Jarin wondered what the sorcerer planned to do with the amulet. To bolster his own waning life force? Or something else?

Artus wanted the treasure to eclipse Jarin and every other pirate. As dangerous as he would be with such power, at least his motives were simplistic. But the amulet in the hands of the wrong sorcerer could be disastrous. Look at what his mother had managed to do, with nothing more than grief and her innate ability.

The trees thinned near the mountain's peak. Jarin and Riella slowed their pace, creeping between trees with hushed determination. The trees gave way to a steep rocky incline leading to the summit.

"Those are the caves," murmured Riella. "They're half open to the air."

Firelight flickered through the gaps in the cave. Jarin's

stomach clenched. Why hadn't they encountered any defenses yet? They'd climbed the entire mountainside unobstructed, except for the grim discovery of the bones.

"You don't recall any fortifications?" asked Jarin as he crouched with Riella behind a fallen log where the tree line ended.

Riella shook her head, absentmindedly stroking the handle of the knife strapped to her leg. "None that I saw. But I was trying to get out of the place, not into it. And I was somewhat distracted at the time." She gestured at the right side of the summit. "That's where the stairs lead to his workshop."

Bent low, he and Riella crossed to the shadowy gap containing the stairs. No gate or fence stood in their way. Would it really be this easy?

"Let me go first," said Jarin from behind Riella, who blocked the entrance to the stairs.

A high-pitched voice called from the caves above.

"Help! Somebody please help me!"

The siren sprang into action at once, trying to enter the stairwell. Jarin caught the back of her blouse just in time to stop her barreling up to the caves. At this rate, it'd be all he could do to keep her alive until the full moon, let alone beyond it.

"It's almost certainly a trap," he breathed in her ear, pulling her back.

"I don't care. I'm not afraid of him."

To his horror, she wrenched herself free and bolted up the stairs.

CHAPTER 26

Riella hurtled up the steps two at a time.

The pure panic in the voice cut straight to her heart and forced her to act. Jarin may've been right about the plea being a trap, but what if it wasn't? Guilt had plagued her ever she left Seraphine behind. Now, she finally had the chance to balance the scales and she was going to take it. She and Jarin came to face Polinth, didn't they? If it was a trap, then he already knew they were present anyway.

The voice from the caves stopped calling, but Jarin's boots thundered on the stairs right behind her. Never did she imagine she'd appreciate a Dark Tide pirate running after her, and yet she wouldn't prefer to storm Polinth's workshop with anyone else. A towering, muscular, invulnerable pirate wasn't the worst accomplice for a rescue mission.

Riella should've asked Jarin if his invulnerability extended to a magical attack, since they were ambushing a sorcerer. But it was too late now, because the cave entrance was in view.

The crash of waves came from the bottom of the cliffs. She slowed near the top, crouching just behind the entryway.

Jarin caught up with her and clamped his large hand firmly around her ankle to prevent her from running. She turned and bared her teeth at him in warning, not wanting to be stopped, but she needn't have bothered.

From inside the caves, a siren began Singing. The sound was intimately and bizarrely familiar, making her pause to listen in disbelief. It was Riella's own Voice.

Jarin buckled and jammed his hands over his ears, his face pained. Riella climbed the last few stairs and entered the mouth of the cave, feeling like she was in a bizarre nightmare. Despite hearing her own lilting, unearthly Song, she was unprepared for what she found.

The water tank where Polinth kept her was gone, along with the workshop table and the Starlight Gardens flag.

Now, the cave resembled something impossible—a place between the ocean and land. Glowing candles hung suspended in midair, casting ethereal firelight. But seaweed also sprouted from the ground, floating and drifting as if in water, only there was none. Multi-colored coral shimmered on rocks covering the floor.

Another Riella danced in the center of the cave on slender legs. At first, she thought she was looking into a mirror, her mind struggling to make sense of the eerie sight. But other-Riella's hair flowed loose as she danced, her black dress flaring at the knees. Her eyes were closed, her face lifted to the ceiling as she Sang. This was no reflection.

Jarin appeared beside Riella, his hands pressed over his ears. If the Song was causing him genuine pain, that meant it really was a siren's Voice. It was *her* Voice, even if the rest was sorcery.

"It's a Glamour!" he shouted over the Song. "She's not real."

Riella blinked, and realized her mirror image was not perfect after all. Other-Riella's figure was bustier than hers, and her facial features were slightly different from her own. Polinth had conjured her likeness from memory and like all humans, his memory was imperfect.

The Voice, though? She was sure the Voice was real. It was the one tangible thing he'd stolen from her and kept.

Jarin's shouts made other-Riella cease Singing and dancing. She turned and smiled at them. The center of her throat glowed with a brilliant blue light.

"Riella," said Jarin with a note of warning, letting his hands fall. "I don't like this. We should leave. Now."

"Not a chance," she replied, not taking her eyes from her crude doppelgänger.

She wasn't leaving without Seraphine. Another opportunity had presented itself to her, as well. She had the chance to reclaim her Voice.

Black vapor rose from other-Riella's shoulders and head in fine tendrils.

"You can't fight a Glamour," said Jarin. "Please, trust me. We need to leave."

Despite her determination, fear trickled down Riella's spine. Jarin's mother was a sorceress—she should probably listen to him. He knew about dark magic.

But she couldn't bring herself to just *leave*. Her days were already numbered, and she'd come all this way. She couldn't turn and flee without trying to find Seraphine.

"The elf could be in the chambers of the caves," said Riella. "And Polinth would need to be nearby to conjure the Glamour, wouldn't he?"

"I don't know, Riella, but I don't think we should stick around to find out. Do you really think he'd let you take your Voice back? He's toying with you."

Before her eyes, other-Riella morphed, the black vapor rearranging itself into another form. Within moments, the figure became the likeness of Polinth. He smiled, wearing a black robe, and he held up a small glass bottle containing the blue glow of her Voice.

Riella went to cross the few paces to the sorcerer. But this time, Jarin was ready, grabbing her around the waist with both arms to stop her.

Polinth laughed heartily.

"You are too late, my dearest," he said in a horrible singsong voice. "I already have what I needed from you." He wriggled the glass bottle. "And I thank you for it, endlessly. I regret that I couldn't meet you at the cave in person, but I have much to do before the royal wedding. I hope you don't mind that I left a Glamour behind to greet you." He chuckled. "Well. Goodbye, now."

His face and body faded, the black vapor overtaking his features. The vapor drifted backward with unnatural speed, as if sucked into a portal. Only the glass bottle containing her Voice remained, suspended in midair.

The bottle was so close. All she had to do was reach out and grab it.

With a grunt, she wrenched herself from Jarin's vise-like grip and lunged for the bottle. The moment her fingertips touched the glass, the bottle vanished, and her Voice along with it. A puff of black smoke was all that remained.

Her shoulders slumped. What a disaster of a mission. The only bright spot was that he obviously didn't know Riella and Jarin had the map. He mightn't even know about its existence.

"The royal wedding," repeated Riella with a frown, remembering the news bulletin they heard at the tavern. "It's being held on the night of the full moon. The night I die."

"Riella, what's that?" asked Jarin in an uneasy voice.

The cave interior had changed. While the floating candles remained, their yellow flames flickering in the breeze, the seaweed and coral were gone. In their place were piles of red sticks with strings coming from the ends, like candles. Polinth had bewitched the red sticks to look like seaweed and coral.

A metallic pungency drifted through the air, mingling with the briny scent of the sea. Was this another Glamour? How could she be certain of anything she saw?

Jarin peered closer at the red piles in the low light. Then, he cursed loudly and skittered backward, grabbing her wrist and tugging her with him.

"I saw these in Hatara," he said. "Run!"

As he yanked her to the mouth of the cave, the suspended candles dropped from the air, landing on the red sticks. The flames spread to the strings protruding from the sticks, sparking them and burning brightly.

Riella went to run down the stairs, but Jarin pulled her toward the cliff's edge.

"No time!" he shouted. "We need to jump!"

He sprinted at the cliff and Riella followed, trusting him. At the black rocky edge, they leaped, his hand locked around her wrist. For a moment, they hung weightless, the sky and sea sparkling with starlight.

Then, the cave exploded.

A deafening wall of orange light and searing heat blew into their backs, propelling them through the air. Riella's skin flamed as she fell, overcome with confusion and fear. Polinth had conjured the sun.

The force of the explosion sent chunks of rock sailing narrowly past Riella and Jarin, splashing into the choppy water below. Her legs flailed as she fell and the churning onyx water sped toward her. An instant before she hit the surface, Riella gulped air, praying their bodies would not be dashed against the cliffside by the waves.

Upon impact with the water, a falling rock broke Jarin's hold on her, sending sharp pain through her arm. She plunged into the sea, rocks hitting the water around her like missiles. She looked wildly for Jarin, but the dark, seething ocean concealed him from view.

Instead of kicking for the surface, she swam deeper, trying to find him. Was he invulnerable to drowning? If he sank unconscious to the bottom of the sea, his body would disintegrate or be eaten, regardless of the curse.

A plume of red floating through the water drew her to him. He'd been knocked out, a deep gash on the side of his head. Riella hooked her wrists under his armpits and kicked upward, gritting her teeth with the strain.

A boulder hit the water directly above, and she dragged his body clear just in time. Her lungs burned and her endurance was waning. If she did not surface soon, they would both perish.

In sheer determination, she beat her legs against the bubbling water. Finally, her head broke the surface. She coughed, the waves buffeting her, willing Jarin to breathe as she held his head above water. The gash was deep and poured blood. If he survived, it would only be due to the curse. Such an injury would kill a normal human.

The orange light was now a faraway glow against the inky sky. The caves were burning. Mercifully, the rocks stopped falling. A whole section of the cliff was missing, leaving behind a crater.

Puffing hard, she struck for the open waters of the bay, where she might catch a wave to the beach. Her progress was slow. The waves kept pushing her backward, and swimming was difficult with Jarin's enormous body in tow. He regained consciousness shortly after she hauled him past the breakers.

Bleeding profusely from the gash, he gazed around blank-faced.

"Are you alright?" she asked, waving her hand in front of his eyes.

He blinked, then winced, placing one hand against his head. "Ow."

To her relief, he started treading water of his own accord.

"Are you alright?" he croaked.

She nodded. Physically, she was alright. But the reality of her situation was so dire that she dared not think about it, lest she lose all hope and offer herself to the sea to escape. She'd vastly underestimated Polinth, and paid the price.

They swam to shore in exhausted silence. Riella crouched on the sand, coughing up the salty water she'd swallowed. Jarin lay on his back panting, his eyes unfocused.

With her remaining energy, she crawled to him and collapsed by his side. The last thing she remembered, as her eyes fluttered closed, was an unusually vivid blue star shooting through the black sky.

CHAPTER 27

*R*iella's head throbbed.

She was lying on her back while being bounced around without pause, making her whole body vibrate unpleasantly. Opening her eyes revealed little. A dark fabric canopy stretched above her, sunshine darting through the cracks. Her pulse quickened. Where was Jarin? Was he alive? Moreover, where on earth was *she*?

"She's awake."

The voice was a man's—quiet and unfamiliar.

Wincing at the ache in her head, she sat up. Three men huddled on wooden benches in the small space. Jarin lay unconscious on one of the benches.

Riella stood to go to him, but fell straight onto the slats of the floor. Through the gaps in the floorboards, the rocky dirt ground moved rapidly beneath them. She was in a cart pulled by horses, whose hooves clopped on the road.

But who were these men?

"Your friend's alive," said one of them. "We gave him a dram for the pain. You can wake him up if you like, but he'll be sore."

She shuffled to Jarin and leaned over him. His chest rose and fell steadily, and there was color in his face. The gash on his head had closed, leaving behind an angry red line.

"How long was I unconscious?" she croaked at the men. "Where are you taking us?"

A bald older man answered, who looked vaguely familiar. "We found you both on the beach this morning, in pretty rough shape. Couldn't just leave you there, but we need to return to Klatos. Been stranded out here in the settlements for over a week now. We thought we'd take you with us."

The other men grumbled something bitter and surly, not meeting Riella's eyes.

The older man spoke over him. "And we're happy to do it, too." He gave her a kindly smile.

"That's a siren," spat one of the others, raising his voice. "And a bloodthirsty pirate. Savages, both of them. We ought not to harbor them. Dunno why you'd take the risk."

"Don't be silly," replied the bald man with a chortle. "Sirens don't have legs. And your so-called pirate won't be thirsty for your blood—not in his condition. We believe in doing good deeds, don't we?"

He winked at Riella and suddenly she recalled how she knew him. This man was the captain of the fishing boat she hauled to shore right before Polinth captured her. Had he recognized her? Was he trying to return a favor?

"Where are you heading?" he asked her. "We've just set off not ten minutes ago. Took us some time to get your friend into the cart, the huge lad he is."

"Oh, um. The pine forest?" She didn't know its name. "It's off the main road, a few hours away. There's a small bay and the trees are dark."

He started nodding before she'd even finished speaking. "I know it. We'll let you out there, no problem." He stuck his head through a flap in the front of the cart and relayed instructions to the driver.

"Thank you," she said when the man retook his seat.

Without anything to distract her, except for the nauseating and incessant bumping of the carriage, Riella dwelled on her imminent demise. Her insides were a tempest of conflict and feeling—for herself, for Seraphine, her siren friends, and Jarin.

In the privacy of her own thoughts, she wished she had more time with him. She'd grown attached to him. It was a new and foreign feeling, and already she grieved that she wouldn't get to explore it properly. There were many things she didn't want to say goodbye to, but Jarin was fast becoming number one. Her heart felt linked to his in a mysterious, invisible way. Death would sever that link, she supposed.

These were perfectly horrible thoughts, so she was glad when the cart finally slowed. The older man poked his head through the back flap before hopping out and tying it open with twine.

"This the place?" he asked Riella.

She peered out at the grim, lonely pine forest, and nodded.

The older man roused Jarin by feeding a few drops of a potion into his mouth. In less than a minute, the pirate was groaning and sitting up. He appeared every bit as confused as Riella had when she regained consciousness.

"These men let us ride with them to the forest," she explained to him. "Are you alright to walk?"

He rubbed his head, which was now fully healed, as if he'd never been hurt at all. "Aye."

The other men in the cart eyed Jarin in silence, much like the stablehand at the settlement. They seemed to have shrunk now that he'd awoken. Riella felt a rather absurd stab of annoyance that the men hadn't feared her as much as they obviously feared him. She was every bit as capable of hurting them.

After he climbed from the cart, Jarin shook the older man's hand in thanks. The man returned to the cart and it set off again, trundling away in a cloud of dust. Riella and Jarin stood in the middle of the road, regaining their balance and inspecting each other for injuries.

Jarin shocked her by spontaneously cupping her face and kissing her gently on the mouth. "You survived that blast, and without the help of sorcery. You are incredible."

She exhaled. "I'm sorry for leading us into danger. I should've listened when you said we needed to leave the caves."

He shook his head and drew her into a tight hug. "It was a trap all along. The moment we set foot on that mountain, Polinth had us."

Riella grunted. "This is probably how I'm going to die. I'll go running blindly into some trap. I won't get a say in how it happens."

"You can't think like that. Just because last night didn't go to plan, doesn't mean it was a mistake. After all, now we can find Polinth. He said he'd be at the royal wedding. And with any luck, he thinks we died in the explosion."

"I hope that's true." Riella looked up at him. "I'm glad you didn't die last night."

He smirked, dark circles under his eyes like shadows. "Takes more than that, siren." He kissed her forehead. "Come, we have to go. The crew have probably returned to the Pandora by now."

The crew was boarding the ship when Riella and Jarin arrived, ferrying themselves to the Pandora in rowboats. Berolt noticed them as he waited on the bank, lifting his hand in greeting. The strain in his expression worried her.

"How was it?" asked Jarin as he piled into the boat with Berolt and Riella and the last of the crew.

"We got plenty of loot," replied Berolt in clipped tones. "Plenty of weapons, too."

"Meet any resistance?"

"Nothing we couldn't handle."

Jarin nodded, frowning. Riella wondered what he was thinking, but dared not ask him in front of the crew. Something was definitely wrong.

No one asked Jarin and Riella how their night went.

Aboard the ship, Jarin did laps of the deck to check on the crew and the cargo. Only once they set sail did Riella begin to realize the problem. Looking around, the deck was far emptier than on yesterday's journey. What happened to the rest of the crew?

She found Berolt and Jarin having a hushed discussion at the helm, steering the Pandora into open waters. Hanging back, not wanting to interrupt, she couldn't help overhearing.

"—as soon as we parted ways with you yesterday," Berolt was saying. "They set off toward Klatos once we left the pine forest. Splintered off from us. Made me real nervous, but what could I do?"

Jarin shrugged and stared straight ahead, gripping the wheel. "No point having a crew who aren't loyal. Good riddance."

"They said they'd not consort with a siren. I reckon they went to join Artus."

"Let them. I'll cut their—"

As Jarin turned to say these words to Berolt, he saw Riella behind him.

She tried to rearrange her expression, so that her concern and dismay wouldn't show. Jarin clearly had enough to worry about already—a good chunk of his crew had deserted him. Because of her, too.

"Riella—"

She shook her head. "I didn't mean to interrupt."

Before he could say more, she slipped away and climbed the rigging.

The desertion of crew members was yet another blow to their cause. Would their luck ever change for the better? Perhaps not, when death was her ultimate destination. No worse luck existed.

With clear blue skies and a calm sea, the Pandora traveled swiftly. Hieros Isle came into view within hours. From her vantage point, Riella was the first to lay eyes on the island.

She squinted, dread creeping up her spine. Splashes of red stained the white sand of the beach.

Then, she saw the body, slumped and broken in the shade of a palm tree.

CHAPTER 28

Riella and Jarin climbed from the rowboat on the beach and rushed to the broken figure beneath the tree.

In the dappled shade of the palm, Ferrante's bleeding body seemed grossly at odds with the picturesque tropical surroundings. Jarin crouched next to Ferrante, touching his shoulder with care. Riella and Berolt stood back, surveying the tree line. The assailants appeared to have departed the island, and recently—drag marks in the sand indicated that a series of rowboats had been and gone.

The Pandora's crew came ashore, armed with the axes and swords and clubs from the slaver's stronghold. If only the ship had returned to the island sooner. They'd missed the attack by a slim margin, judging by the crimson freshness of the blood.

Riella feared for Kohara and the children. Along with Ferrante, they had been the only people to remain on the island after the Pandora set sail. Were they taken as hostages? Or had something worse happened?

Jarin eased Ferrante onto his back. A red bubble

expanded from the old man's mouth, and he groaned. He was alive, but perhaps barely. His face was covered in blistering burns, like he'd been held to hot coals. His legs were heavily lacerated and his skinny right arm was bent at a strange angle, as were several of his fingers.

Riella fought the urge to vomit. Injuring a defenseless blind man was more than she could stomach. To call the assailants animals would be an insult to animals.

"He was tortured," said Jarin in a grim tone, raking his eyes over Ferrante's wounds. "I recognize these methods. It was Artus."

A fresh wave of nausea hit the siren. Why would Artus torture Ferrante? He was trying to find the amulet, surely. Or perhaps glean Jarin and Riella's location to retrieve the map, depending on how much Artus already knew. After being blindsided by Polinth, Riella was reluctant to assume anything.

Ferrante rasped. Jarin put his ear to the old man's mouth, frowning in concentration.

"He says they're hiding. He must mean Kohara and the kids. Riella, see if you can find them. Call out. They'll come if they know it's you. We'll get Ferrante to camp."

She nodded and jogged into the tree line. Berolt and Jarin had begun the delicate process of relocating the old mystic's crushed form. Ferrante's anguished cry reached her from the beach, making her wince with sympathy. It almost seemed crueler for Artus to have left Ferrante alive.

"Kohara!" called Riella as she skirted the sandy path toward the camp. "Nuri!"

The only reply was the hypnotic buzz of insects and chattering parrots. Riella chewed the inside of her cheek. If the pirates would hurt a blind elderly man, she had little faith they'd spare a woman and children.

The absence of blood on the path did give her some hope

that Kohara and the children had successfully hidden before meeting Artus and his vicious crew.

But any hope came crashing down when she reached the camp. The treehouses were torn apart, the shelters surrounding the fire pit knocked over, and the food supply ruined. Hessian sacks of flour and rice were upended onto the sandy ground, and stank strongly of urine—a stench worsened by the heat of the blaring sun.

With fresh fear, she headed down the track she and Jarin had taken to Ferrante's caves. She figured that Kohara and the children may've gone farther inland to hide. The path was relatively undisturbed, suggesting that Artus and his men didn't venture this way.

Riella cupped her mouth to amplify her voice. "Kohara! Nuri! Ruslo! It's safe to come out! The Pandora has returned!"

She searched behind mossy boulders and inside hollow tree trunks, to no avail. But Kohara and the children knew the island far better than she did—if the siren found them, it would be because they wanted her to.

Ruslo dropped from a tree overhead so suddenly that Riella jumped backward.

"Gods, you surprised me," she said.

Nuri leaped from the branch, landing nimbly next to her brother on the path. Their hair was messy and their faces were filthy, but they seemed unharmed.

"Are you alright?" asked Riella. "Where's Kohara?"

"I'm coming, I'm coming," said a voice from within the thick green foliage. A clutch of palm fronds parted and Kohara hobbled out. "I'm not as quick as the little ones."

The older woman tried to smile—for the children's sake, Riella supposed—but her bottom lip wobbled and her brown eyes were awash with grief.

"How is he?" she asked the siren in a hushed tone.

Riella glanced at the children. "He's alive. They're bringing him to camp. Are you hurt?"

She waved her hand and started down the path to the clearing. "Only my heart, dear. Only my heart. I've known Artus since he was a lad, you know."

Jarin and the rest of the crew crowded the camp. They'd cleaned up one of the ground-level huts, its ruined contents heaped in a pile on the sand. Jarin's low, reassuring voice came from inside, murmuring something to Ferrante, who cried out periodically.

Kohara disappeared into the hut while Riella hung back with the children, unsure what to say to them. Ulyss barreled into the clearing, wild-eyed and searching. As boatswain, he'd been below deck when they dropped anchor, and hadn't been on the first rowboat ashore. Ruslo and Nuri ran into his arms and he hugged them tightly, tears wetting his cheeks.

When he finally set them down, he spoke in a strained voice.

"How would you two like to swim in the rock pools with me?" he asked them.

The children nodded eagerly, and he led them away down one of the jungle paths. Riella was glad they'd be distracted while the crew tended to the camp and Ferrante. Children were not supposed to witness such horrors.

Riella helped with the cleanup in subdued silence. Ferrante's cries rang ceaselessly at first, but gradually quieted. She prayed it was because his pain was being eased, not because he was dying.

The camp resembled something habitable when Jarin finally emerged from the hut, ashen-faced and dark-eyed. His hands and the front of his shirt were stained red.

He beckoned to Riella. She followed him a short way to a secluded pocket of the jungle, where they would not be overheard.

"He's alive," said Jarin. He went to rub his sweating forehead with his hand, then caught sight of the blood on his palm and grimaced. "He'll be crippled, though. I'll try to convince him to come to the mainland, but he's a stubborn man, and Kohara's a stubborn woman, and I believe they wish to remain here. He went right down to the beach to meet Artus. He sacrificed himself, so that Kohara and the children would have time to hide."

"He's brave," replied Riella in a soft voice. "What did Artus want?"

"The map. He must've found out we had it, or at least strongly suspected." A muscle worked in his jaw. "Ferrante told them what the map said. Not everything, but enough to sound convincing. Artus knows the full moon is significant, and that a siren is involved. They tortured it out of him. Artus threatened to go looking for the children."

Riella groaned. "What terrible luck, that Artus came while we weren't here to defend them."

"It wasn't bad luck." Jarin flexed his blood-stained fingers. "The deserters from yesterday went right to him. Artus knew he'd have an easier time getting information from Ferrante than me. Why torture a man who can't die when you can just find out secondhand from a frail old man? And you can bet he didn't want to fight you head-on. Not if he didn't have to."

Riella rubbed her temples. "This is a disaster."

"Artus would still need a siren's Voice to access the amulet. And a way to dive deep enough. He doesn't have those means."

"And Polinth? *He* has a siren's Voice."

"But he knows nothing of the map's contents. He doesn't know where to look for the amulet."

For now, thought Riella. How long would that last?

"Then, we find them both," she said, determined to rally. She was going to die soon. This wasn't the time to accept defeat. "It won't be hard, will it? We know Polinth will be in Klatos for King Leonid's wedding. At the very least, I can save Seraphine. And if we can kill him before he can locate the amulet or wreak any havoc, all the better."

Jarin nodded thoughtfully. "Every pirate in the kingdoms will be drawn to the celebrations, like flies to honey. All those drunk wealthy noblemen and docked foreign ships make for easy pickings. I bet Artus'll be there." He frowned. "Unless he's out to sea, looking for the amulet with the bits of information Ferrante gave him."

Riella chewed the inside of her cheek. "Pirates talk, don't they? For better or worse, word travels fast between you all. Can't you plant a seed with your crew that a sorcerer in possession of a siren's Voice will attend the king's wedding celebrations? To bait Artus into showing himself?"

"I bet that'd work, but it's a huge risk. What if Artus manages to actually steal your Voice from Polinth?"

"He won't steal it. We'll stop him." Riella kicked at the sand with her battered boots, tense and frustrated. She couldn't let these horrible people win. Either of them. Why else would her death be prophesied? She was meant to do more with her remaining life than wait around and dread that Polinth or Artus would succeed. "And I don't have time to sail the seven seas searching for our enemies. That could take forever. We have the opportunity to bring both of them to us, in Klatos for the wedding. Let's do it."

"You're right." He touched her arm. "I'll send my men with the biggest mouths to the mainland to spread the word." He paused. "Ferrante wants to talk to you, by the way."

A jolt of alarm traveled through her. "Me? Why?"

She dreaded hearing any more prophecies or vague, eery words.

Jarin shrugged. "Only one way to find out."

They walked back to the camp together. He waited

outside while she entered the hut where Ferrante lay in a makeshift cot. Kohara sat by his side, her back rod-straight.

Riella thought she'd been prepared for how he'd look, having seen him already on the beach, but her stomach still twisted at the sight of his battered face and body. Purple and black bruises covered his exposed flesh, blooming like ghoulish flowers among the blistering burns. His hand and arm had been set, and wrapped in bandages.

He turned his head slightly as she walked in. As she stepped closer, Ferrante's milky eyes somehow managed to lock onto her.

"Jarin said you wanted to speak to me," she said.

Kohara looked up. Riella expected the woman to be tearful, but her eyes were clear and her chin was high. "He went down to the beach to meet them. Can you fathom such fortitude?"

The siren nodded, fiddling with her talons out of nerves. "Jarin told me."

"That's exactly it," rasped Ferrante, showing his gapped teeth. "Exactly what I wanted to tell you."

Riella braced herself for riddles. "That you went down to the beach?"

"No, siren. That I got to choose my fate. There's no greater gift. As I drifted near death, I Saw that if you stay on your path and be brave, in the end, you will get to choose your fate, too."

CHAPTER 29

The roads to Klatos heaved with travelers the day before the royal wedding.

Riella and Jarin had split from the rest of the Pandora's dwindling crew. The pirates would blend into the masses, entering the city in twos and threes. The Pandora was docked leagues north of Klatos, in a secluded bay. Jarin dared not allow the ship anywhere near the city, because the Dark Tide Clan was still very much wanted for plundering the royal ship.

Ulyss and a few other crew members stayed behind on Hieros Isle with Ferrante and Kohara and the children. The old man was recovering slowly, but the worst of his injuries would never fully heal.

When the Pandora finally set sail for the mainland, the siren had mixed emotions. Although glad to take action, she'd spent the preceding days on an idyllic island with Jarin. They swam in the rock pools and explored each other's bodies. During the headiest of moments, when carnal pleasure had altered her state of consciousness, she could almost fool herself into believing her time with him would never end.

But then, night would come. While Jarin slept, Riella lay in his arms, eyeing the moon through the window. Every night it grew fuller, brighter—every night brought her closer to the end of her life.

Spending so much time with him was a double-edged sword, though. Since she would die soon, she allowed herself to be close to him without boundaries or restraint. Caution seemed pointless. The consequence was the explosive growth of her feelings for him. She sought comfort in him, as well as pleasure. It was foolish of her. But then, if you could not be foolish in the face of death, when could you?

Perversely, she wondered if she'd know when she died. Would there be a warning? A slow and conscious demise? Perhaps it would be sudden and without ceremony, the way deaths often were in reality.

Jarin had spread the word about Polinth possessing her Voice, via his crew. They wouldn't know if their plan to lure Artus had succeeded until they entered the city and found him, or at least his men. He'd be free to dock at the Klatos port, since Jarin took the fall for the royal ship scuttling. Jarin believed that Artus was arrogant enough to do little to conceal himself, and Riella prayed it would be true.

"Why's this taking so long?" asked Riella with a groan.

While patience had never been her strong suit, the stress of her impending death and the difficulty of her mission made the siren unbearably restless. She stood on her tiptoes, trying to see past the city wall, to little success. Only the gleaming golden turrets of the palace were visible.

A stone wall, roughly double Riella's height, enclosed the entire city except for the port. They'd approached Klatos midmorning, hoping to avoid the crowds, only to be greeted by a seemingly endless line of people, horses, and carts waiting to gain entry into the city. The queue moved at an agonizingly slow pace.

"The guards are searching everyone before letting them through," said Jarin, whose height allowed him to see farther than Riella. "Ordinarily, we could jump the wall, but there are guards every few paces. I've never seen such heavy security." He lowered his voice. "Not even when my mother was terrorizing the city."

Royal guards in red and blue coats patrolled the wall on foot and horseback. They carried swords and crossbows and interrogated anyone who strayed from the dirt road.

A middle-aged man ahead of Riella and Jarin, who'd overheard part of what he said, turned around. "There's rumor of an assassination attempt on the king before he's wed, that's why. I reckon it's Prince Davron wanting to claim the throne."

"Nay, I heard the king will be slain after the wedding, by the Garstangs," said the woman with him. "So Meliohr can reign as queen alone, and transfer power to Morktland. Her nasty brother's the real puppeteer behind everything. King Reynard."

A young man behind Riella piped up. "I heard it was the High Magus who'll get a blade in the back tomorrow."

She and Jarin raised their eyebrows at each other. Were these rumors the usual chitchat and speculation of humans, or were they based on truth?

"Reynard," repeated Jarin in a thoughtful voice.

"What?" asked Riella.

"My mother knew him when she was young." Jarin shrugged. "She never told me how exactly, but her father was a baron, so she probably met him at some royal event."

"Oh, that's right," said Riella, nodding. "Your mother's from Morktland. Sirens don't swim that far north, because the waters are freezing."

"Wise. Only monsters lurk in those parts."

When they reached the front of the line, Riella was sweating. A scarf was tied around her head, which caused her hairline to itch in the midday heat. Jarin's clothes covered his body entirely, to conceal his Dark Tide Clan tattoos. Neither of them carried weapons.

Their story, should they be asked, was that they were visiting from a small village in the northern mountains, and would stay with Jarin's relatives in Klatos during the celebrations. They'd arrived on foot instead of horseback, which was slower but added credibility to their story of being humble village folk.

The city gate was open barely wide enough for a cart to fit through, and was manned by armed guards. Two of them stopped and questioned every person who entered, and another pair conducted searches of any carriages or carts.

Riella noted with relief that very few people were turned away. One exception was a man known to the royal guards for selling a chewing leaf that induced hallucinations. Another was a woman who tried to bring a live snake into the city, slung around her neck like a scarf. She appeared genuinely confused by the panicked refusal of the guards, and she chose to stay outside the city walls rather than surrender or release the animal.

Finally, it was Riella and Jarin's turn.

"Where're you staying?" asked the guard as he looked Jarin up and down. He'd given Riella a disinterested glance.

"With my uncle," replied Jarin with a distinct note of impatience.

Riella bit back a smirk. As a pirate, he wasn't used to being questioned and operating through proper channels. He'd probably wanted to ditch the line and scale the wall, consequences be damned, even more than she had.

From inside, another guard muttered to a colleague while

looking at Jarin. Then he nodded decisively and hurried away, out of sight behind the wall. Riella suppressed a huff, wishing the guards would wave them through and be done with it.

Her impatience morphed into apprehension when the guard returned moments later with a colleague who was clearly recovering from an injury. He wore a thick bandage over part of his face, covering one eye, and listened intently to whatever the other guard was uttering in his ear.

Jarin had watched this exchange, too. Riella sensed his energy shift, his shoulders stiffening fractionally.

"He was on the royal ship I scuttled," breathed Jarin at Riella, hardly moving his lips.

The injured guard looked up, finding Jarin with his one good eye and squinting. Then his face transformed in recognition, his eyebrow flying up. Riella groaned inwardly. She and the pirate were about to run or fight. Perhaps both.

Sure enough, Jarin reached down and grasped her wrist in preparation for action.

Should they steal a horse from a traveler? Weapons from the guards? Plenty of people around them carried daggers.

But they couldn't fight an entire platoon and hope to get away. It was a risk they couldn't take—far more was in jeopardy than their own freedom. Polinth and Artus were on the loose, and poor Seraphine had no one.

A bang erupted directly overhead.

Riella ducked by instinct, looking around for the source of the attack. More ear-splitting bangs filled the air, accompanied by streaks of colorful light. To her surprise, no one seemed concerned by the assault. The children in the line clapped and cheered.

"Firelights!" one squealed.

The metallic scent of smoke from the so-called firelights singed Riella's nostrils. She craned her neck and spotted

Berolt's distinctive red hair and beard. The firelights came from his direction, and she suspected he meant to provide a diversion.

Jarin ran at the closest guard, hitting him square in the throat, which Riella took as her cue.

The one-eyed guard tried to grab Riella as she dashed past, but he misjudged the distance and nearly fell over. Other guards drew their weapons as a fresh wave of firelights soared overhead and exploded, filling the air with bright lights and blinding clouds of smoke.

Riella sprinted, ramming red and blue coats indiscriminately, making the guards bellow with surprise and pain. They hadn't expected her preternatural strength and had focused mainly on Jarin. Their misjudgment made it easy for her to carve a line through their defenses.

She quickly became separated from Jarin, because the guards had drawn their swords on him and attempted to close in. Once she'd run far enough beyond the gate for the smoke to clear, she cast around for him. If they caught him, he'd be imprisoned and hanged for the attack on the ship. And when they figured out they couldn't hang him, they'd surely do something far more gruesome.

He charged out the smoke unharmed. As he ducked around a flailing red and blue coat, he stole the guard's sword with a deft sleight of hand. From up on the wall, guards sounded the alarm, blowing horns and shouting for reinforcements.

"Follow me!" yelled Jarin, running up the cobblestone street with a small army of royal guards in pursuit.

They'd entered the city in an impoverished residential area, with open drains in the streets, tightly packed houses, and laundry hanging from ropes strung between neighbors' dwellings.

Although the streets were crowded, no one made any

move to intercept the obvious fugitives, nor did anyone assist the guards by making way.

Jarin and Riella ducked around a food cart, and he made a hard left into a cramped alleyway between buildings, only wide enough to enter single-file. They pounded up the uneven cobblestones until they reached another corner, turning into an even smaller walkway.

Drum-heavy music played somewhere overhead and the sounds of the street, including the guards' shouts, became muffled by the density of the buildings.

Jarin stopped at a metal grate that lay inconspicuously among the rough cobblestones. He inserted his fingers between the metal grills and hauled the grate aside.

"You go first," he said.

She looked down into the space he'd opened. A surprisingly fresh gust of air blew up in her face, and she could see nothing but impenetrable black. From the street, the enraged shouts of the royal guards grew louder.

"Jump!" said Jarin. "Trust me."

The siren took a deep breath, and leaped into the darkness.

CHAPTER 30

Riella fell several times her height and landed on something soft.

Jarin climbed down into the circle of light above her. He hung from the sides of the manhole by one hand while dragging the grate back into place. Realizing he was about to jump, she scurried out of the way.

"Are you alright?" he called down, unable to see her.

"Yes! You can jump."

He dropped through the air and managed to land on his feet, unlike Riella.

Already, her eyes were adjusting. She'd fallen onto masses of fabric piled beneath the grate for a soft landing. They were in a tunnel with stone floors and walls. It was large enough to stand in, and branched off in five directions.

"What is this place?" she asked in wonder.

"Asterius. Underground city." He cocked his ear toward the grate, listening. "I don't know if the guards are aware of this entrance, but we should keep moving. There're plenty of places for us to surface, far away from here. We'll meet the rest of the crew at the inn later."

Riella followed him down one of the tunnels. "I hope Berolt and Drue make it past the gate."

Jarin gave a dry laugh, which echoed slightly in the confined space. "After our entrance, I bet the guards are too distracted to pay them much mind."

"How do you know about this place?"

Torches shone from brackets in the walls and the tunnel was remarkably clean. At each intersection, gusts of air blew through the adjoining tunnels. Some brought the briny scent of the ocean, while others smelled like spices or perfume or firelight smoke. Riella tore off her scarf and stuff it in her pocket.

"I lived down here for a while," he replied without turning around. "Back when—" He cleared his throat. "Back before I found my way onto a pirate ship."

"Oh, I'm sorry. That must've been hard."

"Don't be sorry. It was a better education than any other I received. I had no other family, after I lost my parents, and I was a pariah above ground by virtue of what my mother did. But down here, it's different. It doesn't matter where you come from or what you've done."

The labyrinth was extensive, and Riella marveled at how innately Jarin seemed to know his way. Then she noticed hand-painted signs hammered into the walls at each intersection, resembling street signs. She touched one of them.

"They're a mirror of the street names above," explained Jarin. "Still, it's easy to get lost down here. Some tunnels are caved in, some are dead ends. Now and then, when the rains are heavy, the network floods. Most Klatos residents never come down here. But the tunnels have been mighty helpful to the Dark Tide Clan, for transporting goods around the city undetected."

"Do royal guards not patrol them?"

"The tunnels were mostly built by the palace during the Zermes-Morktland war, decades ago. The resistance fighters used them to sabotage and attack the invaders. Since they were made for guerrilla warfare, the royal guards mostly leave it alone. They know a different law operates down here."

He and Riella kept walking, slower now that they'd put distance between them and the royal guards. The walls had been painted in some stretches, depicting magical beasts and poems and warnings about what lay ahead. One rhyme in particular caught her eye and she read it aloud.

"Tides will turn and tears will flow. As above, so it is below." She frowned, feeling vaguely unsettled by the words. "What does that mean?"

Jarin put his hand on the back of Riella's neck, looking over her shoulder at the poem. "That change is constant. And whatever happens on a cosmic scale happens on the earthly plane, too."

She looked at him in puzzlement. "How'd you come to that conclusion?"

He smiled slightly while gazing at the rhyme. "My mother was obsessed with understanding the forces that govern our worlds."

"Oh. Well, I wish *I* understood."

"Don't worry. No one really does." He leaned down and kissed the top of Riella's head. "Come. I'll get us some weapons at the market up ahead. Then we'll go to the surface."

Music drifted through the tunnel, mingling with the hum of many human voices.

Riella and Jarin followed the sound and arrived at a large gallery, held up by floor-to-ceiling stone columns.

The gallery was home to a crowded array of stalls, each

selling peculiar wares and food. Beyond the gallery were countless alcoves, which appeared to be residences. Jarin had not lied when he'd called it a city. There was a whole other world down here, and she would've never known it existed if he hadn't shown her.

No one paid them any attention, except for the odd cursory glance. Holding Riella's hand, Jarin wove through the crowd toward a stall with an impressive weapons display. Daggers, swords, and crossbows lay on tables and hung from a backboard.

"Jarin, old friend," said the stall holder with a grin. He was a skinny older man with dark skin and blue eyes. "Been a while since I clapped eyes on you."

"Aye, that's the truth," replied Jarin.

The men launched into a conversation, catching up on each other's lives. Soon bored, Riella began to wander, the other stalls drawing her curiosity. There was a man selling lithe black snakes, a herbalist whose stall emanated pungent aromas, and a woman selling bottles of what she claimed was the breath of elves.

"The breath of life," called the woman to passersby. "To revive your body and mind."

Annoyance rippled through Riella, thinking inevitably of Seraphine. She hoped the woman was merely a charlatan who sold empty bottles to guileless shoppers, and not some kind of trafficker.

The human preoccupation with harvesting life and power from other creatures—and even each other—was bizarre. They already possessed great magic and might. Why were they never satisfied?

Polinth expressed the desire to conquer the laws of Nature. Sirens were raised to nurture and protect the ocean and all its mystical forces. Aside from anything else, the ocean was too powerful to conquer. It would always humble any adversary, in the end. Perhaps humans were taught differently about the earth.

One stall caught Riella's attention, despite being tucked into a shadowy gap between alcoves. Patterned bolts of fabric were decked above a woman, who sat cross-legged on a cushion behind a tiny stand. On the stand was a candle, glowing tall and bright and still, and a cloudy crystal ball.

She seemed to notice Riella, too, because she followed the siren with her vivid yellow eyes, and then beckoned.

Riella hesitated, glancing back at Jarin, who was still deep in conversation with the weapons merchant. Figuring she had time to pass, she went to the woman, dodging children playing games and elderly folk in chattering groups.

"Hello," said the woman, smiling up at Riella. "You found me."

Her age was impossible to determine—her hair silvery-gray, but her skin smooth and tanned. Riella didn't recognize her accent.

"Are you a Seer?" asked the siren. She patted the pockets of her trews. "I'm sorry, but I have no coin."

The woman shook her head. "You don't need coin. Please, sit."

Riella did not particularly wish to hear any more predictions, after what Ferrante told her, but this woman was clearly telling fortunes for entertainment only. So, the siren kneeled before the stand, sitting back on her ankles and inspecting the crystal ball.

The woman held out both hands, palms facing upward, indicating for Riella to take them. Feeling a little bit foolish, she did. Immediately, the flame of the candle turned blue and flickered.

The woman's eyelids fell closed, her wide mouth slightly ajar. The crystal ball remained unchanged, and Riella wondered how it was supposed to work, or if it even did.

At first, the siren felt nothing except the smooth, cool flesh of the woman's palms. Just as she'd started to relax, her mind wandering, a distinct surge of heat traveled from the woman's hands into Riella's. In the same instant, the crystal ball turned perfectly clear.

Disconcerted, Riella wrenched her hands away. The woman kept her palms facing up and her eyes closed. Riella frowned in confusion. Should she simply get up and leave? This was nothing like her experience with Ferrante. The fortune teller was clearly a time waster.

"You shan't find it," said the woman, her eyelids beginning to flutter violently. "You shan't find it, because another already has. You will lose all you hold dear. You will lose more than you ever imagined you could possess. You will lose your life. You will lose your love. And when—"

"That's enough!"

Jarin appeared beside Riella, interrupting the eery foretelling. A tear had rolled down her cheek and hastily she brushed it away. While he placed a few copper coins on the stand, she scrambled up, glad to be leaving. She shouldn't have stopped here in the first place. Her idle curiosity got the better of her.

The candle had returned to an orange flame and the crystal ball was clouded over. The woman didn't seem offended by the disruption, smiling serenely as she swept the coins from the stand and dropped them into a grubby tin on the floor next to her.

"Ready?" Jarin asked Riella, taking her hand.

She nodded, and didn't look back as they moved through the gallery to a tunnel on the far side.

"Pay no mind to whatever nonsense she spoke," said Jarin, giving Riella's hand a firm squeeze. "It's all smoke and mirrors and darkly vague pronouncements. The con-artists are out in force because of the wedding festival crowds. Plenty of victims around."

"Of course." She forced a smile. "Smoke and mirrors."

The woman's prediction really *had* been vague. Her words could apply to any number of scenarios and appear to make sense. It was a simple deception.

But then, why hadn't she wanted payment from Riella? If the woman was a con-artist, that seemed like a fairly monumental oversight on her behalf.

"I bought discreet weapons," said Jarin, handing her a knife sheathed in leather. "Better to arm ourselves covertly, to avoid attracting any more attention than we already have. We'll change our clothes, too."

Riella tucked the knife into her boot. The farther they traveled through the tunnel, the less shaken she felt by her encounter with the fortune teller. Her impatience to surface increased, like a human who'd been underwater for too long without a breath.

They exited the tunnels on a ladder made of rungs hammered into a wall. At the top was another grate, which Jarin heaved to the side before helping Riella to climb out.

The courtyard she emerged into was blindingly bright after the darkness of the underground, despite being overgrown with vines and shaded with trees.

Riella turned on the spot, trying to orientate herself. The golden turrets of the palace were closer now, as was the sea. Seagulls cawed nearby, and the scent of the ocean was strong.

Jarin hauled himself out, and then kneeled to tuck his dagger into his boot.

"We need to find the rest of the crew," he said, standing. "Or they'll assume we were captured and they'll storm the jail."

The pair left the courtyard and entered the street.

This part of the city was markedly different from where they'd entered Klatos earlier that day. The streets were clean and wide and rather devoid of crowds, which made Riella feel exposed. She'd turned to Jarin to ask about the location of the inn when an irate shout came from a few paces behind.

"Oi, you two! Stop right there!"

CHAPTER 31

Riella prepared to run.

Thankfully, Jarin had the presence of mind to look back first.

"Silas!" he said wryly, looking the unkempt man up and down. "Seems like you found a tavern."

Silas was part of Jarin's crew and he'd entered Klatos earlier in the day than Riella and Jarin. He'd partnered with Drue, who trailed after his drunk crew mate with a resigned expression. The two men caught up with Jarin and Riella, Silas trying and failing to throw his arm across Jarin's shoulders, because he could not reach.

"I've been trying to get him to the inn," said Drue. Out of all of the Dark Tide Clan, he looked the most respectable in regular clothes, and least like a pirate. In his neat collared shirt and trousers, he could've passed for a merchant's assistant. "We're in the vicinity of the inn now, at least."

"Hey, Captain," said Silas to Jarin with slurred speech. "We did what you told us to do. Went to the docks and had a good looksie, didn't we, young Drue?"

Jarin raised his eyebrows at the cabin boy.

"Aye," said Drue. "Artus is in Klatos, it would seem. The schooner he commandeered is docked."

"Along with every other vessel in the seven seas," said Silas with a hiccough. "But we found Tregor. Gave him some coin for info."

"And?" asked Jarin as they rounded a corner.

"Artus'll be at the festival in Creta Square tonight. At least, I think that's what Tregor meant. Hard to understand him, you know, what with the—"

He gestured vaguely around his head, and then at Riella.

"I didn't *personally* deafen him," she said with a sniff.

It was possible she had, actually.

"Anyway—" continued Silas. "Artus'll surely weasel his way into the wedding at the palace tomorrow night. Dunno how he hopes to get an invite, though. Rumors are swirling about assassinations and such. Security will be tight."

"I'm certain he'll find a way, and so must we," said Jarin. "We go to the Creta Square festival tonight, then. Tomorrow, the wedding. We stop him before he becomes more powerful."

Jarin seemed reluctant to mention the amulet in front of Silas, which Riella thought wise. Trustworthy or not, the man was drunk, and drunks had loose lips.

"Stop him?" repeated Riella with a frown. "But what about the blood oath? How does it work?"

"The blood oath states that if I or any Dark Tide Clan pirate try to kill him, we die."

"Even you? Won't your invulnerability protect you?"

He hesitated. "I don't know, to be honest. It's the kind of theory you can only test once. But there are more ways of stopping a person than killing them. And besides, you didn't take any oath. You could still slay him."

"I'd love to."

With an appreciative smirk, Jarin turned back to Silas. "Any word on a sorcerer making trouble?"

"Which one?" he asked in a sardonic tone. "Everyone in the kingdoms will be at the wedding, including the High Magus. If there *isn't* trouble of grand proportions, I'll be flabbergasted."

"Alright," replied Jarin. "Good work." He nudged Riella. "We need to visit a tailor and a dressmaker before the wedding."

She nodded. Her mind was preoccupied with the idea of Polinth attending a crowded wedding. Even without the amulet, his potential to cause catastrophe was enormous. He possessed explosives and could create elaborate illusions at will.

Then again, the High Magus surely held his position for good reason. He had to be a supremely powerful sorcerer himself. If Polinth attacked, Riella wouldn't be the only one trying to stop him.

And stop him she must. The full moon was tomorrow night. This was it—she was out of time.

A pair of royal guards passed by in the street. They cast an appraising stare over Riella and the pirates, but kept walking. News of her and Jarin's entry had obviously not reached this end of the city, but it would only be a matter of time.

"Let's get off the streets until sundown," said Jarin. "We should—"

His words died in his throat, as he inhaled sharply and doubled over. Riella grabbed his shoulder in alarm. Silas and Drue stopped, too.

"Are you alright?" she asked him.

But he did not reply. He only clawed at the center of his torso, grimacing in pain. Had he been poisoned? Should she try to find a healer?

Before she could decide, he abruptly dropped his hands.

His grimace disappeared, replaced by a look of uncertainty, or perhaps even fear. He stared at his hands, turning them over and flexing his fingers. His face gleamed with sweat.

"Jarin?" asked Riella. "Are you alright? What just happened?"

He shook his head, stuffing his hands in his pockets. "Nothing. Too much sun. Come on, let's go inside."

Mystified and concerned, but not wanting to press the issue in front of Silas and Drue, she followed him into the inn.

The woman at the front desk barely looked up from her parchment as they walked in. Jarin paid, and collected brass keys for the rooms. Silas wandered in the direction of the in-house bar, while Drue slumped after him to keep him in check.

Riella and Jarin climbed the narrow staircase. The inn had an air of gloom, despite being quite luxurious. The wood was dark and polished, stuffed animal heads decorated the walls, and chandeliers glittered from the ceilings. She tried not to think too much about how this inn would likely be the last place she ever slept.

Would Jarin be with her when she died? If she had one wish for death, that was it. Feeling his strong arms and hearing his deep, gravelly voice might be some comfort in her final moments. But she ought not to expect such mercy. Most creatures on earth and in the ocean died alone.

Their suite had burgundy linens and carved wooden furniture and a four-poster bed with a canopy of layered red silk.

"Are you sure you're alright?" she asked Jarin carefully, as he kicked off his boots and ran his hands through his hair with a frown.

"Of course." His expression cleared and put his arm around her waist, drawing her close. "Don't worry about me."

She surveyed him, gnawing the inside of her cheek. It was a nervous habit she'd acquired since losing her tail and gaining legs. When she'd been a proper siren, she never had nervous habits. But then, she'd also never had a warm glow in her chest when she was close to someone or thought about them. There were good things to go along with the bad. Jarin had been right about that.

Her face broke into a smile. "I can't believe I'm in a bedroom suite with a *pirate*."

A slow smile crept across his face, his eyes twinkling. "Not the first time though, is it?"

"You really couldn't have imagined any other way to evade the royal guard at Madame Quaan's than to get me on the bed? Or were you being a scoundrel?"

He kissed her forehead. "I wanted you from the moment I pinned your wrists to the wall in the brig."

"You didn't answer the question," she replied, punching his shoulder.

"I did, though." He laughed.

"The siren elders always warned us about evil pirates when we were young—especially the Dark Tide Clan. Their sordid deeds and ugly faces." She put her head on the side. "How best to eviscerate them. I could hardly wait to grow up and join the fighting."

"Let me tell you a secret." He paused, his smile widening. "We never spoke about sirens that way. As much as we hated you, we loved you, too. You could deafen us and mutilate us and sink our ships, but you still entranced us, every time."

Riella smirked. "Yes, well. That was the idea. The elders did lie about something, though." She traced the angular line of his stubbled jaw, her fingertip coming to rest on his chin. "You, for one, are not ugly."

He pretended to buckle at the knees. "An almost-compliment? From a siren? Surely no other man can boast of such an accomplishment. I can die happy now."

His grin faltered as he realized what he'd said.

Riella dearly didn't wish to spend her last days and nights lamenting her death. She put her head to his chest, feeling his invulnerable heartbeat and hoping he wouldn't apologize or try to discuss it. He took her cue and smoothed over the hitch.

"But am I sordid?" he murmured into her hair.

The siren burst out laughing.

"Sometimes." She tilted her head back and bit her bottom lip. "I quite enjoy it when you are, though."

"You are not exactly a sweet little kitten yourself."

With a cackle, she drummed her fingertips against his shoulder, where she often clawed him during sex. She did it on impulse, to vent some of her overwhelming desire for him. Of course, being invulnerable, he always healed within minutes.

"You love it," she replied.

"I do. You have no idea."

Jarin swept her off her feet and took her to the bed. Her physical desire for him flared, and she smiled in anticipation as he lowered himself over her body. But the look on his face made her hesitate. It was as though he was feeling a hundred things at once.

"What is it?" she asked.

He held his weight on his elbows, his body on top of hers. In this position, his gray-green eyes penetrated hers at close range and she couldn't avoid the intensity of his gaze. Not that she wanted to, exactly, but she did not know how to respond to the hurricane of emotion that his attention stirred in her.

He dragged his fingertips across her forehead, moving a

stray lock of hair from her face. "I would kill for you, you know. I would die for you."

She returned his stare. "That's easy to say, when you can never die."

He put his lips to her neck and kissed her soft pale skin, sending frissons of pleasure through her body that were at odds with the sweet pain in her chest. Or perhaps the pleasure was in concert with the pain. When you were a landwalker, it could be hard to tell where one ended and the other began, Riella had learned.

"Never say never," he whispered, tugging the sleeve of her blouse over her shoulder and kissing her décolletage.

"Make me forget everything," she said, swallowing the lump in her throat. "Please, just make me forget for a little while."

She imagined he would ravage her, undressing her roughly and taking her with enough force to render her incapable of thought. And she liked that idea. She liked it a lot.

But what he did instead was somehow better, even though it hurt. Jarin undressed her slowly and with care, covering her body and neck and face in kisses. His salty, leathery scent enveloped her, giving her comfort and inciting her arousal. Her lips grew tender as he kissed her mouth for an inordinately long time—as if they had all the time in the world—before finally pulling back to tug his shirt over his head.

She lay back, naked, her legs splayed before him while he gazed down at her, his jaw clenching and unclenching. With one leg, she reached up and traced his siren tattoo with the tip of her toes, a smile playing on her lips. His skin flamed against her toes, his sun-burnished abdominal muscles rigid beneath her touch.

He took hold of her ankle and, without breaking eye

contact, kissed the arch of her foot. It tickled, but in a good way, and Riella giggled. With his other hand, Jarin eased his trousers over his hips and kicked them off, his huge cock presiding over her eagerly waiting form.

Setting her foot down gently on the bedcover, he leaned forward again, lying over her. This time, she didn't feel nervous and uncomfortable looking directly into his eyes. She felt safe and calm and happy.

He trailed his finger along her ear, then her cheek, and touched her on the tip of her nose. His erection lay hard and heavy against her stomach. The sensation of his body made her pink heat swell and grow slick with longing.

Still staring into her eyes, and breathing deeply in sync with her, Jarin pressed his mouth to hers. She returned his kiss, nibbling at his bottom lip. He probed her mouth, sliding his tongue against hers. She inhaled his breath as they kissed with growing intensity, marveling at how addictive she found his scent and taste.

He paused, his mouth hovering over Riella's, while he dragged the slick head of his cock down her stomach and over her flushed entrance. Her eyelids fluttered with anticipation, her talons finding his shoulder so that she could sink them into his flesh. Aroused as she was, she barely noticed as he reached up and guided her hand away.

She threaded her fingers into his hair instead, holding his head close to hers and kissing him deeply as he pushed the head of his cock into her sodden opening, forcing it to give way to him. Gasping into his mouth, she accepted all of his considerable length and girth into her pulsing depths. Her tight muscles wrapped around his shaft as he drove into her fully.

Riella laced her legs around his waist, her hands still in his hair, and held him tightly as he glided in and out of her.

Every stroke felt like pure heaven and she wondered how it was possible for sex with Jarin to get better every time.

He put his arms around her body to gain better leverage, increasing the speed and depth of his thrusts. Her moans filled the room and her wetness made his steel-hard erection slippery against her flaming walls. Riella felt herself rapidly approaching climax and she longed for him to fill her with his seed.

Determined to send him over the edge, she used the strength of her legs to drill his cock harder and faster into her. Only when his body grew rigid and his teeth gritted did she allow the waves of her own climax to wash over her. She gasped with pleasure, her core surging with heat as he released his shuddering desire into her.

For those long, blissful moments, her mind was indeed blank. All that existed was Jarin and Riella and the sweetness of their mutual ecstasy.

He cradled her face as the waves began to subside, his shaft still encased in her taut depths.

"There's something you need to know," he said as he looked into her eyes.

She blinked. "What?"

"You will survive this full moon, if it's the last thing I do."

Before she could reply, he kissed her softly on the mouth.

CHAPTER 32

Jarin felt the exact moment the curse broke.

Searing pain lit up his solar plexus, and he felt a strange rushing sensation, as if falling from a great height. He was in the middle of the road with Riella and Silas and Drue, and he had to pretend nothing was amiss. But right away, he knew his invulnerability no longer existed.

The dark power that'd flowed through his veins for a decade vanished. He felt lighter, as if he could move more freely, but also far more vulnerable.

Why did the curse end? Most likely, a woman fell in love with the prince. Jarin hoped that was the case, because Davron deserved happiness, after everything his mother had done to him.

But for Jarin, the timing couldn't have been worse. Riella faced death, and he was now far less useful than he'd been a day ago. He could die like any man now. Another stab to the heart would be his last.

Artus, he could deal with. But Polinth? How could Jarin defend Riella against an amoral sorcerer?

His best hope to save the siren was still the amulet. If Artus or Polinth had it already, he could steal it from them and use it to save Riella's life. He was still a pirate, after all. Stealing was second nature to him. Hardly a solid plan, but it was the best he had.

One thing he knew for sure? He wouldn't tell anyone the curse had broken. Riella might act differently if she knew, and put herself in danger. He didn't want her to be concerned for him, especially this close to the full moon. While she was striving to save Seraphine, he would strive to save her.

"What are you thinking about?" came her sleepy voice.

She blinked her eyes open and stretched her body against him.

"You."

The afternoon gradually turned to dusk, making it safe for Jarin and Riella to emerge from the inn. They visited a boutique for new attire and continued to the pre-wedding festival at Creta Square. Most of his crew came along, although some went to the docks to plunder ships instead.

They arrived at the festival as night fell, the stars blossoming silver in the navy sky. Jarin determinedly ignored the nearly full moon. He could not ignore its light, though—opalescent, and edging the city in white.

Riella wore a cobalt-blue dress that showed a distracting amount of her décolletage. The dressmaker had fitted her with a headpiece made from gauzy material and elaborate beading, concealing her distinctive platinum hair.

He chose well-cut black attire for himself, to blend in with the merchant class of Klatos. The city crawled with royal guards, and the last thing he needed was to be thrown in jail the night before Riella faced her fate. The breaking of the curse had been a big enough blow.

Creta Square was in a rough part of the city, spitting

distance from the docks. Tonight, the square heaved with musicians, entertainers, hawkers, and revelers. Lights were strung between the buildings and every few seconds, firelights bloomed in the sky overhead, bathing the crowd in transient colorful light.

Riella stayed close to Jarin, reaching for his hand, which made his heart want to explode like the firelights. Affection from a siren was the most impossibly perfect thing he could've experienced in this lifetime. Nothing was rarer or sweeter or more vicious than Riella. Maybe he truly could die happy.

Sometimes he forgot she'd only been a land-dweller for a very short time. And for most of that time she'd been on Hieros Isle, where she was surrounded by the ocean. To find herself in a drunken crowd of partying strangers must've been surreal and unnerving for her.

"We'll split into pairs," he shouted to his crew over the din. The pirates were in varying states of inebriation, having mostly spent the afternoon drinking. "If you clock Artus, one of you keeps an eye on him, and the other comes to find me. Understood?"

If he could dispense with Artus tonight, that would leave Polinth as the only remaining threat to Riella. As far as he knew, anyway. He didn't have a huge amount of information to go on. Would it have been too much to bloody ask that the fates tell Ferrante *how* the siren might die?

Silas saluted, his eyes unfocused, then plunged into the crowd. A hapless and very sober Drue went after him. The rest of the crew, including an already hungover Berolt, splintered off in different directions.

Jarin guided Riella toward the center of the square, where a tarnished bronze statue of the former King Branimir Nikolaou loomed over the festival. The king who'd ordered the slaying of Jarin's father. The king his mother had then executed in retaliation.

Like Riella, Jarin preferred being at sea. He felt uneasy here, in the place of his family's devastation. If he and Riella survived, by some miracle, he vowed to sail away with her, anywhere she wanted to go.

And if she wanted to resume her siren form and return to the ocean, he'd make that happen for her, too. He'd take her to Starlight Gardens. If Polinth could do this to her, surely someone existed who could undo it.

Standing a head taller than most other people, Jarin surveyed the square. He didn't spot Artus and his crew, but he had faith the chaotic festival would bear fruit. There were too many wealthy foreigners and drunk courtiers cavorting with abandon for the pirates to stay away.

"Riella!"

Jarin whipped his head around. Who on earth would be calling her name? It was a female voice, at least. That made it less likely he'd have to bury his dagger in their gut before they could get near her.

The siren searched for the source of the voice, smiling when her eyes fell on the red-haired woman squeezing through the crowd.

Jarin didn't recognize her at first, but as she drew closer, he realized she was one of the women from Madame Quaan's. She wore an expensive-looking crimson dress and had a dapper older man in tow. The gentleman looked politely uncomfortable and out-of-place, bumping up against the great unwashed of Klatos.

"Sehild!" exclaimed Riella, pulling the woman into a tight hug. "I'm so happy to see you."

Jarin continued scanning the crowd while Riella spoke with Sehild, keeping one ear on their conversation. The older man stood at the edge of the group, twiddling his cane and intermittently bouncing on the balls of his feet.

"Where've you been?" asked Sehild. She surreptitiously swept her eyes over Jarin. "I see you're still enjoying certain earthly delights. Not that one can blame you."

"I've been on an island, mostly. But who's this?" Riella lifted her chin at the older man, whose face brightened at the merest scrap of the siren's attention.

Jarin snorted to himself. The gentleman didn't realize the blonde beauty would flay him alive if Sehild gave even the slightest hint that he was mistreating her.

"This is Olivier," replied Sehild, waving a jewel-encrusted hand in his direction. "We've just been at a salon off the square. They serve the most incredible concoctions. Enchanted with magic, they are. Have you been there?"

Riella shook her head. She started to reply, but Jarin cut her short by grabbing her upper arm. He'd seen two things in quick succession that'd turned his blood cold.

From the northern end of the square, a horse-mounted patrol of royal guards carved a purposeful line through the raucous crowd, heading toward the king's statue. And to their right, on a balcony of a tavern, stood Artus, smirking and looking directly down at Jarin. Several of his crew mates flanked him.

Artus waved at Jarin, then pointed at the patrol. *Dammit.* He should've realized that Artus would've spread the word of Jarin's presence in the city. The old captain would have sent his men out that afternoon to gather information, just as Jarin had done.

If Riella was captured by the patrol and thrown into the palace dungeons, would she die there, alone in a cell? He couldn't risk that happening. He needed to draw attention away from her.

He bent low, speaking to Riella. "Go to the salon with Sehild and her patron. I'll meet you there when I can."

"Why—" she started, shaking her head in confusion.

He addressed Sehild. "Did you hear me?"

Wide-eyed, the woman nodded. "I owe you and Riella my freedom. We'll take care of her, I promise."

Before the siren could argue, he lunged into the crowd. If she knew Artus lurked nearby, she'd go straight to him and kill him. And fair enough, too. But she needed to stay out of trouble, lest anything hinder whatever the fates had in store for her tomorrow night.

Jarin moved diagonally through the writhing masses of people, away from the patrol. The chaos of the music and drunken shouting and exploding firelights did a good job of concealing him. Soon, he was at the edge of the crowd, under the awnings of the shops and taverns surrounding the square.

He looked back, squinting through the smoke and darkness, across the square at the balcony where Artus had been standing. He was no longer there, and nor were his crew.

"Jarin. I'm sorry."

He recognized Drue's voice at once. Jarin turned to find the boy ashen-faced and with a silver blade at his neck. Fletch hovered behind him, grasping the knife's handle, his one beady eye glaring at Jarin.

"Come," wheezed Fletch. "Captain wants a word with ye."

Jarin glanced back at the square, where the royal patrol advanced.

"Let the kid go," he said to Fletch. "Threats aren't needed. I've been looking for Artus myself."

Fletch's eye twitched. After a few moments of contemplation, he shoved Drue away. The boy stumbled, righting himself and watching haplessly as Jarin followed Fletch down an alleyway.

The atmosphere of the dingy alley was in stark contrast to the square. The festival noise became muffled, and the shadows were dense. It was a likely place to be slaughtered like an animal, thought Jarin wryly.

At the dead-end of the alley, Fletch backed away, disappearing toward the street and leaving Jarin alone. Less than a minute later, Artus swaggered down in Fletch's place. Jarin watched him approach with grim resignation.

The captain appeared to be alone, but his lackeys would be waiting nearby for his orders, whatever they may be. Was he after Jarin's head, or Riella's Voice, or the amulet? Likely, he wanted all three. At least Artus wasn't aware Jarin could be killed now.

Unless news of the curse breaking had traveled here from Velandia already? Surely not. For even the fastest vessels, Port Hyacinth was a day-and-a-half-journey.

"Jarin, my boy." Artus grinned, his pockmarked cheeks like the craters of the moon. "Funny meeting you here. Tell me, how's Ferrante? And your lovely siren?"

Anger surged through Jarin's body. Should he slice Artus's throat open right now and be done with it, blood oath be damned? The only thing stopping him was Riella. He couldn't leave her to fend for herself. Therefore, he couldn't kill Artus.

But, what if he did something else instead? Like Jarin said to Riella, there were more ways to stop the old captain than killing him. He could disarm Artus until he could get the siren to safety, far from Creta Square.

Jarin glanced past the old captain. A rickety ladder ran up the rear wall of a tavern, right to the roof. The buildings were crammed close enough that he could run straight across the roofs, evading Fletch and the rest of Artus's crew.

Jarin crossed his arms in front of his chest. "What do you want?"

"Ah, you know what I want, boy." Artus brushed his sun-destroyed hands over the lapels of his black jacket. He, too, seemed to be imitating a merchant. "Ferrante gave me faulty information, lad. He sent me chasing my tail all over the bloody ocean."

"Least he could do. You nearly killed him."

Artus gave a magnanimous shrug. "And your siren stole from me. All I'm trying to do is get my map back and secure her Voice, then I'll be on my way. I'm owed that much, I figure."

"Can't help you. I don't have either of those things."

"Ah." Artus cocked his head, eyeing the younger man. Despite seething with anger, Jarin was immediately wary under Artus's appraising stare. His shrewdness was unmatched. "But you and your siren read the map. And I'll bet she knows exactly where to find the amulet." His gold tooth glinted. "Perhaps she can be my guide."

"If you lay your hand on her, I'll cut it off."

Artus hooted with glee. "Oh, she got to ye, didn't she? That must be one mighty fine magical cunt she has. You're making me regret I didn't—"

Jarin forgot he was newly mortal. He forgot at least a dozen pirates were waiting to ambush him. Or, more accurately, he didn't care.

He strode to Artus, knocked him backward against a barrel, and withdrew a dagger.

Artus hadn't put his hand on Riella, it was true. But he'd spoken foully about her. So, Jarin stuck the blade in the man's mouth and sawed off his tongue. His old captain gurgled and screamed and struggled, but Jarin overpowered him.

The detached tongue fell to the gravel, blood spurting from Artus's mouth.

In the time it took for the older man's crew to register his screams over the festival's din, Jarin had scaled the ladder and disappeared.

CHAPTER 33

Riella followed Sehild and Olivier to the salon. Jarin had vanished into the crowd before she could object to splitting up. Then, she saw the mounted patrol of royal guards heading into the square and understood. He wanted her out of sight and away from trouble.

But where did he go?

"I'm pleased to have run into you," said Sehild as the trio slipped into a quiet side street. "I've dearly missed Yvette and Odeya since they left Klatos. Yvette took off at once to the countryside to study Healing, and Odeya is sailing to Morktland, where she's from. It's a long journey by ship, and far too cold for my liking, but she was thrilled at the prospect of going back."

"That's good news." Riella smiled, falling into step beside her friend. Olivier walked behind them. "Any word of Madame Quaan?"

Sehild grimaced. "Yvette didn't go back for her, I know that much. Certainly, no one has seen or heard from her, nor Gerret. I suppose they're dead."

Olivier held a door open for Riella and Sehild to an

elegant salon. Once the door was closed behind them, the difference in atmosphere and sound was as pronounced as the ocean and earth. Riella exhaled in relief. She'd not realized how overwhelming she found the festival until she left it.

The salon was furnished in brass and jewel-toned velvets. A maze of narrow corridors leading to nooks and intimate bars was lit with chandeliers and candles. The clever acoustics transformed all conversation into an ambient hum. String music played from one of the bars.

"Let's have a drink while we wait for your strapping man," said Sehild.

She winked at the siren, leading her by the hand to a gilded bar. Differently shaped and colored bottles filled the mirrored shelves.

Olivier passed a menu to Riella.

"The drinks here are potions," he explained. "Enchanted by mages. Pick your poison, so to speak."

She perused the list. There were brews promising seductive abilities, but also good fortune or heightened senses or the promotion of healing. What she really needed was the ability to find and destroy her enemies at will, which sadly was not on offer.

"Do they actually work?" she asked.

Sehild shrugged. "They don't hurt, I'll say that much. It's a bit of fun."

"Alright. I shall take good fortune, then, I suppose."

Olivier and Sehild chose the potion that promised heightened physical sensation.

The bartender mixed their drinks, making an elaborate show of shaking and stirring and pouring. He slid a tall glass of sparkly red liquid to Riella, and shots of dark blue to her companions. The trio clinked their potions together and drank.

The drink was sweet, and delicious, but did not feel particularly magical to Riella.

"This place is leagues better than Madame Quaan's," said Sehild, gesturing around the salon. "We work for ourselves, you see. Many of our old clients have drifted over here, which is nice. Although, you've got to be careful who you speak to. There's been some particularly nosy folk around lately."

Riella put down her empty glass. "Nosy, how? And—"

She glanced at Olivier, unsure how much to say in front of him.

He bowed his head. "I'll go and get us a table. Come over when you're ready."

The siren felt a flare of gratitude for his tact.

"Go on," said Riella to her friend when he'd left. "Who's been nosy?"

After what had happened to Ferrante, the idea of anyone asking questions made her uneasy.

"A series of people I've never met." Sehild absentmindedly traced her fingertip around the rim of her glass, making it sing. "Asking about a map."

"Yvette stole a map from Artus, remember?" whispered Riella, leaning close to her friend. "You didn't tell any of these people, did you? Who were they, anyway? Pirates? A sorcerer?"

"Of course I didn't tell anyone." Sehild chuckled and rolled her eyes. "Give me some credit, please. They weren't pirates or sorcerers, that I could tell. Just normal-looking people. I don't know." She downed the last few drops of her drink, giving a little shiver of pleasure. "But I figured it was important, for them to keep trying, so I played dumb. I only talked about the map to Yvette, when she came in a couple of days ago."

"Oh, well, I suppose that's alright." Riella frowned. "But you said she moved to the countryside at once."

"She did. She came back for a patient." Sehild tilted her head, toying with her long red braid. "The patient was with her, actually. An elf, quite near death, sad to say."

The siren swayed on the spot, suddenly dizzy. Polinth. Word had obviously spread about the map, and he'd used Glamour spells on Sehild to get the information out of her. Finally, when he'd impersonated Yvette, he'd succeeded.

"Did you mention to her that I took the map?" asked Riella, her heart thudding.

"Well, I suppose." She arched her brow. "What's wrong with that? Yvette already knew."

Riella felt sick. She and Jarin came to Klatos to ambush *him*, but what if they'd walked into a trap? He already had her Voice. Now he knew she'd read the map, too. He would surely be hunting her.

At least Seraphine had been spotted alive. Riella could still save her. She ground her teeth, a familiar burst of siren rage and determination fortifying her.

Perhaps this was good. She wouldn't need to waste precious time trying to find Polinth, if he was indeed hunting her. Let him come. She wanted to face him, and she would.

But what became of Yvette? To assume her form, Polinth must've met her. Perhaps Madame Quaan survived, and helped him. What a vile thought.

Head pounding with stress, Riella allowed Sehild to lead her to the table where Olivier sat.

"Do you feel the potion working?" asked Sehild cheerfully.

"I don't believe so," replied Riella, sinking into the seat.

She felt the opposite of fortunate. And the room suddenly seemed too small, and strangely airless. Her thoughts would not slow down.

Sehild trailed her fingertips across the back of Olivier's hand while they gazed drunkenly at each other. "I'm feeling it," she said with an impish grin.

"I need a washroom," said Riella abruptly, rubbing her temples.

More specifically, she needed *water*. Cool, peaceful, beautiful water. All she wanted to do was dive headfirst into the ocean, away from her ever-mounting problems. But she could not.

At least not until her death, she thought dolefully. Ferrante said she'd be washed away with the tide. In a bleak way, her wish to disappear into the ocean would be granted.

"I'll come with you, if you like?" asked Sehild, starting to stand.

Riella stopped her, wanting to be alone. "No, stay here."

"Oh. Alright. I'll check on you soon, though. Your pirate friend did charge me with taking care of you."

"I can take care of myself. But thank you."

"Of course you can," said Sehild with a small smile. "But that doesn't stop people from caring about you." She pointed at a door leading to a hallway. "Right down there, and turn left. You can't miss it."

Riella followed her directions, running her fingers along the wallpaper as she walked down the hallway. The potion had been a mistake. Her stomach churned and rocked, like the sea during a monsoon.

It was strange to think that land-walkers cared about her. Would they mourn her death? Would Jarin? He said he'd kill for her. She'd kill for him, too. But then, violence was in their natures.

He also said he'd die for her. Were they just pretty words, knowing he'd never be put to the test, or did he really mean it? Did he care for her as she cared for him?

Riella was so distracted that she didn't register the man in the shadowy hallway until she bumped into him.

Four men flanked him, wearing matching brown uniforms with swords on their hips.

"Apologize this instance!" one of them barked.

She focused her gaze on the man she'd bumped into and she groaned.

It was Count Zemora. He wore green brocade and heavy gold jewelry. The jewels had presumably replaced those Riella had stolen from him, flagrantly, right off his fingers and neck while he was tied to a bedpost. So much for the potion of good fortune. This really was the *worst* luck possible.

She swallowed hard, knowing she should apologize for running into him. Too much was at stake to justify fighting with a courtier right now, especially under the hostile gaze of his bodyguards. Her mouth opened, to say the words, and yet she could not.

"I've never in my life given a fake apology," she said before she could stop herself. "I won't start now."

After all, she was dying tomorrow. She would not compromise her values at this late hour. Especially not for a ridiculous man like Count Zemora.

At once, she realized her mistake. The Count's eyes widened and he began to tremble. His four lackeys moved their hands to their swords in unison.

"I can't believe you," said Zemora, taking a step toward her. "The *trouble* you landed me in!"

Riella balled her fist, preparing to punch him in the face.

"No one has ever treated me so poorly. *No one.* It was marvelous!" He clasped his hands in front of his ruffled shirt and beamed at her. "And look at you! You're as miraculous as ever. Such luck, that I should see you again. I've thought of nothing and no one else since our little rendezvous at Madame Quaan's."

Without tearing his rapt gaze from her, he gave a vague wave at his men. They let their hands drift away from their swords. A pair of them exchanged identical looks of knowing resignation.

"I trust you'll be at the wedding?" asked the Count. "I'd love to see you there."

Riella hesitated. Perhaps the good fortune potion had worked, after all. Count Zemora could make her life markedly easier, if he agreed to her request.

"I'd like to go," she said. "But my friend and I misplaced our invitations."

The Count held up a bejeweled hand. Despite herself, she considered robbing him again, just for fun. He did quite literally ask for it.

"Say no more," he said in a pompous tone. "I will personally see that you, and a plus one, are on the guest list. You know it's a masquerade? Such a pity to cover your face, but alas, the bride and groom have insisted. Rather odd, for a wedding." He bowed deeply. "It will be my honor to serve you, my lady. And an even greater honor to behold you tomorrow night in your finery."

She didn't bother hiding her disgust at this last sentiment, her lip curling. He straightened up, catching her expression, and gave a little squeak of joy.

"May I?" he asked, reaching for her hand to kiss it.

She smacked his hand away. "You may not."

"Ah! Sublime."

He gazed at her with such adoration that she couldn't bear his presence any longer. Forgetting the washroom, she returned to Olivier and Sehild. The two of them were stroking each other's forearms.

"Are you alright?" asked Sehild as Riella sat down.

"Fine," replied the siren.

She really did feel better. The absurd meeting with Count Zemora had realigned her sense of purpose. Tomorrow night was the night that mattered, and now she had access to the wedding.

"Riella."

Her heart leaped at the sound of Jarin's deep voice. He strode to the table, placing his hand on her back. His skin was hot through the thick fabric of her dress and his face was flushed.

"Thank gods you're alright," he said. "Did anything happen?"

Olivier offered him a seat, which he took, pulling his chair close to Riella. He appeared unhurt, although she thought she detected a red smear on the underside of his wrist. In the low light of the bar, it was hard to tell.

He noticed her looking and moved his hand into his lap, out of sight. She decided not to muddy the waters by discussing Count Zemora in front of Sehild and Olivier. Once she was alone with Jarin, she'd tell him.

"Not particularly, no," she replied. "How about you?"

Jarin shifted in his seat. "Uh, not really. Nothing to speak of."

CHAPTER 34

"No, stop. It's too tight."

"Take a deep breath. That's it. Deeper. Good girl."

Riella did as the dressmaker instructed, inhaling until she thought she'd pass out. The bodice was laced so firmly that she could barely move. How could she save Seraphine tonight in such ridiculous garments?

"You'll get used to it," said the dressmaker while he tied the laces. His name was Pierre and he was from Velandia. He had a thin mustache and oiled black hair.

"What? Not breathing?" she retorted.

"The bodice is good for your posture," said Pierre.

Riella kicked her leg to test her range of motion, catching the many layers of her chiffon underskirts. She narrowed her eyes in the mirror at Jarin, who stood behind her, having already been fitted by a tailor. He wore black trousers and a shirt, long black boots, and a smart jacket with gold edging.

"Why can't I have clothes like he's wearing?" she asked with a sigh. "They look far better to fight in."

"We have to blend in with the guests," explained Jarin. "We must look like we belong."

Pierre paused to stare at her. "My beauty, why on earth would you be fighting? It's a royal wedding."

Jarin cleared his throat and gave the dressmaker a pointed look. The pirate had given him a hefty pouch of gold coin when they arrived at the studio, for discretion as much as clothing. Evidently, Pierre recalled the same, because his face colored and he fell silent.

As the dressmaker fussed with her skirts, Riella admired Jarin. He looked incredibly handsome, his stubble neatened with a razor and his hair slick. The formal attire did nothing to hide his broad, muscular frame, and his gold pendant sat on his tattooed chest. The tailor had suggested a ruffled shirt that would've come up to his neck, but one look from the pirate quelled this idea.

Riella's dress was made from silk and was pale gold, with tiny pearl buttons along the sleeves and down the back. She'd met up with Odeya at the salon, who'd arranged the siren's hair in silky waves and enhanced her features with cosmetics. The dressmaker supplied the pair with masks. Riella's was golden and jeweled, shaped like a butterfly with eyeholes in the wings. Jarin wore a black skull mask that left only his piercing gray-green eyes and chiseled jawline visible.

They arrived at the palace as dusk descended, the huge tangerine sun setting the golden turrets ablaze. Riella was grateful for the distraction of her tight dress and the spectacle of the palace entrance, because otherwise she would dwell on the heartache of witnessing her final sunset.

Jarin, who hadn't left her side all day, offered his arm. "Shall we?"

She threaded her arm through his and they began the long walk up the red carpet to the palace entrance. Hoards of rowdy onlookers packed the cobblestone street in front of the palace grounds, jostled by royal guards on horseback. Berolt and Silas and the rest of Jarin's crew lurked among the onlookers, searching for Artus and his men.

"I worry that Artus will talk his way into the palace without an invitation," said Riella.

Jarin snorted. "Trust me, he won't."

"Oh. Right."

Jarin had told her he cut out Artus's tongue, though he didn't say why, and she told him the Count put their names on the wedding's guest list, though she didn't say why.

Neither pressed for details. Believing this to be their last day on earth together, Riella and Jarin came to a silent understanding to do naught except help each other achieve their ends. Whatever else happened, it was imperative to keep the Amulet of Delphine from Polinth and Artus.

Closer to the entrance, Riella and Jarin joined the chattering press of wedding guests. Everyone wore elaborate clothes and masks, and spoke in an array of foreign dialects. Spectacular blue birds paraded around the manicured lawn, fanning their iridescent tail feathers at will.

"Peacocks," said Jarin. "Tempestuous and vicious when provoked, but very beautiful. Reminds me of someone, but I can't think who."

He snorted with amusement while Riella glared at him.

"How about you keep a lookout for Polinth?" she asked. "Instead of teasing me."

"I am. But he'll be masked, at the very least. Or he could've taken on another form altogether. I daresay we won't find him until he wants to find you."

Riella drummed her talons nervously on Jarin's jacket sleeve. "Then, let's hope he does want to find me. At this rate, Sehild may've done me the largest of favors, if she did set him after me. We have mere hours left."

At her last words, the muscles in Jarin's arm stiffened, but he said nothing.

"Name?" asked the royal guard at the door, when it was their turn.

"Uh, Riella," she replied. "And guest."

The guard ran the nib of his quill down a long piece of parchment while she held her breath. What if the Count did not keep his word? Or simply forgot to put her name down?

"Ah, here you are," said the guard, his quill coming to a stop. "Very good."

He gave a small bow and gestured for them to enter.

Like the salon, the inside of the palace reminded Riella of beneath the sea. The ceilings were high, with ornate gold and turquoise-blue accents. Murals of forests and fantastical creatures were painted on wall panels, and balconies oversaw the cavernous foyer. Compared to the outside, the interior was cool and dark and tranquil. She was beginning to realize that peace and quiet were synonymous with wealth in the human world.

With his hand between her shoulder blades, Jarin guided her to the temple where the marriage ceremony would take place. They chose a spot toward the rear, to better survey the crowd of plucked and perfumed nobles. A man in a purple robe presided over a carved wooden pulpit at the front. Thousands of candles lit the temple.

"Is the High Magus here?" asked Riella.

"They're coming in now," muttered Jarin in reply, inclining his head at a side door. "A delegation from Starlight Gardens. He'll be among them."

Royal guards held the door while a group glided into the temple wearing identical black robes. Except for the tallest one, Riella noted, whose black robe had a crimson hood. A hush fell over the room, followed swiftly by ripples of excited murmurs.

The group sat apart from everyone else, toward the front. As soon as they were settled, the ceremony began. A string quartet played elegant music from the chancel.

First, King Leonid was helped to the altar by a pair of footmen. He wore a mask, like the guests, and an intricately embroidered gold and red cape. His posture was stooped, his skin pale, and tufts of hair stuck out from underneath his jeweled crown, which sat slightly crooked on his head.

The bride entered on the arm of an imposing man, who walked her up the aisle to meet her betrothed. Both wore masks and a crown sat atop the man's head. His attire was designed to resemble armor, and his crown was made of silver metal and rose-cut diamonds.

"King Reynard Garstang of Morktland," said Jarin. "Accompanying his sister, Meliohr. Now we know why it's a masquerade."

"I don't," whispered Riella. "Why?"

Jarin lowered his voice farther and leaned into her ear. "Reynard is deformed, and very sensitive about it." He shrugged. "Or maybe they're using the masks to hide Leonid's ailing health."

The young bride had golden blonde hair and excellent posture. Riella gave an involuntary shudder at the thought of having sex with King Leonid, as the new queen would surely be required to do, in exchange for her family's increased wealth and power.

Impatient for the ceremony to finish, she resisted the urge to fidget. The man in the purple robes recited a prayer, then talked about the kingdom of Zermes enjoying stronger new relations with Morktland. Finally, he spoke aloud the vows for the bride and groom to repeat.

" . . . you promise that you will honor and protect her, until you leave this earthly realm?"

A deep heaviness formed in Riella's chest as she listened

to the vows. She tried not to dwell on the pain, but the more she tried to ignore it, the heavier it became. Perhaps Jarin felt it too, because his hand tightened on her own. By the end of the vows, he gazed directly at her through his mask instead of the royal couple. Riella blinked back tears, determined to be strong.

The ceremony ended when the newlyweds walked arm in arm down the aisle and the string quartet filled the temple with joyous strains.

"Thank the gods that's over," said Riella, standing and surreptitiously dabbing her eyes beneath her mask. "Let's go kill Polinth."

The people in the row in front of her turned around in shock. Jarin ushered her along the pew, into the crowd filing toward the temple doors. "As much as I love your enthusiasm, let's try not to get arrested first," he said with a wry chuckle.

Night had fallen, patches of black sky and glittering stars framed by the high windows.

The reception party was held in an enormous mirrored ballroom in the northern wing of the palace, with twinkling chandeliers hanging from the ceiling.

Musicians played in a band on a stage and entertainers danced on platforms. The dancers had painted faces and wore animal costumes. Waiters in black and white suits wove through the crowd, brandishing trays of fizzing wine in crystalware.

In the very center of the room, a grand wedding cake shaped like the golden palace stood tall on a plinth.

The party took off with swiftness and ease. Guests downed flutes of champagne and traded gossip and danced to the spirited music. The High Magus and his acolytes were conspicuously absent, to Riella's disappointment, as were the royal couple. Naturally, though, the one person she did not wish to see was preening himself in the mirrors nearby.

Count Zemora was so absorbed in his own reflection that Riella spotted him before he spotted her. She pulled Jarin into the crowd, out of the Count's line of sight. The last thing she needed was to be waylaid by the fawning of that peculiar man.

"What if Polinth isn't even here?" she asked Jarin in dismay, as she looked carefully at every passerby. "What then? We've left so much to chance."

Jarin's warm palm between her shoulder blades calmed her fractionally.

"Trust that you are where you need to be," he said, his low voice audible under the cacophony of the party.

She sighed. "Perhaps I'm to die by some freak accident that has nothing to do with any greater cause. A falling chandelier, or food poisoning, or—"

A knot of people on the other side of the room parted. Riella's heart missed a beat when found herself staring at Polinth's devious, pointy face. Then, she blinked and the crowd shifted. He was gone.

"Polinth," she said, grasping Jarin's arm. "He's here."

They pushed their way through the carousing guests to the other side of the room, but the sorcerer had vanished. Growing increasingly frantic, Riella barged into circles of partiers in search of him. But if he was using sorcery, he could've taken any form and she'd never know.

"We have to find him," she said, gazing at Jarin in despair.

"We will. Did you see Seraphine?"

She shook her head. "We should talk to the High Magus. If anyone can deal with Polinth, it's another sorcerer."

"Then that's what we'll do." He looked around. "Let's return to the galleries. The Starlight Gardens delegation will be here somewhere."

They made for the closest exit, stepping into the quieter hallways and foyers. Royal guards were stationed every few paces, but several other guests wandered freely and no one tried to stop the pair.

Riella and Jarin were descending a marble staircase, headed toward the temple, when a telltale black robe swept along the deep blue carpet in the hallway below.

"It's one of them!" she said, hurrying down the stairs.

They tailed the acolyte to a gallery and moments later, Riella peered around the doorframe with Jarin at her back. Marble statues populated the room, candlelight illuminating the features of the carved stone faces. People stood amongst the statues, but unlike the ballroom, the gallery atmosphere was subdued.

In a corner, King Reynard of Morktland spoke gruffly at his sister, Meliohr, and the High Magus. King Leonid sagged on a chair nearby, staring at the floor. The kings both still wore their masks, but Meliohr had removed hers, revealing a beautiful face with high cheekbones.

The acolytes drifted between the statues in small groups, murmuring to each other from beneath their black hoods.

"Riella," whispered Jarin. "Guards."

A pair of royal guards were indeed patrolling the hallway. She and the pirate needed to get out of sight, but she was loathe to give up the golden opportunity before her. The High Magus was just paces away.

"Come on," she breathed to Jarin, pulling him into the gallery.

They slid through the inky shadows, hiding behind a towering statue of a man wrestling a three-headed snake.

But then, an acolyte turned and looked right at her.

CHAPTER 35

◈

*R*iella froze.

The acolyte saw her, didn't they? With the darkness of the room and their mysterious hoods, it was hard to be sure.

Heart thudding, she waited for the acolyte to call for guards, or alert their fellows. Riella and Jarin were blatantly sneaking up on two kings and a queen. Their actions were enough to have them thrown in the dungeon, if not summarily executed.

But the black-robed figure merely stared a few moments longer, before returning to the hushed conversation the others were having.

Riella released the breath she'd been holding. With his back against the statue, Jarin moved closer to the Garstangs and High Magus, whose voices echoed strangely in the cavernous room. She frowned, listening to Reynard's icy tirade.

"—consort with filth. I agreed to the match on the condition that sorcery not be allowed inside these walls," he said in a clipped accent. "Your presence is an affront."

Riella raised her eyebrows beneath her mask. She'd never met the High Magus, but couldn't imagine anyone taking kindly to such insult.

"Brother," came Meliohr's smooth voice. "The wedding is a day of pomp and ceremony, you know that. Once the delegation returns to Starlight Gardens, I doubt we'll see the mages at all."

A loaded silence followed.

Reynard sniffed. "Well. I'll be glad to dance on the grave of your foulest pupil, at last. After Tjaele, it's the barest justice I could receive."

Foulest pupil? Riella didn't know who or what Tjaele was, but with such strong talk, surely he referred to Polinth. If so, they might have an unlikely ally in Reynard.

She tapped Jarin's back, which was taut with tension.

"Does he mean—" she whispered.

But her query was interrupted by King Reynard striding away from his sister and the High Magus. Riella cursed inwardly. Should they follow the king and try to enlist his help, or appeal to the High Magus? They were running out of time.

Jarin decided for her.

"I'll follow him," he muttered into her ear. He pulled her around the other side of the gargantuan state, so that they were out of Reynard's sight when he stomped past them toward the doors. "You question the Magus. He's an opaque man but he'll not hurt you, and the queen seems harmless enough. Reynard could go either way. And Riella?"

She looked into his eyes, which were searing and bright behind his black skull mask.

"Yes?"

"I love you," he said.

Then, he was gone, melting into the shadows in the wake of King Reynard.

His words left her strangely breathless. Then, a smile spread across her face beneath the privacy of her butterfly mask. How incredible.

She was loved. Though she would die, she would die loved. Could anyone truly hope for more?

The queen's velvety voice broke through Riella's joyful realization and she forced herself to concentrate on eavesdropping.

"My apologies," she was saying. "He's a bit of a zealot, I'm afraid. Old-fashioned in his beliefs. Given what he's been through, you can understand. But I assure you, I'm far more amenable to the mystical arts than my brother. I hope you and I can be friends, Magus. Just don't tell my brother." Her laughter tinkled. "I've already enlisted the services of Polinth on a little project of mine. Brilliant man."

Riella couldn't believe her ears. Polinth certainly had been busy—he'd already hoodwinked the new queen. Without Jarin to temper her impulsivity, Riella hastened from her hiding spot to confront the queen and the High Magus.

"You're wrong! Polinth is evil."

She faltered as she looked from the queen's surprised face to the High Magus's eyes, which were pale gray and wintry under his crimson hood.

"He seeks the Amulet of Delphine," she tried to explain. "He stole my Voice. And gave me legs. We need your help to stop him."

The acolytes turned their attention to her, listening in silence. In Riella's peripheral vision, royal guards materialized around the room, closing in slowly on her. The queen held up her hand and they halted, but did not disperse.

The High Magus regarded the siren, his eyes not moving from her masked face. "Stop him from what?"

"Well, we don't really—" Riella quailed, aware that she

sounded mad. "He does all kinds of awful experiments. And, he's holding an elf captive! He drains her life force."

"Goodness," said Meliohr, her golden beaded dress glimmering in the low light. "The alcohol certainly has been flowing. Since it's my wedding night and a happy occasion, I shall overlook that you didn't address me in the proper manner."

"What?" asked Riella, nonplussed. "Queen Petra never expected sirens to bow before her."

Meliohr's mood shifted instantly, steel appearing in her gaze. "I am not Queen Petra. Your first clue should've been—"

The High Magus cut in, his voice chilling and low. "Polinth is not my concern. Nor should he be yours. The Amulet of Delphine lies at the bottom of the ocean. Unless you believe a siren will help him, which I highly doubt, all is well. This is not the first time he's made a bid for such an item. He may be eccentric in his academic pursuits, but my understanding is that he has a progressive Rotting disease and is not long for this world. Whatever your quarrel with him, Nature will surely resolve things shortly. Now, leave us."

Eccentric? Quarrel? He was a torturer and murderer.

And it was *Riella* who was not long for this world. The night would claim her before Polinth's disease claimed him. Perhaps she should've pursued Reynard with Jarin. Confronting the High Magus was a waste of her precious remaining time.

"You don't—" she started.

Riella did not hear the High Magus utter an incantation or move his hands, yet he must've cast magic, because a powerful energetic rebuff pushed her backward and made her words wither in her mouth.

She stumbled in her voluminous dress. Meliohr snapped her fingers at the nearest guards and they caught Riella as she fell, dragging her from the gallery while she fought to regain control of her body.

They released her in the hallway and she swayed on the spot while they watched her.

"I'll take her," came a female voice from the doorway.

A black-robed acolyte glided toward Riella. The hood covered her face to her lips, blood red against her snow-white skin.

The guards nodded and resumed their post inside the gallery, leaving Riella alone with the young woman.

"The High Magus sent me," she said in even tones. "I am to lend you whatever assistance you need, courtesy of Starlight Gardens."

Hope flurried in Riella's stomach. "He wants to help me?"

The woman made a small sound in her throat. "*Help* might be too strong a sentiment. He loathes Polinth, and has taken measures over the years to keep him in check. The High Magus is distracted right now with the new queen. The Garstangs represent an existential threat to sorcerers, and having one on the Zermetic throne requires his full attention. But Polinth is a degenerate, no doubt. I'm sure he wants the amulet for his experiments in necromancy. So, let us ensure he does not get it."

"Necromancy?"

Riella thought with dread about the skeletons littering the mountain outside of Polinth's workshop.

The acolyte nodded. "It's why he was expelled from Starlight Gardens. He's been trying to make the High Magus regret it ever since. I'm Neve, by the way."

With a sweep of her hand, Neve pushed back her hood to reveal thick black hair in elaborate braids and an intense brown stare.

"I'm Riella. But I thought the amulet grants life? The Sea

Witch created it with an act of sacrifice. How can such a thing be used for darkness?"

"The amulet allows one to linger in the ephemeral space connecting life and death. The In-Between. With good intentions, you might give peace to a dying creature, or heal a deep wound in someone's spirit, or communicate with a soul as they depart the mortal realm. With bad intentions—" She sighed. "Well, deploying dark magic in that precious space could cause limitless damage. It might dismantle the barrier between life and death altogether."

"You can help me, though? You're a sorceress?"

"I'm an apprentice. I warn that I'm no match for Polinth. My best hope would probably be to Bind him, and we run."

Riella nodded. "Or you Bind him, and I crush his skull."

"That'd work, too."

"First, we need to find my—" She paused. "My friend. Jarin. He's tall, dressed in black, wearing a skull mask. He went after Reynard."

Neve blinked. "Why would he do that?"

"We hoped he could help us with Polinth. He seems to hate sorcerers."

"Oh, that he does." Neve's dark eyes narrowed. "Do you?"

"Gods, no. Except Polinth, because he captured me and experimented on me."

Her expression softened. "Sorry. The presence of Garstangs has us all on edge. Alright, well, let's search the galleries. I'll do the bottom level, you search this one."

With a flick of her robes, she descended the marble staircase, leaving Riella alone.

The siren searched in a rush, wrenching open every door she passed. Partygoers in various states of undress occupied many of the rooms. The full moon winked at her through high windows.

Would Reynard help Jarin? Neve didn't seem to have a

high opinion of the Morktland king, and Riella understood why. But if he truly hated Polinth, he certainly had the power to do something about the sorcerer.

She'd just closed a library door when she caught sight of Seraphine, making her heart leap.

The elf wore a silk dress, her face paler and more sickly than the last time Riella saw her. Seraphine swayed, alone, at the quiet end of the corridor, silhouetted by candlelight. Was Polinth nearby? The siren waved at Seraphine, who responded by shuffling sideways until out of sight.

Riella hesitated, glancing over her shoulder. Where was Jarin? Her stomach dropped as she considered the possibility that she'd said her final goodbye to him without realizing.

And he loved her. Suddenly, she desperately wished she said *something* back to him. Before she departed the mortal plane, she wanted him to know what he meant to her. That she liked him, and wanted him, and perhaps even needed him.

But the desires of her heart did not matter. Not when Seraphine was in danger and Polinth was on the loose. She couldn't forsake the elf, who had no one, for more time with Jarin. She'd made a promise.

Riella ran down the corridor, the skirts of her dress billowing around her, dodging drunken revelers. She turned the corner where Seraphine had disappeared, to another long hallway. The chandeliers were dark and the only light came from a few sputtering candles in the sconces on the walls.

"Seraphine?" called Riella.

Riella tugged off her mask and tossed it onto a console. Perhaps the elf had not recognized her.

This part of the palace was empty and as she walked farther, the laughter and music of the party faded.

Despite fearing for the Seraphine's safety, Riella's familiar predatory instinct kicked in, her senses becoming razor-sharp and her fingers flexing. Polinth had to be here, somewhere. If she was doomed to die, she would take him with her, piece by bloodied piece.

With another step, Seraphine's face came into view. The elf stood in the shadows ahead, staring with unfocused eyes. Her mouth moved as she tried to speak, but no sound came out. Polinth had drained her nearly completely of life.

With another step, she saw him.

The sorcerer lurked behind Seraphine, a ghoulish leer on his face and one skeletal hand around Seraphine's neck.

"Let her go," said Riella, fighting to keep the rage from her voice.

"I will," replied Polinth, smiling wider. "But you know what I want in return. Take me to the amulet."

"Give me Seraphine."

"Take me to the amulet," he repeated with a sigh. "We could do this all day—go back and forth. But, one of us doesn't have time for that." His hawkish eyes gleamed. "Take me, and the elf will live. Is this not why you came all the way to Klatos? To redeem yourself after abandoning Seraphine, like a coward? You left her behind to save yourself."

Riella's head pounded with anger and shame. "You are one to speak of cowardice. You hide behind her, even now."

"Yes, or no?"

The siren considered her choices. Mostly, that she had none. As much as she hated him, Polinth was right. Her life was already forfeit, and she owed Seraphine.

Could she really let Polinth have the amulet? If she could even find it. She didn't know if she could swim deep enough, or locate the right spot.

But, at least she'd be in her own territory, out on the ocean. Powerful though he was, she had a better hope of catching him off guard and killing him on the open water.

After all, the moon was still high, glaring at her through a window like an accusing eye.

The night was not over, yet.

"Fine. I agree." Riella dug her talons into her palms with the effort of keeping her voice steady. "I'll take you to the amulet."

CHAPTER 36

Jarin stalked King Reynard from the gallery like a shadow, his blood simmering with anger.

His mother, the sorceress Levissina, was born and raised in the icy northern village of Tjaele, Morktland. The grave on which Reynard hoped to dance was Levissina's.

Did the king kill her?

Jarin assumed the curse broke because a woman fell in love with Davron. It didn't occur to him that Levissina might've died in the process. She always seemed bigger than life and death.

Could Jarin confront the king? Reynard might indeed be able to help with Polinth, given how much he loathed mages. Jarin could send the king and his men after Polinth like a bloodhound after a rabbit.

He had to try, for Riella's sake.

Reynard swaggered down the corridor, away from the party. His crown caught the light, shimmering like ice and snow atop his mountainous form. None of his flesh was visible, not even his hands, which were covered by leather gloves.

Jarin quickened his pace, his breath shallow with anticipation. Within moments, Reynard would reunite with his cache of guards, and the pirate would lose the ability to speak freely with the king. So, speak he must, regardless of how ill-prepared he was for the confrontation.

"Garstang!" he shouted, his deep voice filling the high corridor.

That was all he had. Jarin didn't know what to say next. Reynard turned around slowly, like he didn't fear a thing in the world. Jarin strode within three paces of him.

Reynard squared his shoulders, squinting at Jarin's masked face. The pirate was close enough to make out the king's mismatching eyes. One was clear and pale blue, and the other was nearly closed over, the flesh red and scarred.

"The sorcerer Polinth seeks to assassinate you this evening," said Jarin.

The lie came to him so easily. If a man like Garstang cared about anything, it was his own hide. Even if he doubted Jarin was telling the truth, the king hated mages enough to act on suspicion alone, surely.

"Then, he ought to join the queue," replied Reynard with a growl. "And who are you?"

Jarin hesitated. Should he tell the truth about his identity? He wanted answers about his mother, and Reynard might have them. But tonight was about Riella.

Tonight could *not* be about Levissina, who forfeited her right to piety when she slaughtered innocents. He knew that. He just had to know one thing.

"Did you kill her?" he asked, trying to keep emotion from his voice. "Levissina."

Garstang stepped forward, regarding Jarin with genuine curiosity. "Who *are* you, that you would care about that demonic wench?" He put his gloved hands on his hips. "Remove your mask."

Regret flooded Jarin's entire being. What had he done? Riella needed him.

"No," he replied.

"I am King Reynard Garstang of Morktland and if you do not obey me, I will have you beheaded this very night." From behind his mask, Reynard's eyes drifted to Jarin's chest, where his mother's gold pendant gleamed in the candlelight. "Remove your mask," he repeated.

With one hand, Jarin took off the black skull.

"I thought as much." Garstang snorted. "You are your father's twin. Well, I'm thrilled to inform you that your mother is dead. Gutted like a fox. I expect you'll be relieved, no? You can crawl out of hiding now."

The air left Jarin's lungs. His feelings about his mother had always been an incomprehensible mess of anger and love and resentment and sadness, and hearing of her death only amplified these emotions. For all her crimes, she died alone and by violence in a foreign kingdom, like his father.

With both parents gone, and Riella living her final night, Jarin felt profoundly untethered to this world.

The sensation was oddly freeing. He had nothing to lose. With his invulnerability gone, it was almost like fate was daring him to offer himself in Riella's place. Why else would the prophecy exist, unless someone was meant to subvert it?

Neither of his parents would sit idly by while the person they loved was in peril. They'd fight with everything they had. Perhaps they watched him from the Beyond now, urging him onward, and would lend him aid on his mission. If he succeeded, he'd meet them again soon.

Fate demanded a life tonight? Let it be his. He who'd never belonged. He who carried the weight of his mother's crimes like lead in his blood.

"I'd ask if you ever faced her in a fair fight," said the pirate to the king. "But I believe I can guess the answer."

He tossed aside his skull mask, turned his back on Reynard, and went to find Riella.

"There is no fair fight where demons are concerned!" called the king after him. "But justice will always be done, in the end."

As he strode in the direction of the ballroom, Jarin privately agreed. He, the son of a renowned murderess, would save a siren—a defender of innocents. Vengeance would not come into play. This was about justice. And he was prepared to take anyone with him who tried to stand in his way.

"Are you Jarin?"

A black-robed acolyte stepped into his path, her hood down.

"Who are you?" he asked.

"I'm Neve and the High Magus sent me to assist Riella. She's looking for you. And Polinth."

"Well, where is she?"

The acolyte gave a faint smile. "She's very precious to you."

"More than you know." He exhaled. "I must find her."

"And we shall. I was with her just minutes ago. Follow me, I'll show you where."

He accompanied Neve to a hallway over the main gallery, littered with partiers and empty champagne flutes.

"We'll check every room," he said to the acolyte. "We don't stop until we find her."

Jarin banged the doors open, not bothering to be subtle or close the doors afterward. He barged in on drunken guests, some passed out and others mid-copulation. After scanning the room and finding no Riella, he'd move on.

Finally, he reached the end of the hallway. There he stood,

considering the shadowy labyrinth of walkways and halls and galleries comprising the rest of the palace. The place was enormous, and she could be anywhere by now.

From the corner of his eye, something glimmered on a console partway down the darkened hallway. He frowned, walking over. Riella's butterfly mask lay discarded on the marble top.

"Riella?" he called.

He went to the balcony railing, and shouted her name again. There were only drunken shouts in return.

Neve appeared at his elbow, her face pinched. "You found her mask?"

He nodded and gave it to her wordlessly, a concrete block forming in his stomach. He was too late. Something had happened to her.

The acolyte held Riella's mask, waving a pale hand over it.

"I might be able to pick up her essence. Her energetic signature." Neve frowned in concentration, staring into space as she continued waving her hand. "This isn't my specialty, but if I can detect it, we can follow it."

"What is your specialty?" asked Jarin, hoping it was something like vanquishing dark sorcerers with the snap of her fingers.

The corner of Neve's eye twitched at his question, but she didn't answer.

Unable to stand still, Jarin paced, running his hands through his hair in frustration. What if he'd seen Riella for the last time? He couldn't believe he voluntarily walked away from her.

Neve drifted toward the nearest staircase.

"She went down here." The acolyte jerked her head, as if catching a scent or hearing a sound. "A mage was with her. There's a strong imprint."

"Gods," said Jarin with a groan. "Polinth has her, and he wants the amulet. He'll be taking her out to sea. Let's go."

The streets were feral with revelers in the humid night. Berolt and Drue spotted Jarin from the porch of a tavern where they'd been waiting for his instruction. They ran to catch up.

"Where're we off to, Captain?" asked Drue.

"To get ourselves the fastest vessel we can find. We're going after Riella."

The four arrived at the docks, which were eerily quiet compared to the chaos of the city. There was no movement or sound except for water gently lapping against hulls.

"Are you sure she came down here?" asked Berolt.

Jarin boarded a cutter, leaping onto the sleek vessel directly from the dock and climbing over the railing. He slammed down the gangway for Neve, Berolt, and Drue to board. At the helm, he found a spyglass and scanned the shimmering indigo horizon. The moon splashed silver across the water, illuminating a lone vessel sailing away mid-distance. He squinted. Was that Polinth and Riella?

Movement on the side of the vessel made his heart drop. Half a dozen pirates scaled the hull with ropes, having snuck aboard. Polinth may've been a powerful sorcerer, but he knew nothing about checking a ship for stowaways or pirates.

Artus and his lackeys had beaten Jarin to the punch. Artus, whose tongue Jarin had cut out, would want more than just the amulet—he'd be out for revenge. Jarin's beloved Riella was on a ship with a deranged Polinth and barbarous Artus, and no one to help her.

He would not let her die alone. He would not let her die at all.

"Haul the anchor!" he roared over his shoulder.

CHAPTER 37

Jarin and Drue pulled the rigging.

Soon, the cutter sped through the water in pursuit of the other ship.

"Arm yourselves!" he commanded as they steadily gained on the other vessel.

Berolt found a weapons chest on the stolen cutter and he distributed crossbows, daggers, and swords.

"You can stay on board," said Jarin to Neve. "This'll be dangerous."

She selected a sleek silver sword, moonlight sliding over the blade. "No, thank you."

The acolyte uttered an incantation and the sword glowed red, illuminating her pale face.

Jarin shrugged, and armed himself with a dagger and sword of his own. "The more the merrier."

The four of them gathered at the bow, watching the other ship grow clearer.

"The element of surprise is probably too much to hope for," said Jarin. "They'll see us coming long before we can draw level."

"I could try a Cloaking spell," said Neve. "Mine don't last for long, and I've never tried to Cloak anything as big as a boat, but I can try."

He nodded. "Do it."

She recited a spell, her fingertips resting on the cutter railing. When she drew her hand away, a translucent, shimmering bubble encased the ship.

"Wow," said Drue, staring around.

"It's not very steady," said Neve. "I don't know how long it'll last."

Berolt took charge of the rigging and Jarin steered. They drew close enough to discern movement on deck, at both the stern and the bow. From a distance, the moonlight made the figures look two-dimensional, like silver-and-black shadow puppets.

Jarin pressed steadily onward until nearly upon the ship. Disembodied voices traveled from its far side. When close enough, Jarin and Berolt lashed ropes between the railings of both vessels. As the hulls bumped together, he winced. Even with a Cloaking spell, Polinth and Artus would feel and hear the vessels colliding. They had to move fast.

"Come on," he said, sword in hand, leaping to the other ship's deck.

He landed on his feet, then moved aside for his collaborators.

Neve arced through the air, her flying robe like a specter. The moment she landed, the Cloaking spell failed, the translucent bubble disappearing.

"Dammit," hissed Neve. "Sorry. I didn't realize that would happen."

"Doesn't matter," said Jarin, looking back and forward, trying to discern Riella's location. "I want Artus and Polinth to know I'm here now."

He sprinted along the deck toward the stern, only to

round a bend and crash headlong into a man. Jarin grasped the man by the throat and threw him against the wall.

"Lovel," he spat.

"Artus!" yelled Lovel. "Artus, he's—"

Jarin head-butted him, blood exploding from Lovel's nose. Two pairs of hands grabbed Jarin from behind, hauling him off Lovel. Artus was in his face, snarling at him with bared teeth, his eyes hard and cold. They shoved Jarin against the railing near the stern.

"You best hush," said Terrick, his bald head shining in the strident moonlight. "We're tryin' to keep a low profile. Gots a nasty sorcerer on board, and he doesn't know we're here yet. We're gonna relieve him of the amulet, once your girlfriend collects it. Nice and easy."

Another three of Artus's men emerged from the shadows, swords drawn and faces ugly with hate.

Lovel staggered on the spot, holding his nose. "We're gonna cut your girlfriend wide open. Hope you know that."

Artus directed a grunt of warning at Lovel, which Jarin supposed was all the noise he could make without his tongue. Lovel turned just in time to see Drue sneaking up on him, dagger in hand.

Lovel wrestled with Drue, subduing him, while Berolt went after Terrick and locked him in a fight. Jarin swung his elbow, aiming for Artus's face. But the older man, as wily as a snake, ducked around him with a flash of silver.

It took several moments for Jarin to realize the flash of silver had been a knife and Artus had stabbed him.

At first, the wound didn't hurt. The side of his body simply felt wet and strange. Then, he looked down and saw dark red spreading across his shirt.

He hadn't meant to die *yet*. Drue and Berolt and Neve were in danger, and he hadn't even set eyes on Riella. Where was she? What if she was already dead?

All he could do now was go out with a fight.

He lunged at Lovel and tore him from Drue. Artus's other men were upon Jarin at once, wrenching him back to the stern. Jarin managed to bury the blade of his dagger in the chest of one and elbowed another in the face. He couldn't seem to stand straight or catch his breath. It was a decade since he'd been injured and not begun healing right away. His strength was waning at an alarming rate.

The blade of a sword sliced so close to his face that he felt the air move. Jarin punched the pirate holding the sword in the stomach, then picked him up and threw him to the deck, unconscious. He couldn't see or hear Drue and Berolt anymore, which surely meant they were dead or gravely injured.

Jarin struggled against Artus and Lovel as they closed in on him. He threw off Lovel, but Artus bore down on him before he could regain his footing, trapping him against the railing. He groped for the handle of his dagger, but Artus stuck a blade in Jarin's back while holding him in a grotesque bear hug. The older man withdrew the blade rapidly, plunging it straight into Jarin's other kidney.

Jarin stumbled, the sky and the vessel and the captain's face beginning to blur and swim before him. He was losing blood, and lots of it. Death was so close that he could feel the promise of its warm embrace.

Through the darkness, a luminous angel came toward him. Then he blinked, and realized it was Riella in her pale-gold dress, running along the deck, completely unarmed. A terrified female scream came from the bow—Seraphine or Neve. The two were on their own against Polinth. Jarin had to make Riella leave. His life was already over, but hers wasn't.

"Jarin!" she yelled.

Lovel pounced on her. She ripped her talons across his

face, making him yowl. With his last drop of strength, Jarin swung his fist at Artus. Jarin connected with his jaw, but not hard enough to do real damage.

Terrick closed in on Riella, as did a bleeding Lovel and the other men. They knew Jarin was Artus's kill, and had gone for the siren instead.

"Riella, get out of here!" said Jarin with a rasp. "Go save Seraphine and Neve!"

"But you . . ." she said.

Her blue gaze met his, the siren torn between saving them and helping him. But he couldn't let her remain here. With Jarin on the verge of death, Artus and these ghouls could very well overpower her.

"Go!" he shouted. "I can't be killed, remember! I'm right behind you."

He fought to make his voice strong and even. Another scream came from the bow, which tipped the scales. Riella had seen Jarin survive a shard of glass to the heart. She trusted him to live. He hated lying to her, but this was the last gift he could give her. A final act of love.

To his staggering relief, she turned on her heel and sprinted toward the scream.

Artus stood directly in front of Jarin. Lovel and Terrick flanked their captain, grinning like hyenas, the third man leering farther back. Artus held his sword at his side.

"We heard a whisper on the docks earlier, all the way from Velandia," said Lovel with an excited, high-pitched laugh. "We heard your dear old mother died. Ended the curse." He pointed at the wooden deck, where Jarin's blood steadily pooled. "Looks like condolences are indeed in order."

Jarin closed his eyes, the life draining from him like sand from a broken hourglass. Had his actions been enough to disrupt the prophecy? Had he taken her place by saving her just now? She had outlived him, at the very least. That was something.

Artus struck as Jarin opened his eyes again. The long blade plunged into his stomach, burning like fire. With a determined gleam in his eye, Artus leaned into the hilt, making Jarin's insides rupture and implode.

Absurdly, he wondered how he was drowning even though he wasn't in the water. Then, he coughed. Blood streamed from his mouth, and didn't stop. His chest rose and fell in vain, his vision fading, and he knew he'd never take another breath.

Lovel and Terrick rammed him. Artus gripped the sword handle and when Jarin fell backward, the blade tore violently from his stomach. He tumbled over the railing and crashed through the surface of the water. His body sank quickly and silently, pulled under by the powerful current.

The last thing he remembered was endless dark blue and his love for Riella and a hauntingly beautiful Song that seemed to emanate from the waves themselves.

CHAPTER 38

Riella sprinted back to the bow, knowing Jarin could survive anything.

The screams came from Neve. Her sword, which glowed red when she came to Riella's aid, lay dull and discarded on the deck. She was sprawled on her back, grimacing in pain. Seraphine convulsed against the railing, so weakened that she couldn't stand. The elf was a whisper away from death.

Polinth stood over Neve, his face alight with power and glee.

The arrival of Jarin's vessel had distracted Polinth only momentarily. During the journey, he held Seraphine close to keep Riella at bay. He was adamant she needed to dive down and fetch the amulet before he'd release the elf.

That was before she realized Dark Tide Clan was on board. Jarin would kill the pirates, of course. All she had to do was stall until he could help her with Polinth.

But stalling was going poorly. Neve's arrival both invigorated and incensed Polinth, who took it personally that a mage had been set against him. Before knocking her to the deck, he demanded to know what the High Magus said about him.

"Stop!" shouted Riella.

She shoved the sorcerer, but a deflective enchantment encased him and it was like hitting a sheet of metal.

"Careful, siren," he said, his eyes narrowing to slits. "The only reason you're alive is because I need the amulet. Now, hurry up and get it for me."

"Alright, I will," she said. "We're at the right place. There's no need to hurt Neve."

Riella was lying. The underwater caves from the map were many, many leagues away. The ship would never make it before dawn. Even now, the horizon lightened to purple. Her death was close. The only remaining questions were how it would happen, and whether she'd manage to take Polinth with her.

"My patience grows thin." Then, his pallid head whipped around at the male voices coming from the stern. "Who else is here?"

She waved her hands, desperate to distract him until Jarin neutralized his peers. "Doesn't matter. Pirates fighting among themselves."

"Well, then, what are you waiting for?" asked Polinth, redirecting his rheumy gaze to her. "Swim down and collect the amulet."

"But I can't access the place where the amulet lies without my Voice," said Riella. "Remember? That's why you took it, didn't you?"

He considered her. "If you procure the amulet for me, I will not only return your Voice to you, I will grant you life."

Despite her dire situation, she seethed at his arrogance. "*Grant* me life?"

"Yes, of course. I am your god, your creator, your master.

You are an experiment. And a splendid one, but just an experiment, and even I can't work against the laws of Nature forever. From that first night, you've only ever had until the next full moon. But, attain the amulet for me, and saving you will be my first act." He indicated the lilac horizon with one gnarled finger. "Without my help, you have but minutes to live."

He withdrew a small glass bottle from his robes and held it aloft. Riella's Voice glowed blue behind the glass. Before she could reach for it, he uncorked the bottle and threw it overboard. The glass hit the surface of the water with the tiniest splash.

"Off you go." Polinth made a shooing motion at her with his hands. "Fetch."

Riella rushed to the railing. The glowing blue shot from the bottle in tendrils, merging with the ocean. In her heart, she knew her Voice would never return to her. Some things could not be undone.

"Are you going, or not?" asked Polinth, standing over Neve. "Because if I can't have the amulet, I'll happily use the sorceress as an energy source. It's usually so hard to steal them away from under the watchful gaze of the Magus." Neve clawed at the deck, trying to stand. "She'll be my compensation for you wasting my time."

Riella dug her talons into the railing, frozen with indecision. She'd accepted her own life was over, but she'd not reckoned on Neve dying, too.

Seraphine pulled herself to her feet, her eyes dull and hazy but determined. She went for Polinth, raising her arm to strike him. Before she could make contact, he blasted her back against the railing with a casual flick of his fingers.

Heavy boots thundered on the deck, making the siren's heart leap with hope. Jarin was coming. He would help.

But Artus, Lovel, and Terrick rounded the corner. Lovel's face bled profusely where she'd scratched him.

Confused, she peered past them. Where was Jarin?

Terrick leered at her. "Your beau is dead. Fish food."

Nausea rose in Riella's throat and her ears rang. That was impossible, because Jarin couldn't die. Terrick must've been lying.

But then, where was he?

Before she could shout his name, the ship lurched. Everyone on deck stumbled, Neve falling onto her back and Seraphine grasping at the railing for dear life. Then, a beautiful and unearthly Song filled Riella's ears.

"Sirens!" shouted Lovel, shoving his hands over his ears. "Sirens incoming!"

Artus and Terrick and even Polinth covered their ears. Terrick whirled around, trying to pinpoint the source of the Song. But the infinite sapphire ocean appeared empty. It wasn't, of course. It never was, no matter how much it may've looked that way.

Riella pulled Neve to her feet.

"Bind him!" she instructed the acolyte. They had moments before the sorcerer would recover from the surprise and block the Sirensong with magic. "Bind Polinth, now!"

Neve frowned in concentration and moved her hands in circular motions in front of her chest. A black mist appeared between her palms, like a miniature hurricane. She flung it Polinth. The black mist exploded in the center of his robed chest and expanded, like a net, covering his entire body. He roared, stumbling backward. Seraphine dodged him as he lurched into the railing.

The pirates drew their weapons, having shoved candle wax into their ears, and stared around wildly in anticipation.

Thera burst from the ocean, raining water on the men as she soared through the air and landed on the ship. Her powerful pink tail swept the deck, knocking Terrick off his feet.

Lovel lunged, attempting to stab her. The siren picked him up with a scream of fury and threw him against the helm. His bones cracked and his lifeless body fell to the wooden deck.

Artus swung his sword at her while Terrick attacked her from behind. Riella ran at Terrick, slamming him onto the deck. He scrambled to his feet, sword in hand, and aimed a hacking blow at Riella. She dodged the blade and snatched him up by the throat, his boots kicking uselessly in midair. With a twist of her hand, she broke his neck, leaving his eyes to stare blankly at the expansive sky.

Thera fought Artus. He was a tougher opponent for the young siren, who'd never faced off with humans before. The disgraced captain was a veteran of the war and fiercer than his underlings.

Riella went to assist her, but Neve shouted. "Riella, help! The Binding won't hold much longer!"

Polinth struggled against the spell, grunting and snarling. The black mist flickered and began to fade. In the water behind him, Riella glimpsed dark blue shadows swimming swiftly in wait.

He was backed against the railing and she strode to him. He'd lived for long enough. Ever since he kidnapped her, she'd waited for this chance.

Fear crossed the sorcerer's wizened features for the first time as she approached, her eyes full of fury and determination.

"Stop!" he shouted, trying in vain to raise his hands against the Binding. "If you kill me, you'll die. I can save you, I swear it."

"But if *you* die," she replied, balling her fists. "Your hold on Seraphine will break, will it not? She'll be free."

"She's an elf!" spluttered Polinth, his watery eyes bulging. "She's practically dead already—no good to anyone anymore. But you are a warrior. You can save countless lives, if you survive. That's why sirens exist, is it not? I understand you, you see?" He jerked his head at Seraphine, who struggled for breath on all fours. "Think of the greater good, my dearest."

Riella sighed, tilting her head back to gaze at the sky one last time. The stars faded now, the moon setting. Ferrante had been right. She would get to choose her fate. What a gift. And if Jarin had indeed perished, she would be with him again very soon.

She almost felt sorry for Polinth. He believed that power was the most important thing in the world, but he was wrong. It was love, and all of the infinite, colorful, wonderful, messy, big, small, and precious forms it took.

It was Kohara's calm presence, Berolt's kindness, Nuri and Ruslo teaching her to dance. It was Yvette's strength, Sehild's loyalty, and Odeya's gentle heart. It was Seraphine returning to save her, Drue teaching her how to sail, and Neve coming to her aid. It was Ferrante's faith. Galcil and Thera and Mareen searching long and hard for her when she disappeared, and aiding her now, even though she was a land-walker.

It was Jarin. A man, a pirate—who possessed her whole heart.

Her blue stare drifted back to the sorcerer. "You don't understand sirens at all."

She held her skirts and kicked Polinth hard in the chest. He flew backward over the railing, still tangled in the flickering Bind. Mareen emerged from the water with her flaming red hair, her icy gaze fixed on him. Something metallic glinted from her neck.

Mareen caught him before he hit the water, sinking her talons into his flesh. She wrapped her tail around his torso and jerked it, breaking his spine. Helpless and immobile, he shrieked as she scalped him with her razor-sharp talons, his bald head turning to red ribbons. The screaming only stopped when Mareen dragged him beneath the surface.

Riella watched from the railing as he disappeared into the sea. Moments later, a dense cloud of blood ballooned to the surface. Mareen had always liked to rip her prey apart completely.

On the deck, Artus locked Thera in battle. He sliced the air with his sword, as she nimbly avoided the blade. But his attacks were furious enough to prevent her from getting a clear shot at him.

Distracted by Artus's onslaught, Thera had stopped Singing. Riella remembered what it was like, when she first began to fight. She'd be so caught up in combat that she forgot she had a Voice.

"Thera!" called Riella. "Sing to him! Extra loud!"

A smile flashed across Thera's features as she recognized her oversight.

Then, she opened her mouth and Sang, filling the crystalline pre-dawn air with haunting Sirensong. She increased her volume to penetrate the candle wax in Artus's ears. He flinched, then buckled in pain. Blood trickled from his ears.

Thera seized the moment and punched him square in the chest. His sternum cracked loudly and he flew backward, skidding across the salt-crusted deck. His dead body came to a halt at Riella's feet, its chest caved in.

Her beautiful face alight with success, Thera surveyed the deck for threats, but no more existed. She nodded to Riella before diving into the water, leaving the land-walkers alone. Neve crouched over Seraphine, who had collapsed. Riella hurried to them.

She and Neve helped Seraphine to stand. Riella laughed in disbelief at the transformation happening before her eyes. The elf's skin had a healthy peach glow. Her hair turned lustrous and thick, the color of honey. And her bright green eyes were full of life and feeling.

Seraphine took a step toward the railing. "I shouldn't rejoice in death, but I do rejoice in the triumph of the light."

Her voice was sweet and soft, like a lullaby. She looked around in wonder, inhaling deeply. Only when her gaze rested on Riella did she falter.

"Are you alright?" Seraphine asked the siren.

"Oh, Riella." Neve grabbed her elbow in alarm. "Your face is gray."

Riella was not bothered, or afraid. She'd done exactly what she set out to do. And now it was time for her to rest.

The sun broke over the horizon, turning the ocean to brass. Riella's vision began to fade, and her heartbeat slowed. She would reunite with Jarin very soon. Perhaps then, she could finally tell him what she learned about herself, and her feelings, and what it meant to know him.

Neve frantically cast spells at the siren, moving her hands and chanting words. Riella wanted to tell the sorceress not to worry—that all was well—but she was beyond speaking. She ambled across the deck, climbed the railing, and plunged into the water.

The ocean embraced her, enveloped her, and she sank into the sapphire abyss. Gravity ceased to exist and she hung suspended, waiting for whatever came next with acceptance and curiosity.

Dark blue shadows swirled beneath her, rising.

"I can't believe I'm saving a *pirate*," Sent Galeil.

How strange, thought Riella. Was she hallucinating?

Mareen's cloud of red hair rose from the depths, the siren stopping level with Riella. Around her neck, hanging from a chain, was an intricate gold pendant with a blue stone in the center.

Riella tried to Send, or move, but found she could not. She couldn't feel her body at all.

"We heard your Voice," Sent Mareen. "We came to investigate, and good thing we did. I had fun slaughtering the mage."

Thera swam toward Riella, her opaline body and pink tail undulating through the water.

"We found the amulet with your instructions." She giggled. "Mareen's been itching for a reason to use it."

"I have not!" Sent Mareen.

"Can she even hear us?" Thera tilted her head at Riella. "She looks dead."

"Because she is! We're in the In-Between, but I don't know how long we have. Now, stop chatting and let me concentrate. I need to call forth the Sea Witch before they pass into the Beyond." She held the pendant and a searing blue light ignited in its center, illuminating her face. "Galeil, bring the pirate here."

Galeil swam into Riella's field of vision. In her arms, she held Jarin's unconscious body. Blood spiraled from the injuries in his back and he looked very much deceased. But apparently, Riella was, too.

"I hope you know what you're doing, Mareen," Sent Galeil. "The elders said the sacrifice had to be voluntary for the Sea Witch to grant them life. Are you sure that's what happened, Thera? They both died for another soul?"

"I'm sure. He gave his life for her, and she died to save the elf."

Behind her friends, an enormous shadow loomed, tentacles reaching toward Riella and Jarin. Far from scaring her, the mysterious presence flooded Riella with gratitude and joy. The other sirens didn't seem to notice the shadow or the tentacles, as if only Riella could perceive the Sea Witch.

"Wait," Sent Thera. "Ask the Sea Witch if you can restore Riella to her original form."

"Is that even what she wants?" Sent Galeil. "She seems very attached to this land-walker."

"Well, we can't very well ask her," Sent Mareen, exasperated. "She's dead."

"We should—"

"Hurry!" interrupted Thera. "The water's starting to—"

A flash of blue light blinded Riella and silenced her friends. She was driven upward by a roaring tornado of white water for what seemed like an eternity. The siren could do nothing except be borne on the water, glimpsing tentacles as she whirled higher.

Then, all at once, it stopped. She was underwater, near enough to the surface to see shafts of sunlight. The current buffeted her sideways.

"What happened?" Sent Jarin.

With a jolt, Riella turned in the water, kicking her legs. Jarin floated in the water before her, apparently healed. And . . . able to Send to her.

Jarin looked around in confusion. He seemed completely at ease, and she realized he could breathe underwater. And so could she, although her tail and Voice had not returned.

"My friends recovered the Amulet of Delphine," she Sent to him, making him start with surprise as he experienced telepathy for the first time. "They used it to save our lives. I believe the Sea Witch imparted some siren traits to us, as well."

"You're alive," he Sent, sheer relief overcoming his features.

"We both are."

"But *you're* alive. Riella, all I wanted was for you to live, with or without me."

"And I want you. I need you. Jarin, I have so much to tell you."

His face broke into a huge smile. He swam to her, grabbed her waist and kicked upward. Together they broke the surface of the ocean, water streaming from their hair.

In the golden light of a new day, they kissed.

EPILOGUE

Old Cove was the last stop for Riella and Jarin before they were to board the Pandora with Berolt and Drue and the rest of the new Dark Tide Clan.

The first stop had been Klatos, to return Neve to her Starlight Gardens cohort. The mages greeted her rather indifferently, Riella thought, considering the danger the young sorceress had been in. Before saying goodbye, Riella and Neve swore allegiance to each other, should either of them ever need help.

Next, they traveled leagues inland to the Emerald Mountains, where Seraphine lived. The elf was welcomed home with warmth and relief. Patrols of elves had been searching for her fruitlessly, Polinth having concealed Seraphine with sorcery.

Riella then insisted they find Yvette, who was studying Herbalism and Healing at an academy in the countryside. She was bemused to meet Riella again. Polinth had come to the academy to question her about the map's whereabouts, but she'd been canny enough to reveal nothing. Yvette had a new healthy glow, not unlike Seraphine. She spent her days learning from books and foraging for medicinal plants and tending to the infirm.

And finally, Riella and Jarin arrived at Old Cove, in the far northern reaches of Zermes.

The graveyard was easy to find. It sat atop a hill in the seaside hamlet, birch trees standing guard over the smattering of headstones. The leaves of the trees were turning orange, as summer gave way to the first breaths of autumn.

Riella and Jarin dismounted their horses as they approached the gates of the little cemetery, walking the rest of the way on foot. His parents' grave was in the center. The headstone was hewn from white marble, brand new and elegant, naming Malakai and Levissina.

One grave was covered in thick velvety grass, and the other was piled high with fresh soil.

Jarin stood at the foot of the grave, his arm around Riella.

"Davron and Amelie brought her body here," he said. "I can't think why they'd do that, after everything."

"Perhaps simply because they are decent people."

"Then I pray they stay far away from Klatos and the throne, for their sakes." He heaved a sigh. "I'm afraid death would await them."

"But Davron is the rightful heir. I can't see how anyone could stop him, should he wish to return."

"The Garstangs are shrewd and cruel and power-hungry. They would not relinquish their newfound hold on Zermes easily."

"I don't know." Riella leaned her head against Jarin's shoulder, thinking of Polinth. "The shrewd and cruel and power-hungry have a way of plunging to their deaths."

"I don't believe I have to worry about Davron telling the Garstangs the location of my mother's grave, at least. The Nikolaous and Garstangs are no friends to each other. My parents can finally rest, together."

He and Riella lapsed into silence, gazing at the headstone. Overhead, a pure white dove arced in the blue sky. The breeze carried the sweet, musky scent of roses, which was impossible, because none existed nearby.

As the afternoon grew longer, the pair descended the grassy hill to the cove. The pale yellow sand was warm, and the turquoise water lapped gently at the shore. Berolt and the rest of the crew would arrive at dusk to collect Riella and Jarin.

Until then, they reclined together on the private beach, Jarin running his hand up Riella's lightly tanned leg.

"I'm looking forward to being on the water," said Riella.

"Oh, aye. Me too. And what fun it will be, to rob and plunder slavers."

"Especially now that we can Send and breathe underwater. They won't know what hit them."

"I still can't believe you convinced your siren friends to create an alliance with us against the slavers."

"Are you kidding? They can hardly wait to wreck ships. Nor can I, truth be told. I'm so grateful the Sea Witch restored my full strength."

Jarin sighed. "She could've given me some."

"You're plenty strong already. And besides," said Riella with a cheeky grin. "Now I can overpower you whenever I like."

She swung her leg over Jarin and straddled him, pinning his wrists over his head. Her name adorned one of his biceps, and her portrait covered the other. The tattoo artist had taken great care to ink an accurate depiction.

"No complaints here. I'm all yours, evermore."

"Jarin."

"Yes?"

"I love you."

His breath caught. She'd never said those words to him.

Although she'd felt them for some time, she wanted to be sure she knew exactly what they meant before expressing them. She wanted to understand the complexity and depth and utter sweetness that was love. Now, she did, and it was Jarin who'd shown her.

An ancient hurt in his eyes melted away, like ice after a long winter. Waves crashed on the beach and the sun warmed her back. She leaned forward, her hair falling around his face, and kissed him.

※

Are you ready for the grand finale?

The sorceress Neve struggles to evade a ruthless assassin. She doesn't know why there's a bounty on her head, but when she finds out, both her life and the course of the Zermes kingdom will change forever.

The Sorceress and the Spider King, the final installment of the Fairytales Forever trilogy and a retelling of Snow White, is available for preorder now:

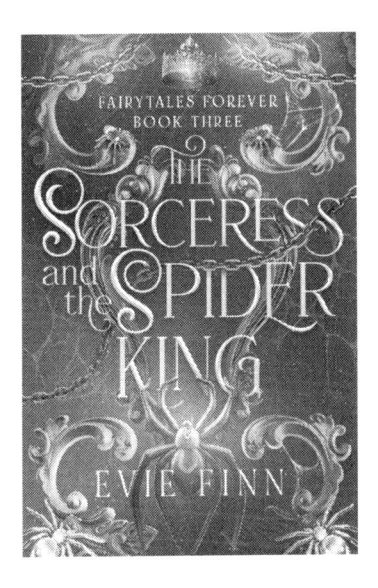

Subscribe to Evie's newsletter and receive a FREE Fairytales Forever ebook. This prequel novelette tells Levissina's origin story, including her courtship with Malakai and her fateful run-in with King Reynard:
eviefinn.com/newsletter

SOCIAL MEDIA:
instagram.com/evie.finn.author
facebook.com/evie.finn.author

IF YOU ENJOYED The Siren and the Dark Tide, please consider leaving a rating or review.

ALSO BY EVIE FINN

Fairytales Forever Trilogy:

The Curse and the Silver Rose: Book One
The Sorceress and the Spider King: Book Three

Dawn of the Dark: Prequel Novelette

ABOUT THE AUTHOR

Evie believes in magic, especially the powerful magic of escaping to another realm via a book. When she's not writing or reading, she explores the world outside, eats good food, and cuddles her beloved cat.

Printed in Poland
by Amazon Fulfillment
Poland Sp. z o.o., Wrocław